ONE SMALL STEP FOR MAN . . . ONE QUANTUM LEAP FOR MANKIND

Theorizing that a man could time travel within his own lifetime, Dr. Sam Beckett stepped into the Quantum Leap Accelerator—and vanished.

Somehow he was transported not only in time, but into *someone else's* life. . . .

And the Quantum Leap Project took on a whole new dimension.

QUANTUM LEAP

Now all the excitement and originality of the acclaimed television show are captured in these independent novels . . . all-new adventures, all-new leaps!

OUT OF TIME. OUT OF BODY. OUT OF CONTROL.

QUANTUM LEAP
PRELUDE

A NOVEL BY
ASHLEY McCONNELL

**BASED ON THE UNIVERSAL TELEVISION
SERIES "QUANTUM LEAP"
CREATED BY DONALD P. BELLISARIO**

ACE BOOKS, NEW YORK

Quantum Leap: Prelude, a novel by Ashley McConnell, based on the Universal television series QUANTUM LEAP, created by Donald P. Bellisario.

This book is an Ace original edition, and has never been previously published.

QUANTUM LEAP: PRELUDE

An Ace Book / published by arrangement with MCA Publishing Rights, a Division of MCA, Inc.

PRINTING HISTORY
Ace edition / June 1994

ISBN: 0-441-00076-2

ACE®
Ace Books are published by The Berkley Publishing Group,
200 Madison Avenue, New York, NY 10016.
ACE and the "A" design are trademarks
belonging to Charter Communications, Inc.

PRINTED IN THE UNITED STATES OF AMERICA

10 9 8 7 6 5 4 3 2

AUTHOR'S NOTE

I would like to thank Lisa Winters for providing the title of this book and awkward details, Linda Young for reminding me of the meaning of the Vietnam Memorial to a hero who lost his brother in that conflict, and Pathman Ed and Claire from GEnie's Medical RT for details about cell cultures. Special thanks also go to Claudia DeGailler for invaluable and voluminous research on Navy retirement ceremonies, Ginjer Buchanan for excellent suggestions and more awkward details, and Charlie Grant, who traded the earthquake for gravity. Any mistakes that appear in this work are mine, not theirs.

Synchronicity happens: the August 1992 issue of *Discover* magazine featured an article about Masuo Aizawa's work at the Tokyo Institute of Technology on combining nerve cells with electronics. My conception of Ziggy as a neural "hybrid computer" predated this article by over a year, and Ziggy is, of course, several generations beyond Aizawa's work, but it's fun—and a bit disconcerting—to find yourself writing science fiction when you thought it was fantasy.

Several fans have noted a discrepancy between the *Quantum Leap* books as I write them and the series as it's presented on television, to wit: in the series, Sam's body Leaped, and the person he replaced appears in the Waiting Room. In the books, Sam's mind Leaps and his body stays home, to be occupied by the mind of the person he replaces. All I will say in defense of this is that in the first season of the series, the distinction wasn't clear, and I made my choices based on the inherent dramatic opportunities involved, and have remained consistent with them thereafter. It may help the determined purist to consider the books an alternate-universe version of "Quantum Leap."

In that spirit, therefore, one might take *Prelude* to be the story, not of "how things happened," but one version of how things *might* have been. . . .

SUMMER, 1990

Theorizing that one could time travel within his own life-time . . .

He reads much; he is a great observer, and he looks
Quite through the deeds of men.

—William Shakespeare
Julius Caesar, I, ii, 200

CHAPTER
ONE

The morning paper had announced that Iran blamed the United States for the recent earthquake. A Navajo student attending the University of New Mexico had found a "New Gap to Bridge" that was, in fact, as old as the clash of cultures. A New Mexico man had been elected President of the League of United Latin American Citizens. It was going to be another hot, dry, sunny day in Albuquerque.

Admiral Albert Calavicci was nearly as white as the sheets he was lying on, his eyes closed and his left arm dangling from a traction hook to keep it elevated.

"You know, that stunt last night really took it out of you," his visitor continued. The kid couldn't take a hint in a package. "You're going to have to take some time to get back on your feet."

The eyes snapped back open, challenged. "What, you think I'm some kind of old man?"

The young man—Al decided grudgingly that he deserved that—lifted his hands in protest. "No, no, no, nothing like that. It's just that, you know, lots of things are changing for you now, and you've got this broken arm. Makes a great excuse for sitting back a little and taking some time to think about things. You should take advantage of the opportunity."

Al's eyes narrowed. "What do you know about what's changing for me?" Pushy, this kid was. Poking in. Interfering. Of course, if the kid hadn't been there to apply pressure and

3

all of that stuff, Al might be dead right now instead of in the hospital with his arm hanging from a bunch of wires and pulleys. On the other hand, if it hadn't been for this kid, Ross Malachy, he wouldn't have gotten shot in the first place. It served him right for barging in on a robbery in progress.

His attention had been attracted to the situation in the first place because he recognized Ross. It wasn't as if Ross Malachy were a friend; he was just the kid who worked for Stephen Wales, and Stephen Wales was the guy who led the encounter group Al had gotten mixed up in. But he'd recognized the kid when he'd seen him in the notions store, and then seen what he was trying to do: disarm another kid armed with a gun. Al didn't really *know* Ross; he would have provided a diversion for anybody under the same circumstances.

Of course, *he* was the one who got lucky and caught a bullet. If he wasn't so hazed out from pain medication, he might get a little ticked off.

Ross shrugged. "I dunno. I heard it somewhere. That you were retiring from the military, and . . . that you were retiring. I knew somebody once who was retiring from the military. It wasn't easy, being a civilian all of a sudden."

Al studied him. Ross had a really dumb grin on his face. In fact, he was acting like he had some kind of secret, some surprise he was hugging to himself. Al didn't like surprises. But aside from that, he was the first person who really seemed to *understand*. Getting shot, hey, that could happen to anybody. But retiring from the only life you'd known for thirty years— that *meant* something. His suspicions thawed.

"Well, I can't stay *here*." He glanced up at his arm in disgust. "This really sucks."

"You know what I think you should do?" Ross said, the picture of innocence. "Since you really shouldn't stress yourself any more. Right now, I mean," he added hastily. "With a bullet wound. You ought to take some time. That's serious stuff."

"Yeah, kid, what do you think I should do with all this time you think I have?" The words were heavily laced with sarcasm, but not too heavily that it wasn't clear Al was curious about the answer. He tilted his head, watching as Ross came around the bed and adjusted the wires and hooks and trappings so the arm would hang more comfortably. The kid was deft and professional about it, and the changes helped considerably.

"I think if you've got any friends in this part of the country, you ought to give them a call," he said. "I'll bet they'd be glad to see you. I'll bet they want to see you."

Al opened his mouth to dismiss the idea, then closed it again, slowly. There *was* somebody—and he *was* somewhere around here. "Yeah. I guess I could do that, come to think of it."

"Sure you could. He really wants to hear from you. Like his life depends on it," Ross said cheerfully. "And you wouldn't want to disappoint an old friend, would you?"

"No, I guess not. . . ." Al watched him, confused and wary.

"Oh, and I got you a present. Call it a get-well, thank-you-for-saving-my-life, welcome-to-retirement kind of thing."

"Oh yeah?" Presents were always good. This explained that air of glee, too. Suspicion wiped away, Al smiled, and tried again to sit up.

"I'm gonna have to open it for you," Ross warned. He took out a narrow, flat box. "There's a card, see?"

The cover of the card featured a crudely drawn cartoon of a man fairly mummified in bandages. Al opened it with his free hand—"I'm not helpless!"—and read it aloud. " 'When you leap into the unknown, make sure you've packed your parachute! Get Well Soon!' "

"You didn't sign it," he said. But he was distracted by the box, and set the card aside, watching eagerly as the gray satin ribbon slid off, finally taking the box away from Ross to open it. "What the—"

He held up a tie—a fine silk tie, heavy, expensive, beautiful, fluorescent purple with tiny bright pink squares and circles.

"Oh boy," Al said, awed and appalled in equal measure. "Hey, I'm in the military. I don't wear anything like this."

"You will," Ross assured him.

5

• • •

Three weeks later, having finished a course of IV therapy to prevent possible bone infection and having tried (and failed) to make dates with every female nurse in his ward, Al was released from the hospital with a sling, a recommendation for physical therapy, and an abiding distaste for civilian hospitals. By rights he should have been transferred to the Kirtland Base hospital, but a snafu in the paperwork had kept him where he was while surgeons repaired the damage caused by a bullet in the upper arm, a trifle too close to the shoulder for comfort. A fraction of an inch closer and it would have ripped out an artery and he would have bled to death. Ross Malachy had shown an uncanny knowledge of emergency medical procedures, the doctors said later. It kept the damage from being permanent. He'd get back full use of the arm if he did exactly what he was told.

Come to think of it, doctors in military hospitals said the same kind of stupid stuff. When he got out of the hospital after getting back from 'Nam, they'd given him a list of things to do and let him go, too. Doctors were the same everywhere. It was the same now as it had been more than twenty years before—out of the dim shadowed lobby and smell of antiseptic into blazing sunshine and an empty feeling that he didn't quite know what to do next. He squinted and looked around for the taxi that was supposed to be waiting for him. There was no taxi.

Heroes on TV could take a bullet in the arm and keep on going like the Energizer Bunny. He'd been pushing to get out of the hospital since he woke up from the anesthesia. But he sure as hell wasn't going to stand around in hundred-degree, July-in-New Mexico summer sun until a taxi showed up.

Unfortunately, there wasn't any place to sit down, and it wasn't as if he could stroll over to Central Avenue and flag down a cab. For one thing, his flagger was temporarily out of order, and for another, taxicabs weren't all that common in Albuquerque. Come to think of it, the only place he could ever remember seeing one was at the airport. He was contemplating going back into the shadows and sitting down for a while when Ross Malachy came out of the hospital entrance behind him. The kid was visiting Wales's wife, Al remembered.

"Admiral?" Ross was different somehow. A moment after he'd given Al the tie, he'd stepped back, blinking, and backed out of Al's room, confused. Probably a little self-conscious about giving a guy a present, Al figured. He still had that look—younger somehow, less self-assured. As if when the gift left his hands, something else did, too.

Weird present, too, but the more he'd looked at the thing— a horrendous pink-and-purple creation—the more it grew on him. It appealed to the somewhat warped sense of humor the military had never quite managed to get rid of. So, now, he nodded and smiled, acknowledging the greeting.

"Did they release you, sir? Is your arm okay?"

Al glanced down at the white sling and forced himself not to shrug. "Yeah, it's fine. They just let me out. There should be a taxi any year now."

"Do you need a ride back to your hotel? I can take you." The offer was instant and without strings, an impulsive generosity Al had found in only a few people.

Being less generous himself, he was inclined to take advantage of the offer. "Sure," he said promptly. "God knows when a taxi will show up. I *guess* I still have a room."

"If you don't, the hotel will still have your things," the kid assured him. "I'm sure the cops or somebody let them know what happened."

"Speaking of the cops, are you okay?"

The blue eyes clouded, as if Ross were having trouble remembering. "Oh, sure," he said uncertainly. "They said I'd have to testify, but then Stenno pleaded guilty, so I guess that's it. Lisa wasn't even charged."

Lisa must have been the girl in the store, Al thought. When he'd walked by and seen the boy pointing the gun at Ross and the store owner, Lisa, Stephen Wales's daughter, had had a look of sheer horrified enlightenment on her face. Al had been willing to bet that she didn't really know what she was getting into. It was nice to know that she wasn't going to have to pay the price.

Ross led Al over to a red Blazer, and Al settled back with a sigh of relief. The arm was hurting more than he wanted to admit, and the interior of the car was an oven. The warmth felt great.

They were more than halfway to the hotel before the air conditioning kicked in. By that time the cool air felt great, too. Thunderheads were forming over the Sandia Mountains, but the rain wouldn't hit until later. Now, the heat was still shimmering off the asphalt, blurring the cars in front of them.

Ross left him in the vehicle, air conditioning running on high, while he checked with the front desk, without suggesting that Al didn't look quite ready to walk the dozen yards to the lobby. When he came back he had a key and Al's battered leather suitcase.

"They gave you a new room on the ground floor," he said. "The public relations lady was at the front desk. She was really nice." His dark eyebrows were knotted, as if once again he was trying to remember something. "I'll drive you around."

He not only drove Al around, he unlocked the door and carried the little black suitcase in. Al wondered if he was expecting a tip. But Ross only smiled awkwardly, waved, and then got back into the red Blazer and pulled away, leaving Al wondering what had caused him to change.

The hotel room was identical to the one he'd had before, decorated in Pueblo Deco, with an imitation R.C. Gorman print next to the bathroom and walls that were painted brown and orange, presumably to evoke thoughts of a desert sunset. The bedspread was gray and black and brown and cream, reminiscent of a Navajo rug; the carpet was standard hotel-room mustard yellow. Everything was faded out by years of dust and wear. He lay back carefully on the bed and stared up at the ceiling and wondered what he was supposed to do now. He could have a cigar, he supposed. They wouldn't let him smoke in the hospital.

He'd called Washington already. The final separation papers had been filed while he was in the hospital, and his office had postponed his last debriefings yet again. He'd asked for, and received, two more weeks of leave. He wasn't sure what he was going to do with them. But once they were gone, he'd be going back, finishing up the last bits of paperwork, getting ready to turn over his "command" of the current projects. His life was winding down. He wasn't sure what lay beyond retirement; the military had been his only home for too many years. Even when he was a POW, he'd been a member of the United States military, and he'd known exactly who he was. He hadn't always liked it, but he'd known. A few months from now, he wasn't sure what he'd be. He exhaled a stream of pungent smoke toward the ceiling.

He didn't want to go to any more encounter groups.

He was really, really tired of moving around from station to station, of having no home but military housing.

Maybe it was better than not having a home at all.

Maybe not.

There was always Ross's suggestion.

Well, why the hell not.

But he *wasn't* going to tell Sam about parading around with his shirt off, participating in a men's encounter group. With luck, Sam'd never find out. It was just too embarrassing.

He reached over, wincing as he stressed the injured arm, and picked up the phone.

CHAPTER
TWO

"Now, Dr. Beckett," the senator said, looking up from under beetling brows, "tell us again about how this idea of yours is going to pay off for this country." He leaned back in his leather executive chair, causing it to roll away from the cherrywood desk. The chair squeaked against the floor mat, and the senator swiveled back and forth, repeating the sound, smiling to himself.

Sam Beckett sighed and sat up to go into battle again. The other senator, a motherly type seated not quite behind the desk but definitely on her colleague's side of it, smiled in a non-motherly fashion. Sam failed to notice. He, unlike the senators, was seated in a straight, uncomfortable suppliants' chair, and as he opened his mouth he looked over his audience's shoulders at the glass-fronted bookcases. The glass was shining clean, evidence of recent dusting. He wondered sourly if the dusting hid the fact that no one in this office actually read the books behind the glass.

"It's essential research, first of all, Senator Bantham." Sam was repeating himself, and he knew as well as anybody that you couldn't make someone understand an explanation by simply repeating the same words over and over, as if repetition would make them magically understandable. But he had worked so hard on this presentation, and the image of the words on paper wouldn't leave his mind. He'd hoped they would sweep the committee away.

He hadn't expected to meet a snake and a . . . he didn't quite know *what* to make of Senator Judith Dreasney. There was no committee, no hearing. Just two senators and their aides. He wasn't even sure if this was legal or not. Committee meetings weren't usually held in private offices with rubber tree plants—fake rubber tree plants at that—in the corners. It was a very nice office, other than that, he admitted. Broadwood floors and heavy rugs and a very expensive desk set that must have set a few taxpayers back. It smelled of very stale cigar smoke, and he wondered if Bantham observed the rules about not smoking in government offices. Maybe he didn't think of it as a government office. Maybe he thought it was *his* office.

No computers, though. He wondered how the Senate got any work done without computers.

"Yes, Dr. Beckett?" Bantham prompted. "You were saying?"

Sam dragged himself wearily back to his argument. "In order to do applied research, Senator, such as we were trying to do on Star Bright, you have to do the basic work first. That work may appear to have no relevance to the lay observer; it may even appear frivolous; but you can't ever get to a final product unless you have a complete foundation to build on."

"Oh, I see. Foundation. And empire for Dr. Beckett, no doubt?" Bantham slanted a glance at Dreasney, inviting her to share the joke. Dreasney, clearly not a science fiction aficionado, looked blankly back. Bantham snorted and turned back to Sam, letting a thick drawl color his words. He was just a good ol' boy, sure enough. "So you came in on Star Bright, decided it didn't have itself a good foundation, proposed to shut it down so you could go do something else?

"Now, I do respect your intelligence, Dr. Beckett. It's damned hard, I tell you, to ignore a Nobel Prize winner when he comes into my office, hat in hand, to ask for funding for a pet project." He paused to enjoy the look of incredulous irritation beginning to bloom on his visitor's face as the fact that he'd been insulted sank in. "But I've got to keep in mind the best interest of the American people," he went on. "This budget you've drawn up, well, Judith and I have gone over it, and it's just way too much money. What you're asking for here, why, do you have any idea how many children we could feed for that kind of money?"

Sam looked from Bantham to Dreasney and back again. The fading sunlight lit them unevenly, like a Lucifer and his shadow, and he wondered momentarily what he was going to be tempted to now. Sam Beckett as Dr. Faustus, perhaps?

"It's a shame that we can't find *some* kind of practical application," Judith, shadow, said. She was smiling again, uneven white teeth showing.

It was always this way, Sam thought. He'd been coming back to Washington from New Mexico at least once a week, every week, for almost a year now. Star Bright had been shut down because there were just too many things they didn't know, and Sam Beckett had been the one to say so. Then they'd asked him to put together a project proposal, given him just enough seed money to get started. Now they were reexamining the proposal. They were interested, all right. They just didn't want to pay for it.

"This is based on Hawkings's theories, isn't it?" Bantham mused. "So you could say, in a sense, that Hawkings did the basic research. You could take his work and . . ."

"No, Senator. I don't want to mislead you," Sam said. "We're actually extending the scope of Hawkings's work. We're taking it into a whole new area, integrating it with Lotfi Zadeh's work in fuzzy logic . . ."

"You say you can build a computer that can handle 'a greater level of complexity than heretofore achievable,' " Bantham interrupted, with the air of a man cutting to the chase. "We've got a dozen computers that can handle complex problems. Now if you had one that could handle the deficit, you might have something there." He chortled, would have dug an elbow into Dreasney's ribs if the woman had been close enough. She drew back an inch, not sharing his camaraderie.

"It's not just a matter of complexity," Sam said wearily.

"You've tried pitching this to the Energy Department, I assume," Bantham said. "They seem to be getting into weird stuff these days. Maybe they can find a weapons application, or something."

"I thought that would be Defense," Dreasney said thoughtfully, as if Sam weren't present.

"Nah. They only use the stuff. Energy does the research." Bantham set his elbows on the desk pad, swiveled his head around vulturelike to give his full attention to her.

"There's that new department," Dreasney suggested, unperturbed. "Nobody seems to have figured out *what* they do yet. And they're certainly interested in new projects. They might have some stray budget money they haven't committed yet."

"That's possible," Bantham agreed, picking up a pencil and tapping it against his teeth.

Sam closed his eyes. He'd have to go back and write up his proposal again and haunt somebody else's halls for financial support. And it was so simple, really. Just a matter of building a computer.

Not multitasking, not parallel processing. A computer with inspiration. A computer that could dream.

A computer that could send Sam Beckett into the past, to see and understand what *really* happened: when the Kennedys and King were shot, when Marilyn died, when all the mysteries happened. When Donna left him at the altar.

He got up and left the office, leaving the senators squabbling behind him, and wandered down the halls, thinking. It was one of the things he did best, and he stepped around a line of schoolchildren, not noticing when the teacher recognized him and spoke excitedly to her charges, not aware of the second glances and sharp looks from the people he passed. He'd been getting those looks ever since the *Time* cover. It made his mother proud, he supposed, but other than that it wasn't important.

He hadn't had a chance to do more than think since he'd given the final briefing on Project Star Bright. He wanted to work. He wanted to build that computer, to see his theories take shape. He'd been working on this since . . . he couldn't remember when he'd started thinking about time as a string. He'd been watching television, he knew that. And he knew if

13

he really tried to remember, he would.

Often enough he didn't bother to try to remember. It was too easy, for one thing. And for another it made him feel a little more like a normal person.

He was not a normal person.

He wanted to build that computer.

He wanted to walk into the past and find out what went wrong, and *fix* it.

Once he understood the past, he could go back to Star Bright and deal with the future. *First* time, *then* space.

Unfortunately, in order to do all that he had to deal with politicians and money people and others who wanted concrete results, right now, so the world could beat a path to their doors. Not one of them could appreciate the sheer fun of scientific research.

He wandered out of the building and down the marble steps and up the street, ignoring the traffic and noise and humid haze of a Washington afternoon. He could have been anywhere. It didn't matter. He was lost in the calculations, the theory.

A message was waiting for him when he got back to the hotel that night, after a late dinner and a show. It hadn't been difficult to get a single ticket to the Performing Arts Center. It usually wasn't. He always tried to attend at least one concert, one musical when he was on the East Coast; it was his private reward for having to be there at all. He checked at the desk when he came in, hoping forlornly that perhaps Dreasney, at least, had had a change of heart and that all was not yet lost.

The message was from Al. He grinned in delight, and practically ran to the elevators. He fumbled for the key to his room, slid it into the door, and lunged for the phone.

He'd already dialed before the familiarity of the area code registered, so when the phone was picked up on the other end his first words were, "What the heck are you doing in New Mexico?"

"Hello to you too," came the familiar, raspy voice. "I'm recovering from a gunshot wound. How's *your* day been?"

14

"You *what*?"

And then there were explanations and amazement and recriminations and laughter, and two old friends trading stories and recent events.

"What are you doing anyway?" Sam said at last. "Were you out at the Labs? I wish I'd known—I was going through there just a couple of days ago."

"Two days ago I was doped to the gills in a hospital," Al growled, exaggerating only slightly for the sympathy effect. "Where were you?"

Sam took a deep breath. "I was out at the project." *What I hope will be the project*, he amended mentally.

"Ah?" Al was trying to pretend he was only casually interested. He wasn't succeeding. "This is the new deal you're working on? So, what's going on?"

"I can't talk about it over the phone," Sam said, belatedly remembering the limitations. "But listen, when are you going to be coming back to Washington?"

He could hear movement on the other end of the line, as if Al were shifting, a grunt and a sigh. Sam's nose wrinkled automatically at the memory of cigar smoke.

"I think I might want to stick around here for a few more days," Al said at last. "I'm probably going to go stay on the base, in Bachelor Officers' Quarters."

There was strain in his friend's voice, and he wanted to ask if Al was okay, but something told him the question wouldn't be welcome. Al was his closest friend, but he didn't confide much. If he'd been badly hurt, he'd joke about it. Saying he'd stay in New Mexico was tantamount to admitting he was in pain.

"Okay," he said. "That'll work too. I'm going to spend a couple more days here and then I'll be going back to—" He hesitated. He couldn't tell Al, not yet. And he certainly couldn't tell him over the telephone. "I'll be in New Mexico. So stick around, and I'll take you to Sadie's or the Sanitary Tortilla Factory for dinner."

"Deal," Al said. "Let me give you the base locator number."

Information exchanged, Sam hung up, a smile beginning to spread across his face as he considered the possibilities. Al Calavicci, in New Mexico. Right on the verge of retirement—he'd be looking for something to do with himself. And Sam had something in mind. Sam Beckett needed a shark for the Washington waters, and nobody fit the bill better than Al Calavicci.

"Oh boy oh boy oh *boy*!" he crowed, delighted.

CHAPTER
THREE

The next day Sam headed for the Library of Congress to spend a few hours checking out the latest journal articles. Afterward he had lunch with colleagues also visiting the capital in the endless quest for government funding, and gently turned down an invitation to come join them at their various institutions of research and/or higher learning.

"What's the matter, you going to Los Alamos?" one, a bearded, slight man who stooped even sitting down, asked.

Sam grinned and shook his head. "Nope. Got some other irons in the fire."

"Like what?" another man wanted to know, pushing his glasses up on his nose.

When he wouldn't say more, the bearded man traded knowing glances with his two friends. Refusal to talk about work in public meant secrets, and not just industrial secrets, either.

The third man, the only one at the table not wearing a tie, changed the subject immediately. "So, Sam, how d'you like being the patron saint of the Nonluddites?"

"The what of the who?" As a subject-changing tactic, it worked beautifully. Sam set aside the fork with which he'd been digging into his salmon and took a long swallow of coffee. He'd better get funding soon, he thought irrelevantly. He'd have to bring his own lunches otherwise.

"The Nonluddites. That technology-no-matter-what bunch." The bearded man stabbed at a lettuce leaf. "Just when DOE is making our lives miserable with the Tiger Teams looking for safety and environmental problems, this group pops up and starts proclaiming the gospel of Build that Computer, Kill that Spotted Owl."

"I'm all for the Build that Computer end of it," his bespectacled compatriot smiled. The others, including Sam, nodded enthusiastically. "But you'd think they could give the bird a break. It's the visible symbol of the ecosystem—"

"Okay, Shelby, enough already about the ecosystem," the bearded man interrupted. "He was lecturing to us all the way out here about the damned ecosystem," he informed Sam.

"Sam knows what I mean," Shelby protested.

"The point is, these Nonluddites don't. They think more machines, more factories, more industry, more jobs. They don't think it through." The bearded man was visibly angry.

"They don't *need* to think it through," the man without a tie said. He was the only one who didn't have a meeting with a politician that day, and could afford to go casual. His name was Yen Hsuieh-lung, and rumor had it that he was the next candidate the Nobel committee had had in mind the year Sam Beckett won the Prize. "Why should they? The thinking has been done. Anyone with the eyes to read an economic forecast can see they're right."

This evoked an immediate storm of protest from Shelby and the bearded man, whose name was Whitsunder. Sam sat and listened until other diners started staring pointedly in the direction of the debate, and then raised his hand. "How about we all calm down and listen to what Hsuieh-lung has to say?" he said gently. "Or at least calm down?"

"Thank you, Sam," Hsuieh-lung said politely. Whitsunder and Shelby grumbled, but shut up.

"The Nonluddites are regrettably extreme, it's true," he went on. "But one must admit that they are correct in that a pristine old-growth forest provides comparatively far fewer jobs and far less to the nation's wealth than the same land converted to factory production of, let us say, computer chips." He nodded to Sam. "Their support would have been useful when we worked on Star Bright."

18

"I'd rather drink from the stream running through that old-growth forest than from a stream into which the waste from that factory had been discharged," Shelby said.

"Personally, I would prefer to have the water treated in either case," Hsuieh-lung riposted. "Proper utilization of resources, however, demands the factory."

"Do you agree, Sam?" Whitsunder demanded. "You're being awfully quiet."

"Yeah, what's this 'patron saint' business?" Shelby followed up. "Are you a Nonluddite?"

Sam chuckled, shaking his head. References to the Prize, or his own fame, always made him uncomfortable, particularly from the scientists he regarded as his peers. He knew many of them, especially the older ones, were jealous; he wanted to think that the ones closer to his own age were more supportive, but he knew that wasn't true, either. He found himself being very quiet in conversations rather than remind others of his expertise in so many different fields, gained in the same period of time others had taken to gain mastery of only one. Lack of practice in social conversations with fellow scientists often made him appear awkward.

Before he could answer, however, Hsuieh-lung interjected, "Sam has the academic background—six doctorates, isn't it?—and the notoriety, with the Nobel Prize. Besides, he's young and personable, a former child prodigy, and looks good on the cover of *Time*. His personal beliefs are of no consequence. According to yesterday's *Wall Street Journal*, his achievements should be every thinking man's aspiration." The man smiled thinly at Sam and folded his napkin neatly beside his plate. "You're a symbol, nothing more. Your active cooperation with the group would probably be appreciated, but isn't in the least necessary."

"I'm not sure I'm all that comfortable being a symbol," Sam objected, feeling heat creep up his face. "Especially when I don't share those ideas." He couldn't figure out why Hsuieh-lung kept pushing; he wished the other man would stop.

19

"What, you're a back-to-nature enthusiast?" Shelby challenged, changing sides with blinding speed.

"No, I'm not. But there has to be a way to achieve the technology and the industry and the jobs and not completely destroy that old-growth forest in the process."

"Old-growth forest, old-growth ideas. You might consider at least meeting with the Nonluddites, Sam; they might surprise you." Hsuieh-lung glanced at his watch, a gleaming gold Rolex. "If you'll excuse me, please, I must go. It has been a most enjoyable interlude." With that he stood, extracted three ten-dollar bills from his wallet, tossed them on the table, and left, before they could even offer to shake hands.

"That guy is *weird,*" Whitsunder said. "And cheap, too. That salmon was twenty-seven ninety-five, and with the tax it doesn't leave much for a tip—"

"It probably killed his per diem," Shelby remarked. "So, you're a hero to the Nonluddites, Sam. How does it feel to be a hero?"

"I'd rather be a hero to my budget coordinator," he answered. All three men laughed, and conversation moved on to another subject, much to Sam's relief.

That afternoon Sam had another meeting, with yet another federal agency, the one Dreasney had suggested. This one was willing to listen to him, which made him a trifle nervous to begin with; he was reminded of the old Groucho Marx joke about not wanting to belong to any club that would have him as a member. But they had money to spend, and liked the idea of the computer, and were impressed by his credentials. They promised to review the proposal. When he left, late that evening, he felt that he had at last the real beginnings of a new Project.

He stood on the steps of a nondescript office building and breathed deep, enjoying the fresh air, the relative quiet of post rush hour, and a bubbling feeling of delight. He was going to do it. He was going to build it. He was, even if his sponsors didn't know it, wouldn't believe it, going to travel in Time itself. He was going to be able to *see* what really happened. All the confusions, all the mistakes, all the uncertainties would vanish. He could actually be there and see what happened.

Whether the government believed it or not.

He had one more thing to take care of before going back to New Mexico and getting together with Al—the first step toward building the team. A new team, handpicked. He'd find what's-her-name, that ditzy redhead, Martinez-O'Farrell, to design the computer architecture—she was brilliant if you could get her out of the mall long enough. And Gooshie from Star Bright could program anything, and he was bored with his current job.

Sam grinned. The computer he was planning would cure any programmer of boredom, and probably give him night-mares to boot. He couldn't *wait* to spring the design on all of them.

Perhaps it was the broad grin that attracted the attention of the young blond man coming up the steps. In any case the man changed direction and approached Sam directly.

"Dr. Beckett?" he said, holding out his hand. There was no real inquiry in his voice. The immediate neighborhood was empty; Sam's car was parked across the street in a parking garage, and a few people walking across a lawn several hundred yards away were the only others in sight.

Brought back to the here and now, Sam blinked and shook hands automatically. "Er, yes?"

"I'm Chris Jancyk, Dr. Beckett, from the *News*. Perhaps you saw my profile of the Democratic committeemen last month? Or the study of the Washington subway system? That one ran last year."

"I'm sorry," Sam apologized. "I'm afraid I didn't see either one."

Chris Jancyk smiled, showing perfect teeth. "That's quite all right, Dr. Beckett. I do understand." And he did, in fact, because there had never been any profile or study, at least not under his byline. "Do you have a few minutes, sir? I'm a great admirer of your work."

"Ah . . ." Sam was vastly uncomfortable, as always around reporters. He couldn't help but wonder, in an Indiana farm boy sort of way, why on earth people thought he was so *interesting*. His work was interesting, but *he* was just another scientist. . . .

"Just a very few minutes, sir. A couple of questions for a sidebar in our series on new developments in physics."

Sam's eyebrows knit. "I'm afraid I couldn't give you anything new."

"Then perhaps a new slant on old material. If you don't have any plans, in fact, I could buy you dinner."

Sam paused. He did have one more task to fulfill, but it wasn't one he particularly looked forward to. On the other hand he didn't much want to go out to dinner with this man; he had a gut feeling that there was something fishy about him. "I'm sorry," he said. "I'd like to, but I have other commitments."

"It wouldn't take more than an hour or so," the other man coaxed. "And there are some people who'd really like to meet you." He was standing too close. "I've promised to set it up."

That did it. Reporters were rarely interested in facilitating meetings. There was something wrong here. But he *was* polite.

"Not this time," Sam said firmly. "I'm sorry, but I really do have other things to do right now."

Jancyk nodded understandingly. "I understand. Could you give me a telephone number?"

"Oh, sure." Sam reached into his suit coat pocket, fumbling for the cards his new sponsor had given him. He was looking away from Jancyk; he never saw the gun butt that smashed into his left temple.

He was spinning into a featureless globe of blue-white light glowing with pain. No, he thought. This isn't right. This isn't the way it's supposed to be. I've got something to do. I'm almost there. It can't go wrong now.

Somewhere else, far away, sirens screamed, and Chris Jancyk stared panicked at what he had done. The sirens came closer. Jancyk cursed and ran away, leaving the crumpled body of a world-famous physicist crumbled in a spreading pool of blood on the marble steps.

22

CHAPTER FOUR

"What do you mean, you hit him?" Yen Hsuieh-lung snarled. "Why?"

It was dark now. The night breeze, coming through the screened window, did little to relieve the sullen heat of the day. It stirred the dull-gold curtains and touched at the backs of the necks of the people who met in a certain room of a certain building, unremarkable on a side street in Georgetown.

"He wasn't going to come with me," the man who had called himself Chris Jancyk protested. "I was going to, to knock him out, to make him come. But I heard sirens and I thought—"

"You're a fool and an idiot," the scientist said. "You're the son of fools and the father of fools. What made you think it was so essential that he come tonight?"

The others in the room nodded to themselves.

"But you said he *had* to meet with us before he left Washington. You sent me to bring him here—"

"You can't convince a man like Beckett by violence, and now you've destroyed our opportunity to persuade him by reason. You're a liability to the entire movement." Yen Hsuieh-lung was seated in an antique chair, his knuckles white against the polished wood. The others in the room, two men and a woman, kept well apart from him and the object of his anger.

"I did what I thought was best at the time!" Jancyk was sweating, his body jerking as if the urge to pace were nearly irresistible. His hands moved in wide gestures, unrelated to his words.

"The fact that you could not think of anything better is all the proof we need of your incompetence." The more tightly coiled Jancyk became, the quieter Yen Hsuieh-lung was in response, and the more the audience edged away.

"What are you going to do to me?" Jancyk challenged, looking from the Chinese-American scientist to the others in the room. They stared back at him silently, letting Yen Hsuieh-lung act as their spokesman.

"*Do?* We shall do *nothing*," he said. "Violence is *your* means of expression, not ours. But we have no use for you any longer. Go away, and don't come back."

Jancyk hesitated, looking from one person to the next, hoping for some sympathy, some reprieve. None was forthcoming. They were so many statues, their eyes like glass eyes of brown, of blue, of gray. Were it not for the quiver of a muscle below the eye, the lash-shadow of a blink, they might be statues indeed.

"If he'd come here, he'd have had to listen," he began. No one responded. Jancyk licked his lips and swallowed the rest of his justification, reached for his briefcase.

"You will leave that here," Hsuieh-lung said implacably.

The briefcase fell out of his hand as if the handle had burned him. He jerked his head in a staccato nod, scanned the others, looking for and not finding any support, and turned and walked very quickly out of the room.

There was no movement, no sound from the assembly until the footsteps in the hallway paused, and the front door opened and closed. The four people remaining in the room looked at one another.

"Definitely a liability," one of the men said. "I'm sorry we ever brought him into the group."

"And he's a reporter, too. Not wise to antagonize writers, is it? He might write something about us instead of *for* us, next time."

"It *is* fortunate," the sole woman, a short, emaciated redhead, observed tranquilly, "that Washington has such a very high murder rate, isn't it?"

"Indeed," Hsuieh-lung said, and favored her with a thin-lipped smile. "Sometimes the results are tragic. Sometimes less so. You will see to it, I trust?"

She smiled brilliantly in return.

"Meanwhile," someone else noted, "let's see what advantage we can make from this, and what lessons we can learn. Nothing is without use, after all."

After a moment, Yen agreed.

"Oh, shit, I just hate it when they're famous," Weasel Mikowski said, holding his hands up in the air and shaking drops of water from them. "Give me an unknown and a grieving family every time." He leaned forward to give a particularly short scrub nurse some assistance in fastening the mask over his mouth and nose, turned again to let another assist him in putting on surgical gloves. "But the famous ones, holy heaven, you might as well have the press right there taking pictures over your shoulder."

The loose green scrubs, mask, and cap made him look like someone wearing a disguise. Everyone else looked exactly alike, wearing the same garb. He had to recognize them by the way they moved, by the stations they took up. But they all knew where they were supposed to be and what they were supposed to do.

"Is this guy famous?" the second nurse asked. "I never heard of him."

"You never *heard* of him?" Weasel was stunned. "He won the Nobel Prize a couple years back. He was on the cover of *Time* and *Newsweek* and *Rolling Stone—*"

"Get my picture . . ." someone caroled.

Weasel gave the culprit a withering look, the effect of which was largely spoiled by the fact that only his eyes could be seen. "The slab of meat on this afternoon's table, ladies and gentlemen, has more degrees than all of us put together. He sings. He dances. He does physics. He's only one of the smartest men in the world!"

"Not any more," the scrub nurse said. "Not with a depressed fracture of the skull and subcranial bleeding.

He's going to be lucky he doesn't end up a babbling idiot." She counted sponges and instruments and made a note of the total.

"Now Zelda, cut it out. It's not that bad," Weasel chided her as they pushed through the swinging doors into the surgery. "I hope," he added, looking down at the man lying before him.

Sam Beckett had IV needles, BP gauges, tubes down his throat, fluids going in and going out. Sensors were taped to his head, wires trailing over the edge of the operating table to be caught up neatly in a plastic tube. His chest rose and fell in a steady rhythm. His eyes weren't quite closed. The machinery hummed and wheezed.

Zelda, whose first name was not Zelda but whose last name was, unfortunately for her, Fitzgerald, sniffed.

"Let's get cracking, shall we?" she said. "I've got a date tonight, even if nobody else does."

"Yeah, you're bragging," Weasel jeered. But his attention was still on the surgical field. He was standing at the head of the table, and sterile sheeting was draped over everything. The man on the table was no longer famous, no longer Sam Beckett, no longer even a man, but an area of prepared, shaved scalp turning black and blue, with a clearly visible depression in the middle of the bruise. "Vitals?"

In moments the surgical ER was all business, punctuated by the occasional off-topic remark on just what it was Zelda had managed to get a date with. The machines hummed to themselves, making sure that breathing and heartbeat and blood pressure and blood gases remained steady. It might have been moments, but was probably longer, before Weasel laid bare the skull beneath the skin. The bone was pink.

It looked as an egg would, if someone had struck it hard with a pencil: a shallow, concave area, a well filling with blood, visibly cracked, with one or two slender fragments missing. Missing, the surgeon feared, because they had been driven into the brain beneath.

Weasel probed the depression carefully, and grunted with dismay when a fragment of bone shifted under the tip of

26

the scalpel. "I think I'm going to have to go in here and maybe take a bit of a look to see what shape the dura's in," he muttered, almost to himself. "How are we doing?"

"Just fine." Perry James, the anesthesiologist, was paying more attention to his instruments than to the patient. "We're steady and within limits, seventy-five over one hundred ten." As the words came out of his mouth, the machine squawked. "Oh, hell. Oh, *hell*. This is not good. BP's dropping—"

The team swung into emergency status. A controlled frenzy came over them as each person in the room, save one, took the necessary steps to try to bring the patient on the table back from the brink. The clock ticked. They worked. The electroencephalograph readings, reflected on a monitor overhead, jumped and slid crazily. Only one of the operating team happened to be looking at it at the time, and she was too busy to comment.

There was darkness. Pressure. Pain.

It was . . . light, where he was now.

I don't know, Sam said silently. I don't know what I want. I don't know who I am. Where I am or what I'm doing.

I know this is right. I know this has to happen.

But what is "this"?

He was floating in blue-white light, seeking some thread back to reality. For part of him there was no sensation, no weight, scent, taste, nothing but the light surrounding him, bearing him up.

At last the anesthesiologist said, "I've got pressure."

"Stable?"

"Pretty much," the anesthesiologist said. "I think I can keep him going until you close, at least."

"I thought we had flatline," Zelda muttered.

Weasel looked down at the open surgical field, the cracked and splintered bone, the gleam of brain tissue peeking through.

"Get me RPMI," the surgeon said abruptly.

"Get you *what*?" Zelda was incredulous, talking even as she moved. "That's cell-culture medium. What do you want that for?"

27

"I dunno," Weasel said, as he exposed more of the dura mater, the tough membrane surrounding the brain. Meningeal fluid ran along the blade as he sliced through, widening the tear enough to see how deep the splinters went. "Seems like a good idea. I want to . . . I want—"

For another part of him there was the sharp, not unfamiliar smell of antiseptic and sweat and worry, and the relief of someone patting the perspiration from his forehead so it wouldn't run into his eyes and blind him. He had to be able to see. Had to be able to know exactly where the blade was. He could feel the resistance of the membrane before it parted, hear the exclamations as blood under pressure spurted along his thumb and up his sleeve. But the blood didn't go far, and there wasn't too much of it, he thought. Was there?

What am I doing here? he asked silently. What is this? I don't understand!

And answer came there none.

"We'd better put in a drain," Weasel said. "He's got himself quite a hematoma here. Come on, damn it, I asked for some RPMI."

"I'd have to go to Pathology for it," the scrub nurse working with Zelda said.

"Then, damn it, go!"

The other occupants of the surgery exchanged glances over their masks, but the scrub nurse handed a suction tube to Zelda and left, the surgery door sighing shut behind her.

"What, you're trying to clone yourself a Nobel Prizewinner?" the anesthesiologist smirked after a moment.

"I don't know," Weasel said, trying to work an apology into his tone of voice. He *didn't* know. He wasn't even sure what RPMI was. It was as if someone else had spoken through his mouth, asking for something he'd last heard of in medical school. He was a neurosurgeon, not a pathologist. His concern was the brain.

"One more 'I don't know' and we'll get ourselves another neurosurgeon." Zelda's hand hovered over the instruments laid out in a shining row on the sterile white towel. The instrument cart was a little less than elbow height, so as not to

28

be hit accidentally and yet have everything accessible. "Poor baby. I guess maybe he won't get any more Nobel Prizes after this, will he?"

"I *told* you I hated doing the famous ones," Weasel said. "But this one—" he teased a bit of tissue away, looked up at the monitors and allowed himself a sigh of relief—"this one has somebody looking after him. Doesn't look too bad. Not at all."

Zelda slid a glass tube with a screw top, half filled with viscous pink liquid, onto the instrument table beside him. Weasel glanced at it, confused. The pink stuff, that was culture medium. The stuff you grew cells in. Brain cells? You couldn't grow brain cells in culture. Weasel looked again at the brain exposed beneath his knife, the glistening gray matter that controlled breath and movement and life and maybe even that disputable entity called a "mind," and had the kind of flash he always hated having in the middle of an operation: Who was this man? Did he have a wife? Children? Did he love music? Did he have thoughts he was ashamed of, or did he create beautiful things?

That was the problem with the famous ones. You knew the answers.

He knew that if his knife slipped, the sum of human knowledge could be reduced perhaps irreparably. The left temporal lobe controlled speech, the voice. He could suffer seizures for the rest of his life—chronic temporal lobe epilepsy.

Or nothing might happen at all. Nothing noticeable, anyway. Some of the lobe was . . . well, no one quite knew what it was for. You could excise it and never see a difference in the way the patient acted, talked, responded.

No one could really be sure about how they thought, of course.

Light. A tunnel. Wasn't there supposed to be a tunnel, with God or Fate or something at the end of it? There was no direction where he was now. He had no perspective. No way to tell where he was, what he was, who he was. . . .

He reached out, and Zelda slapped the opened tube into his palm.

He teased away a fragment of bone lying across the tear in the dura mater. The fragment was dull with cells.

Cells. Tiny scraps of life.

The scrap of bone dropped into the tube. "Seal that," he said, and held it out, knowing there would be someone there to take it.

There was something about the cells, glossy in the pink fluid sloshing gently in the glass tube lying on the towel— something he needed to do with cells. He needed cells. Any cells would do, but these—these would work best of all.

He couldn't remember what he wanted them for.

The hotel room had cable. The mugging of Dr. Samuel Beckett, noted scientist, Nobel Prizewinner, the man widely regarded as the most intelligent in the world, rated news flashes on all the networks and fifteen minutes on CNN, most of which was taken up by a review of his academic and scientific accomplishments. Al Calavicci tuned in on the last three minutes of the CNN report. He was on the telephone thirty seconds later.

He reached the hospital receptionist, was unable to get a status on a patient in surgery, hung up and tried a flank attack. Years of experience in dealing with the nozzles in Washington bureaucracy came to his aid; two hours and several pulled strings later, a call back told him that Sam was out of surgery and in the recovery room. All his cajoling couldn't get the status of the patient, though.

That was fine. Sometimes a flank attack worked, and sometimes a direct approach was best. Al's next call was to the local air base to find out when the next space-available flight was to Washington.

CHAPTER FIVE

Having an arm in a supported sling turned out to be the perfect disguise for a hospital. Al couldn't quite bring himself to dress in a hospital gown, however, and he was stopped halfway down the surgical ward. To add insult to injury, he was busted by a nurse six feet tall with a thick, ragged reddish mustache.

"Excuse me, sir, can I help you?"

"I'm looking for Sam Beckett."

"Yes, sir. Dr. Beckett isn't receiving visitors yet. Unless—" the nurse looked Al up and down, doubt clear on his face— "you're a family member?"

"Sam Beckett would say so."

The nurse nibbled at the hair over his lip. "I'd ask him, but he isn't in shape to answer just yet."

Al's eyes narrowed. "Just what does that mean?" he said quietly, in a tone of voice that he didn't have to use often. When he did, it sent chills across flight decks throughout the Sixth Fleet.

"He's in Intensive Care, sir," the nurse responded. "He isn't really up to talking."

"I don't have to talk to him. I just want to see him." They moved aside to allow a patient dragging an IV pole to move past them. Family members hovered after.

"Sir, he's getting the very best care, really. He's worked with the doctors here. We all know him." *But we don't know you,* the sentence concluded, unspoken.

Something deep inside Al flinched at the reminder that he really *hadn't* known Sam all his life; it only seemed that way. Sam had friends and acquaintances in whole other universes. Of course the doctors would know him. Sam was a doctor, too. And a classicist. And a physicist. He'd know people in all those fields, from studying with them, reading their research, and having his read by them. Maybe it *was* presumptuous for Al to claim to be as close to him as a member of his family.

Though come to think of it, Sam wasn't all that close to his family in the first place. His mother lived with his sister and her family in Hawaii; there was affection there, but some kind of awkwardness, too. Al wasn't sure about the details. He knew Sam's sister Katie was married to a Navy man, a Lt. Jim Bonnick, and had a couple of kids. Sam rarely spoke of them, giving Al the impression there had been some philosophical conflicts with Bonnick along the way. And Sam had told him once that he'd missed his own father's funeral because of work on a project—not that he was proud of it, he wasn't, but it had happened, and he seemed in some way bewildered and hurt that things hadn't worked in such a way that he could have been in two places at once.

That was all right. There was quite a bit Sam didn't know about Al, either. It didn't matter; they were *friends*. The details were just history. Sam was as close to family as Al had, and he knew Sam felt the same way about him. Yeah, there were some people who might consider that presumptuous.

But Al Calavicci had been presumptuous all his life, and he wasn't about to stop now. "Let me in for just a couple of minutes. I won't disturb him. Hell, I've been a patient myself—" he nodded toward the support splint on his arm— "I know what it's like to want peace and quiet. This is for me, not for him."

"Okay," the nurse said at last. "This way.

"We've had to keep the reporters out," he went on as he led Al down the hall. "It's as much as my job is worth, you know."

32

"That's okay," Al reassured him. "I'm not going to tell the world." They entered a small private room toward the end of the hall.

Like most other hospital rooms, the predominant theme was white. White curtains half-open over the picture window. White walls, white sheets, white metal furniture, white privacy drapes to pull around the bed. Al had eyes for none of it; he was focused on the white bandage covering most of Sam Beckett's head.

"We're keeping a really close eye on him," the nurse whispered, as if the man on the bed would awaken. "He's doing fine, really."

He didn't look fine. He looked as if a vampire had been at him, draining every drop of color from his face, except for shadows like bruises under his eyes. He looked shrunken and vulnerable. One hand lay lax outside the sheet, an IV needle taped into place, a spot of blood on the skin where someone had had to probe twice to hit the vein. Tubes hung from an IV tree, dripping clear liquids into his system. More tubes entered his nostrils, and a larger one entered his mouth, causing a line of spittle to dry on his chin. His lips were dry and cracked.

Wires came from beneath the bandages, from metal disks taped to his head, and led to a strip recorder on a table beside the bed. A cardiac monitor beeped steadily over his head, the spikes and daggers in an ever-repeating pattern of bright green lines on a gray screen. Al had to drag his eyes away from the hypnotic repetitions, as if the sound and pattern were the cause instead of the effect of Sam's still being alive.

"Oh, Sam," Al breathed. "What the hell have you gotten yourself into now?"

He moved awkwardly past the visitor's chair to the side of the bed. The nurse made a protesting noise and subsided. Al looked down at his friend, unable to think of anything more to say or do. He felt almost as helpless as Sam looked, unable to do anything except talk, unable to do anything to affect events. All he could do was watch. Sam lay still, remote.

"They can hear people while they're unconscious, some-times," the nurse offered. "If you want to tell him you're here."

Al seized on the suggestion gratefully. "Sam?" he said quietly, as if still afraid he'd wake the patient up. "It's Al, buddy. I came back after all. Looks like you can't keep out of trouble without me, kid. You need somebody to look after you."

A muscle in Sam's face twitched.

"Do you really hear me?" Al said, wonderingly.

A muscle twitched again, deep in Sam's face.

"He's coming out of the anesthesia," the nurse said, in practical fashion. Moving around to the other side of the bed, he checked the IV flow and the blinking buttons on another machine Al didn't understand, took a swab out of a box on the table and dabbed lemon-smelling gelatin over the patient's lips.

"Already?" It didn't seem possible that someone could have brain surgery and be awake only hours later.

"Well, he isn't going to be on Jeopardy for a few days," the nurse said, coming around the bed again and making a notation on the chart. "But we don't want him to go into a coma, either. Would you like to talk to his doctor?"

"Hell, yes!"

"Well, please don't let him know you've been in here, okay?"

"Yeah, sure." Al paused, studying Sam for more signs of alertness. "Who did this, by the way? I heard it was a mug-ging. Did they catch the—"

The nurse snorted with laughter. The laughter was quickly stifled when it was clear Al wasn't sharing it. "Sorry, sir. It's just that they never seem to catch muggers. Nobody knows who does this stuff. I heard he wasn't even robbed."

A definite grimace twisted across Sam's features.

"Sam?" Al whispered. "Sam, are you in there? Can you hear me, buddy?"

The nurse was looking anxiously at his watch. "Sir, I'm sorry, but—"

"Shaddup!" Al leaned forward, awkwardly. Sam's eyes were opening.

They couldn't have been open for more than a few seconds, and they remained unfocused and glazed with pain. But they were open. Then they closed again. But at least now they didn't look quite so permanently closed.

Al leaned back, weak with momentary relief. "Hey, I better get out of here, huh?" he said, his voice hushed. "Don't want to get you in trouble." He stepped away from the hospital bed, edging back around the visitor's chair, and paused in the doorway. "Better close those curtains," he advised. "He's not going to want a lot of light right at first." As the nurse complied, Al took a quick look at the chart, ignoring the cryptic scribbles to note the surgeon's name, carefully typed in the upper left-hand corner.

With that, he was gone, heading back down the hall to the elevators. He couldn't do anything more right now for his friend.

But he could by God find out everything there was to know about what had happened to him.

The surgeon was Dr. Robert Mikowski, a well-respected neurosurgeon who had years of experience. Al got a summary of Mikowski's qualifications from a starstruck nurse—"He even operated on that Nobel Prizewinner they brought in last night!"—and got the rest of the OR team's names while he was at it.

Mikowski's office was tucked away on the third floor. Al found it by dint of much glaring and well-practiced throwing-around of rank, and caught him as he was getting ready to go home. It was very late by then, and the man was tired; so was Al, and his arm hurt besides, and he didn't give a damn.

Mikowski didn't want to go into details. Al made it clear that he wanted details. Mikowski tried to snow him under with technicalities. Al demanded English.

"There *was* some brain damage," Mikowski admitted finally. He slumped back in his chair and stretched hugely, settled back again, and picked up a gold pencil from the cluttered desk. His desk was piled with books and journals; he had no window. There wasn't room for a window; the parts of the wall not hidden by bookshelves and diplomas and certificates were covered by some very nice landscapes. Original art, Al was sure. "Some swelling, some bleeding. Bone penetration. But we got it under control fast, and the operation went very smoothly."

"I heard you almost lost him on the table," Al said bluntly.

Mikowski blinked, chagrined. "Where did you hear that?"

"It doesn't matter where I heard it. Is it true?" In fact, he'd grilled the scrub nurse. She was sure he was a reporter for one of the tabloids, and had given Weasel a "heads-up" call to warn him. Mikowski knew better, but recognized in his visitor the same dogged determination to find out.

Mikowski took a deep breath and kept his eyes on the pencil turning over and over between his fingers. "Admiral Calavicci, I don't normally have discussions like this, and I don't believe I'm required to answer your questions. What did or did not happen in that operating room is insignificant beside the fact that Dr. Beckett is now responding very well."

He looked up. "Believe me, Admiral, we are giving Sam Beckett the very best care there is. Nobody in this hospital wants to lose him. Not just because we don't want to see headlines saying, 'Nobel Prize Winner Dies at Our Lady of Mercy.' But because a lot of us know him personally, and we know what kind of man he is. We have doctors here who were in medical school with him."

Al raised an eyebrow. "Were you one of them? Did you know him?"

Mikowski shook his head. "No, I didn't have that privilege. I wouldn't have been the one to operate on him if I did. But I assure you I did the best job any neurosurgeon could do, and the patient's response shows that." He set the gold pencil down on the green felt desk pad and knitted his fingers loosely together. "Will that be all?"

"You said there was brain damage. Does that mean . . ." Al paused, unable to formulate the next thought in words. The image of Sam Beckett living life as a vegetable was more than he could stand.

The surgeon sighed a little. It had to be the fear every patient, every patient's friend and relative had when they spoke to a man who took knives to the brain. "We can't tell at this point," he said. "There was some swelling, yes. But it and the damaged area were in a part of the brain we call 'silent,' meaning we can't identify any particular cognitive function which it controls. In addition, the damage which was suffered—we call it the 'insult'—was much less extensive than you may have heard. There may be no aftereffects at all. Certainly motor skills shouldn't be affected, and things like speech, that kind of thing."

"But you don't know where Sam Beckett's genius resides, do you?" Al challenged. "You don't know if he'll still be able to do the kinds of things he did before."

Mikowski pursed his lips, giving himself a more than fleeting resemblance to a ferret or other small predator. "Admiral, we don't even know what the hell genius *is*. Give me a break here. All I can address is how well the operation went. Yes, we did have a scare, though if you ever tell anybody I said that I'll deny it. I don't know what makes a human being a *particular* human being, and I don't think anybody else does either. Some of my colleagues think that we're biological organisms, period, and what we call "mind" and "soul" is just a function of the gray cells. If that's true, then there might be changes. There'd almost have to be. But if the human mind is more than the sum of the axons and neurons and proteins and all of that—then you're talking to the wrong kind of doctor. I'm a mechanic, Admiral. I can guarantee you that the engine's going to keep on running, absent any more disasters. It's going to look the same. Whether it *is* the same, now, that's metaphysical, and if you've got any more questions in that area, the chapel's down the hall."

He set down the pencil with a snap. Al studied him a moment longer, evaluating what he'd just heard, and then got up, thanked him, and left.

37

Behind him, Weasel Mikowski picked up the gold pencil again and tapped it against his teeth. Maybe the chapel was where he ought to be going, too. He had some questions about that operation himself. The cell cultures now safely residing in nitrogen carriers in the Path lab were among them. Why did he take those bits of bone, anyway? Normally they were just thrown away, biowaste, detritus of human tragedy. Something else had made him preserve it. Some urge to save something of the original Sam Beckett? Zelda had teased him about cloning, but—not out of brain cells. He'd read somewhere, in one of the journals sliding off the top of his desk, about some progress in preserving adult brain cells, but they couldn't be coaxed to reproduce yet. Could they?

He dug out the latest *Journal of Neurology and Psychophysiology*, curious suddenly, and skimmed the close type of the table of contents.

There *was* an article. "Some Observations on a Computer Simulation Study on the Preservation of Mature Brain Cells in Specialized Culture Media."

By Samuel Beckett, M.D., Ph.D.

Mikowski shuddered and pushed the journal away. It was very late, and he was going to go home and go to bed.

Three days later, the Nonluddites had issued a press release about the savage attack on a man who represented the hope of the human race, who had achieved the "present pinnacle of human achievement, without whose unceasing work on technological advances the sum of human happiness would be unacceptably reduced." Al Calavicci read the edited version in the *Washington Post* and shook his head. Boy, was he going to give Sam all kinds of hell on this one. "The sum of human happiness"? Sam Beckett? The guy who made him swear off boilermakers?

There were other remarks too, some obviously made before the interviewee was quite sure whether Sam would make it or not. They had a distinctly elegiac tone to them.

The word triggered a flood of memory. Al sagged back against the straight-back chair in his temporary quarters and closed his eyes, surrendering to it as he rarely allowed himself to surrender.

"Elegiac." That was a word Sam had defined for him once, poking gentle fun at his engineering vocabulary. "A poem, expressing sorrow or mourning, in classical distichs, with the first line in dactylic hexameter and the second line in pentameter. From Greek, Al. *Elegeiakos*. *Gray's Elegy in a Country Churchyard*. C'mon, Al."

"Give me a break, Sam. If I can't fly it, what do I care?"

And Sam had laughed and listened to him talk about astronaut training. Really listened. Sam could have recited every word of the conversation verbatim a year later, if he wanted to. He had one of those photographic memories. He'd had the funniest-looking office at Project Star Bright; it had no books. None at all. And no reports, no stacks of papers.

Once Al had realized what was different, he'd asked Sam. Sam had been a little embarrassed about it. He didn't need the books and reports, he said. He'd read them. All he had to do was read something once, hear something once, and he could remember it forever.

Al had made him recite six pages of the last budget report verbatim before he'd believed. And for months after that he'd challenge him, try to catch Sam off guard. It never worked.

But one day he'd caught Sam reading a science fiction novel he was sure he'd seen him reading before. It was a collection of short stories by Heinlein.

"That's different," Sam had tried to explain. "I'm not trying to remember it. I'm discovering it again."

He'd tried to explain the story—something about bootstraps—but Al was too interested in the idea that Sam could turn his memory on and off. Al had done that a time or two himself, and found it very convenient when dealing with angry ex-wives, but Sam shook his head. No. He *always* could remember. He was just choosing not to.

Al hoped the surgeon was very lucky. The alternative was that Mikowski was wrong about how successful the operation was, and if that was the case Mikowski would be very *un*lucky. And that would be a real shame, but Al Calavicci had certain ancestral standards that he could draw upon when it came to friendship, and in this case he would.

He shook himself. This wasn't the time or place for dark bloody thoughts of revenge on the *surgeon,* for Chrissake. Mikowski had done his best. He had to accept it. His sources said Sam was clinically dead for a while there, on that operating table, and Al wanted somebody to pay for that. But there was no sense in taking it out on the man who saved his life. Sam *was* getting better, Al could tell. Al checked on him, in between visits to the Washington police department to review the case file and harass old friends on the police force.

He still had business of his own to take care of while he was in Washington, too—some trifling nonsense about finalizing a financial settlement, retiring from the Navy. It was going to take some time. But he added at least one more task to his personal agenda: If there was any way to find out what really happened to Sam Beckett, to make sure that it really was nothing more than a stupid and irrational incident, he was going to do it. He was owed some favors by people who were good at finding things out. He was going to try his best to collect.

Sam was awake most times, and could even talk a little, phrases and short sentences that left him white with exhaustion. The third time Al had come by, Sam wanted to know why he was in the hospital. He couldn't remember the attack. For a moment Al had panicked. Mikowski, standing at his elbow, tried to assure Al that it was normal to lose short-term memory after such a trauma, but it wasn't until Sam recited, slowly and with much effort, the relevant pages of the textbook at him that Al relaxed—and he'd checked the book in Mikowski's office before he'd left the hospital to make sure. He'd be on the phone yet again to Sam's mother and sister in Hawaii, giving them daily updates on how he was doing. They were concerned, of course, but Al was trying his best to assuage their fears, convince them that the news media had exaggerated. Unless Sam was actually at death's door, he didn't think they'd come out to see him. It was a long way, after all, and Mrs. Beckett was in her seventies, and frail. And Katie would want to stay with her.

But if Sam's priorities had held him to his work when his own father died, it wasn't too surprising that now his mother and sister were reluctant to travel halfway around the world to be with him when Al was doing his level best to convince them that Sam was really just fine, it wasn't nearly as serious as it sounded, he was okay. . . .

He would be, Al swore fiercely. He *would* be.

Sam seemed to think it was interesting *not* being able to remember something. Trust Sam Beckett to find something intellectually challenging about getting mugged. . . .

But he should never have had to go through this mess to begin with. Al Calavicci didn't have so many friends in the world, either, that he could afford to lose one to as stupid and irrational an incident as this one. Nobody did. And he wasn't going to lose Sam Beckett, not now to a mugger, not ever, damn it.

CHAPTER
SIX

Judith Dreasney followed the reports on Sam Beckett's medical condition in the morning paper as they progressed, as the weeks passed, from front page to a small paragraph on the bottom of the last page of the local section. She drank in the news with her first cup of coffee, from "critical" in July to "guarded," then "stable" in August, to "expected to be released momentarily" as the Labor Day holiday came and went. Her aides learned to circle the updates and have the paper open to the appropriate page.

"It would be observed favorably," Yen Hsuieh-lung remarked to her during a meeting in the Senate Office Building one week before Sam Beckett's scheduled release, "if you were to provide tangible support to your belief that Dr. Beckett's faculties have been unimpaired."

Dreasney snorted. "What kind of 'tangible support' would that be?" she wanted to know. Every once in a while Yen Hsuieh-lung seemed to think he was Fu Manchu instead of a product of third-generation Chinese-American parents and an education at UC Berkeley and Stanford. It was extremely irritating.

"Dr. Beckett's proposal for the supercomputer, of course." Hsuieh-lung lit a cigarette, in defiance of the rules against smoking in government buildings, and smiled thinly through a veil of smoke. "You should support this."

"Dr. Beckett's proposal has been classified topmost secret," she retorted. "Nobody'd be *able* to observe my support, favorably or otherwise. It wouldn't exist."

"*I* would know," Hsuieh-lung pointed out. "And I have influence in certain . . . quarters."

Dreasney stared at him. "Why? What are you getting out of this? I thought you hated his guts, ever since he killed off Star Bright."

Hsuieh-lung tilted his head back and gazed dreamily at the ceiling. "Ah, what I think of his guts does not matter. We disagreed profoundly about Star Bright, true. But what matters is his mind and what he can do with it, and I stand second to no man in my admiration for his mind. No one else can develop this computer."

"If it *can* be developed," the woman said, shoving aside a stack of summaries. "I think it's bull, myself. Cancer cells, or whatever it is, in computers—ridiculous."

His head tilted forward again. "Do you really think so, Senator? Do you have the background in medicine, in physics, in mathematics, in philosophy to begin to be able to make such a judgment? No one else in the world has the particular combination of disciplines to be able to visualize this concept. In fact, I would go so far as to say that to Dr. Beckett this may be a relatively trivial project."

"What's *that* supposed to mean?"

Hsuieh-lung exhaled a stream of smoke directly into her face, causing her to sneeze.

"I mean," he said imperturbably, "that everything Sam Beckett has ever done, his life long, has built toward something. Something incredible. And I do not believe that inventing a new kind of computer is his final goal."

"So what do you think his final goal *is*?" she demanded, waving smoke away. "And why do you want me to support it?"

"I don't know," her visitor said at last, unwillingly. "But I am, shall we say . . . most anxious . . . to find out what, given sufficient resources, Sam Beckett is capable of.

"I don't think he knows himself. But whatever one man can discover, another can use. It has always been so, has it not?"

43

He smiled gently. Mysteriously.

After a moment she smiled too. You little slimy monster, she thought. You think you're good enough to take and use what John Beckett's boy can create? We'll see. We'll just see about that.

THE SUPERINTENDENT OF THE

UNITED STATES NAVAL OBSERVATORY

AND ITS STAFF AND CREW

REQUESTS THE PLEASURE OF YOUR COMPANY

AT THE RETIREMENT CEREMONY OF

REAR ADMIRAL

(ASTRONAUT)

ALBERT M. CALAVICCI

UNITED STATES NAVY

ON FRIDAY, THE SEVENTH OF SEPTEMBER

AT TEN O'CLOCK

CENTER COURT YARD, U.S. NAVAL OBSERVATORY

34TH AND MASSACHUSETTS AVENUE, N.W.

WASHINGTON, D.C.

R.S.V.P.   UNIFORM:

CARD ENCLOSED   FULL DRESS WHITE

It was hot and miserably humid in Washington, D.C., on September 7, 1990. The National Weather Bureau had been promising rain, or at least clouds, for the past week, but the temperature had stayed obstinately in the high eighties. It reflected the temperature of world events, Al thought, as he checked his dress sword once more. Al Calavicci had taken a long thoughtful look in the mirror that morning. He still *looked* like a military man, with the medals and the cap and the spit-shined shoes and the white gloves and the dress sword. He looked like the kind of man who ate shavetail lieutenants for breakfast, and picked his teeth with their commanders. He looked hard and tough and sure of himself; a leader of men, a commander of ships, a pilot of jets, an astronaut. He had to resist the urge to salute himself. As he'd realized it, he'd grinned, and the illusion shattered. This was it. Retirement day.

Still, with war ready to break out in the Middle East, maybe this wasn't such a good time to retire after all.

Oh well. It was too late now. When the President of the United States made a special point of stopping off in between his Maine vacation and flying off to a conference in Helsinki to meet with Gorbachev, you didn't mess with the schedule. Besides, the Exec was asking the guests to rise and render honors, and that meant it was *really* too late to back out.

They piped Rear Admiral Voss aboard—well, aboard the stage, at least—and then it was Al's turn, followed by Hollings, Trost, Senators MacBride and Glenn, and then the President; they all stood at attention for the Parading of the Colors, the National Anthem, and the Invocation, and then the Exec introduced Voss and they finally got to sit down.

And then, of course, the speeches, from Trost, Glenn, and finally Bush. They were short, at least. Trost and Glenn managed not to make any embarrassing personal references, and the President kept his remarks to a minimum, probably worried more about Saddam Hussein than a soon-to-be-ex-Rear Admiral (Astronaut).

And then they called him front and center, and Master Chief Yeoman DeGailler nobly refrained from taking her last chance to publicly give him hell for all the grief he'd given yeomen all through his career—not that she would, of course, not in such a solemn, official occasion, but when she presented the flag and a shadow box on behalf of the Star Gazer Chief Petty Officers and stepped back to salute, she winked at him, and he grinned despite himself.

And then the plaques, the reading of the citations, the presentation of the Navy Commendation Medal. Al listened with half an ear for his next cue. It had been a long and distinguished career, all right. Twenty-nine years, starting out as an enlisted man, coming up through the ranks as a mustang, getting an education the hard way. He'd lost six of those years as a POW, and that loss would always mark him. But it was a career that had taken him all the way to space, and he couldn't regret it.

The audience was made up of friends and acquaintances he'd acquired over the length of that career, with one notable exception: no matter how hard he'd argued, the hospital hadn't released Sam yet. Monday, they said; but regs said he had to retire the first week of the month, and that was that. He'd wanted Sam to be there, a kind of witness to a rite of passage, but neither the Navy nor the hospital was inclined to cooperate. He sighed. The President, sitting to his right, heard him and made some inconsequential remark.

And now it was his turn to stand before the assembled visitors and make his own speech. A short one, mercifully, with references to the changing global tensions and the need for eternal vigilance, his pride in service and his confidence in the officers and men—and women, he amended hastily, Claudia was gonna kill him after all—of the United States Navy.

And then the Executive Officer read his orders, and he requested permission to go ashore for the last time. Permission granted, the Executive Officer announced to the assembly, "Rear Admiral, United States Navy, Retired, departing."

And DeGailler rang six bells, and the Boatswain's Mate piped the quarterdeck as he walked between the side boys rendering his last official salute, and the bell rang again.

There was the benediction, and the colors were retired, and the band played Anchors Aweigh, but it was already done. It was over. All but the shouting, as his father used to say.

Well. Except for the parties, of course.

It was late, very late. Or very early, if you wanted to look at it that way. It was still hot and muggy, even at 0300 hours, and the dress whites weren't nearly as crisp as they'd started out to be, the morning before.

He was proud of himself, though. For years he'd believed that his retirement party—the real party, not the official reception—would be the biggest, most drunken, loudest blowout party he'd ever hosted. And it was, too. He was willing to bet that if he hadn't been an admiral, the SPs would have arrested everybody in sight. But *he*, Al Calavicci, had had *one* glass of wine, and he was by damn sober. This time, he'd gotten to see everybody *else* making fools of themselves.

And now he'd send the uniform out one last time, get it cleaned, and put it away in blue plastic in the back of the closet. It would come out again only on the most special of occasions. He started removing the medals, the Navy Cross with the combat V, the Distinguished Flying Cross, Purple Heart, Air Medal, commendations, achievements, citations, multiple awards. His fingers paused and fumbled a bit at the P.O.W. Medal, then moved on: National Defense Service, RVN Campaign, all the rest. Four rows of medals across the left breast, a row of ribbons, three across, on the right. And the Medal of Honor, of course, depending from the ribbon around his neck. A "distinguished career" the speakers had said, over and over again. Damn right it was.

Shaking his head, laughing at himself, he peeled off the gloves and began to strip down. In a very few minutes the dazzling uniform was a pile of clothes on the iron-frame bed, lying in a heap beside a much more carefully placed sword and stack of citations, certificates, and of course the shadow box.

It wasn't his uniform anymore. Well, in a way it was; he'd have salt in his soul for the rest of his life. The Navy did that to you, claimed you for its own and never really let go. But he was a civilian now. A *civilian*.

Civilians were alien beings, and now he was one of them.

It was the end of a lifetime, and the beginning of a new life.

He paused in the process of removing the honors and insignia from the jacket to wince and rub his arm. It still ached. He'd finally gotten out of the cast and splints and associated supports only a month ago. He still, four months after the injury, had a physical therapy routine to follow; it left the arm shaking with fatigue, the muscles quivering. But it was getting better, and he wasn't going to quit until he had the full use of it. He finished removing everything that could be removed and carefully stored it all away in a satin-lined box.

He had a room in Bachelor Officers' Quarters for the night. He was footloose, fancy free, no commitments—except to make sure the Washington police department didn't move Sam's case to the back burner, which it seemed more than likely they were trying to do—and his retirement was committed to his ex-wives. He needed a job.

But he had plans.

So did Sam.

He swept the uniform, now completely denuded of spinach, off the bed in a gesture that he would have considered shockingly disrespectful the day before, shifted the sword and the presentations to one side, and flopped down to think. He had to go shopping, first of all. He had to . . .

It was very late, or very early. In moments, his thoughts were punctuated by snores.

"Well, buddy, today's the day. You ready?"

Sam smiled wearily. "I guess so."

Al surveyed him critically. Sam's hair had mostly grown back to its accustomed medium length, but now there was a streak of white in the brown at the left temple. He was pale—he'd been in for quite a while, longer, maybe, than strictly necessary, and out of the sunlight. For the last month, Sam had been on his feet, wandering unsteadily around the hospital, talking to the surgeons, popping up in the most unexpected places. Even in Pathology, the nurses had told Al. He'd spent a lot of time down in Pathology.

He was thinner than usual, too, which meant he was very thin indeed. Al decided their first stop would be a really good restaurant. Always assuming, of course, that they made it through the gauntlet of reporters outside.

"What are you staring at?" he asked, abruptly registering the look on Sam's face.

"You," Sam said simply. "*What* are you wearing?"

"A tie. You like it?" Al held out the purple-and-pink creation for Sam to examine. Sam declined, an appalled expression on his face. Overreaction, Al thought; the purple matched his shirt exactly, and was one shade darker than his suit. It

48

coordinated perfectly, and he saw no grounds for criticism. So it wasn't white or navy blue—that was the point, after all.

"Amazing," Sam muttered.

"Yeah, isn't it?" Al said happily. "Here, let me take that bag. And what's that thing?"

Sam was holding a small blue plastic box, perhaps six inches on a side, very close to his chest. "Some cultures," he said briefly.

"Well, let me take it."

"No. No, thanks, I'll carry this one. I'm not helpless." Sam looked uncharacteristically awkward. He was dressed in the clothing Al had rescued from his hotel room, so many months before, and it was a bit large for him now. That, plus the box, made him look younger than his years, like a kid with a security blanket.

"Okay." Al switched the bag to his right hand. "Have you gotten your release?"

"Signed my life away," Sam snorted. "Yeah, let's get this show on the road."

Al waved to the nurses as they went past the station, and Sam gave them a grin, and they applauded as the two men went down the hall and into the elevator. Once in, Sam leaned back against the wall and let out a deep breath.

"Lord, I'm glad to be out of here," he said. "And Al— thanks."

Al shrugged, instantly uncomfortable. "For what? I didn't do anything. Listen, I know where we can—"

But the elevator doors opened, and they stepped out into a crowd of reporters and photographers, glaring lights and cameras and microphones held up into their faces.

"Dr. Beckett! Dr. Beckett! Do you feel you've completely recovered?"

"What progress have the police made—?"

"Have the police identified your attacker?"

"Will your injury affect your research?"

Sam was speechless, holding one hand up to protect himself against the lights and clutching the box to his chest with the other.

49

"Hey, back off!" Al was in front of him, quivering like an enraged terrier, and even Washington's press corps backed off half a step before surging forward again.

Half a step was all Al needed. He used elbows and shoulders without fear or favor, and Sam, still silent, kept close behind.

Behind them, set up as a diversionary tactic, Weasel Mikowski was talking about a press conference, holding official-looking papers—blank forms—up before the slavering pack. At least a third of them decided to go for the easy prey, and that was enough for Al to get Sam out the door and into the waiting limousine.

They sprawled back into opposite seats as the car pulled away, and grinned at each other. After a moment Sam laughed. "I haven't had that much attention since I went to Stockholm," he said. "I hope it won't always be like this."

"Nah, you're the flavor of the month," Al said. "If Millie the Mutt has puppies, those nozzles will be beating down the White House doors, and you're nothing."

Sam shook his head, still chuckling. "Okay, now what?"

"Now you're going to get a decent meal. Then you're going to go back to your hotel—they kept your stuff for you, but it's a different room, of course—and you're going to get some rest without a nurse hovering over you." Al looked over his friend critically. "You feeling okay?"

The chuckle softened to a smile; the smile faded, and one lean hand came up to brush against his left temple and the streak of white that marked where he'd been struck. "I'm okay," he said. "A little tired, that's all."

"Well, relax." Al checked his watch, touched a lever to lower the window enough to peek out and sniff the breeze. He wanted a cigar in the worst way, but he'd wait. It probably wouldn't be fair to subject a convalescent to an El Supremo. "It's going to be a good twenty minutes before we get where we're going."

"Okay." Sam put the box down on the floor of the vehicle beside him and lay back on the seat. He kept one hand on the box at all times.

Twenty minutes later, as promised, the limo purred to a stop. Sam had fallen into an uneasy doze, and Al nudged him awake with some reluctance.

"Hey, pal, rise and shine. We're here."

"Where's here?" Sam mumbled.

"Best Italian restaurant in Washington, D.C."

It was, too. It was a hole-in-the-wall place, with spotless linen tablecloths and the back wall covered by a wine rack— "That's the *vino di casa*, Sam, the really good stuff is in the cellars." Al was on a first-name basis with waiters, cashiers, owners, and probably the dishwashers, and rattled on in fluent Italian with everyone who came by the table to say hello. Greetings were brief, though, and they were left alone. Even the other diners only glanced their way and kept their distance, much to Sam's relief. He settled into the dimness, listening to Verdi piped softly over hidden loudspeakers, and allowed himself to relax a little at last, luxuriating in a place that smelled of something besides antiseptics and sick people.

The waiter came by with a basket of bread, laid open the covering cloth to let the warm odor of garlic fill their nostrils. Al rattled off an order, not bothering to ask Sam what he wanted. Sam watched with something like horror as Al poured a small pool of extra-virgin olive oil in his butter plate and sprinkled pepper on it, dabbed the crusty hot bread in it and ate with a look of sheer bliss on his face. "Hey," Al said, once he opened his eyes again. "You butter *your* bread."

"That's pure cholesterol!"

"It is not," Al responded indignantly. "The lasagne, now, *that* might be. But not this." He sopped another piece, offered it to Sam.

Sam tried it, grimaced, and went back to his own, plain piece. It was good bread, even without butter. "I appreciate your doing all this, Al," he said hesitantly. "I mean, spending all that time and . . . everything."

"I didn't spend *all* that time," Al corrected. "I went to Perliasca's banquet. I did stuff of my own. Hey, most of

51

it was here in Washington anyway. Don't flatter yourself, buddy."

"Memorial . . . ?"

Al filled him in on the past few months, distancing himself even more from the image of Italian mother guarding sole offspring. Sam listened, absorbed. He hadn't paid much attention to current events while in the hospital.

"Okay," Al concluded. "That's what's been going on. Now that you're out of sickbay, can we have that discussion we were going to have back in June? What's this project about, anyway?"

Sam closed his eyes. "The project that's gone down the tubes by now, you mean? They've probably canceled the whole thing."

Al took a sip of Chianti. He had allowed himself a single glass, to celebrate, and was rationing even that. "I wouldn't bet on that. Tell me."

Taking a deep breath, Sam leaned forward. "It's a proposal out of Star Bright. You remember those equations I was working on?"

The waiter came then, with orders of lasagne and fettucine con pollo sprinkled with pine nuts, and they changed the subject while the server fussed with plates. He left, and they resumed their conversation.

"Good grief, which equations?" Al said, digging in. He was no longer playing the role of buddy who was conveniently around when needed; it was an image that had never fitted him anyway. He was interested, intensely so. "You were always working on something."

"The computer, Al. The computer that can—" he whispered the words—"can trace time."

His companion froze for a moment. "I thought that was just a joke. That you were putting me on."

Sam shook his head. "I don't joke about things like that. I can do it, Al. I know I can. It's going to be a quantum leap forward in our understanding of time, of entropy, of artificial intelligence. It will use a new way of organizing reality. It's what we needed *before* Star Bright, why I couldn't get Star

Bright to work. I didn't realize it then, but we needed a computer that wasn't constrained by binary logic, by existing languages. We really needed the computer I always wanted to build anyway, one that can measure probability sets instead of just probabilities, one that can work the way the human brain works. It's *important*, Al." His voice was low, intense. It made Al draw back.

"No computer can see the past," his companion muttered, stabbing a scrap of pasta. "Parallel processing won't do it. It can't be done."

"*I* can do it," Sam said. "If I can get the support. The funding. I can do it."

"You can do almost *anything*. If they don't go for this, there are lots of things you can do."

"You don't believe me, do you?"

There was a long pause as Al scraped cheese to the center of his plate. Finally he capitulated. "I believe you can do anything you say you can. If you say you can build a computer that lets us see the past, the real past as it happens—" he sighed—"then you can do it, that's all. Even if it sounds crazy."

Sam heaved a sigh of relief.

"I just don't understand *why*, that's all," Al added.

Sam took another piece of bread, dipped it in the remains of the olive oil on the plate beside his friend, and bit into it without a hint of distaste. "Sometimes you just have to know what happened before to understand what's happening now," he said at last. "There's so much to explain." He took another bite. "I talked to the administrative people, but I'm not good at that. I need your help, Al. I can't do it without you."

Al looked at the bread, dripping yellow oil, and Sam, and his mouth twisted. "Yeah?"

"Yeah." Sam put the bread aside. "Help me, Al."

"So what d'you think I've been doing the last three months?" Al said, smirking. "I've got some contacts. There are meetings lined up. . . ."

CHAPTER

SEVEN

There was one more thing Sam Beckett had to do before leaving Washington, the same task he carried out every time he came in. Everything else was done. Al had come through in royal fashion, performing miracles and slaying dragons in the dungeons of bureaucracy, and somehow had found adequate funding and personnel for the next fiscal year. He could go to New Mexico and get started, taking the Star Bright site and going into Phase-I construction on his new project. It was going to be more than top secret, if there was such a thing; the government patrons of Project Quantum Leap probably had visions of military uses.

That wouldn't happen. It was *his* design, and they weren't going to be able to use it for military purposes. He was going to maintain control of this computer as no scientist had ever been able to maintain control before.

The air was beginning to cool with the first hint of autumn. He lifted his face to sniff the breeze, trying to smell something, anything past the pervasive odor of water and automobile exhaust. The cherry trees on the Mall were losing the rich green of their leaves. Soon the leaves would turn yellow and sere, loosening their grip on the branches, swirling in the wind like unheard answers. The sky was cloudy after weeks of relentless sunshine.

He spared a thought to the last time he'd stood alone outside a building in late afternoon, and glanced around. But there were people around this time. He wasn't alone. He wasn't vulnerable. Not the same way he'd been before.

It was a long walk down the Mall, past the museums and the monuments, the slowly trolling tourist cars, across Seventeenth Street, on the grass between the Reflecting Pool and the lake. Long familiarity with the path told him that the route he followed took quite a while. He could have driven, or taken a cab.

He always walked. It was a way of delaying things, he supposed, when he allowed himself to think about what he was doing, where he was going. He tried not to think; he occupied his mind instead in reviewing the equations, the drawings, the plans. It was a source of intense frustration that he could see it all, *there,* complete in his mind, and yet he was going to have to wait for concrete and silicon and paper—and, yes, other people—to catch up to him.

It had always been that way. He'd learned early, so early, not to show impatience with other people. The high school teachers, trying to teach him how to do the calculus he'd been doing since he was five. The music teachers, giving him tips on how to remember long pieces when he'd *seen* them once and could recall them ever after, like a sharp, clear photograph in front of him.

And the other kids, who thought he was showing off, being teacher's pet because he couldn't help knowing the right answer every time. He'd learned, finally, not to have all the answers all the time. But it was still hard to talk to other people. It would always be hard, he supposed, even if he couldn't understand why he couldn't quite seem to connect. He couldn't with his father, finally. He couldn't with Donna.

Sometimes, even with the IQ of a certified genius and six doctorates, fluency in seven modern languages and four dead ones, "that's the way things are" was the best he could do for an explanation.

It wasn't enough.

He could see his destination now. It was deceptive, from this angle, looking as if it were farther away than it really was.

55

The main processing chips would be different, really different. They wouldn't even look like normal chips. He'd use a diamond substrate. There were still some problems, though. He'd have to think it through. *If* the cultures were still working . . .

He hugged the blue box closer to himself. It was never out of his sight, out of his reach. It was the key. Slender cylinders in liquid nitrogen, holding pinkness and rare earths. Holding gray cells.

Conventional wisdom said that what he had planned couldn't be done, that it was flatly impossible. Maybe it was; he hadn't had a chance to examine the cultures yet. Something could have gone wrong. If it had, he wasn't sure *what* he would do; he'd never have a chance like this one again—he hoped.

He was only a stone's throw from the Potomac river now, walking through Constitution Gardens.

A few other people were scattered here and there, not paying any attention to him. He passed one woman of his own age or a little older, holding a fistful of daisies and crying softly, standing in the middle of a patch of grass. Normally he would have stopped, gone over to her and asked her what was the matter, how could he help. Here, he knew what the matter was. He knew that nothing could help. Nothing could change things. Not here.

He kept going, walking toward the white statue of the seated man, his fingers white too where he gripped his plastic box.

It began out of nothing, out of the earth, a fault in the land where the ground dropped abruptly, leaving the sheared surface glossy, smooth, black. It kept rising, the gloss interrupted by lines. Letters. Words. Names. Hundreds, thousands of names. Names separated only by the larger numbers that were the years, 1965, 1966, 1967 . . . He kept going.

The grass was clipped even and close along the narrow gutter at the base. Out of the corner of his eye, as he passed others come to see, to touch, he could see himself reflected in the polished darkness, a blur without substance, as if only the Wall itself had reality in this place. Someone had stuck a scrap of paper in a seam in the stone. Someone else had left a pair of baby shoes, nestled in the lawn like an Easter egg treasure waiting to be found. There were many, many flowers.

He began reciting log tables to himself, sing-song under his breath, trying to keep the image of the table six places ahead of the numbers he was whispering. It was difficult to concentrate. He kept seeing a smiling face in front of him, but no one here was smiling.

There were children, teenagers, standing back awkwardly while their parents—mostly their mothers, but some fathers, too—stood silent in front of the monument. The teenagers were too young to remember. They hadn't even been born yet. Some of them were even old enough to be parents themselves, and were bringing a third generation to look and wonder. One man held up a little girl to stretch, to press her fingers against cool stone. Grandchildren, he realized with a familiar shock. Grandchildren are making the pilgrimage now. Farther away some played tag among the trees, their laughter a dissonant music in this place.

He swallowed a surge of irrational anger that he had no children to bring. There had never been a chance for children; the laughter represented one more lost opportunity, one more empty future. He paused between steps to control the sudden rage, knowing anger was easier to feel than sorrow.

A man in late middle age and a wheelchair rolled by, his empty gray tweed pants legs pinned up to keep them from flopping into the spokes. Sam stepped aside to make way for him. The man had neatly trimmed hair and a short beard and wore aviator glasses, hiding his eyes; he had an open whiskey bottle cradled in his lap. He paused by the wall and stretched up, his fingers brushing against the black stone. Settling back with a sigh, he took the bottle by the neck and upended it, pouring perhaps an ounce of whiskey into a brown patch of grass. Sam had seen him there before, always performing the same libation, always in silence. Having made his offering, the man backed the chair around with the ease of years of practice and pushed away, still in silence.

57

Someone had left a medal case at the base of the wall, propped open to show a bald eagle circled in barbed wire, depending from a ribbon with a wide black band down the center and alternating thin stripes of red, white, and blue on either side. Next to it was someone's combat boot, a hole ripped in the side. Some distance away a bearded, bald man wearing jungle fatigues kissed an envelope and wedged it into the crack separating the panels. He was weeping.

It was his turn, now. He had no rituals to perform here, except to come, and stand, and like all the others to reach out and touch the name carved silver in the black stone. The stone was cold. With the feel of it, he had to remember, and mere numbers could not keep the memories back.

Basketball. That was always the first memory. Team practice and Coach bringing in someone new to play, someone wearing a gorilla mask to show them they shouldn't be intimidated by mere looks—the important thing was always the person behind the mask, behind the appearance. And the hug, when the mask came off and he could see who the other man really was—he could still feel the hug. His brother's hug. Brotherly love.

It wasn't all happiness. He could remember too the fights, wrestling across the barn floor practically under the cows' udders, and the time he'd been beaten so badly Tom had been ashamed, had taken him for his first lessons in jujitsu.

Tom had been sorry for that, the next time they wrestled. Sam could still see the expression on his face.

He remembered teaching his older brother to play chess.

He remembered his older brother telling him how to handle himself on his first date, with Judy Engstrom.

He remembered it all, all of it, too damned well. He hated it, he could pick any image, any memory out of the past and see it, see it as clear as if Tom were there, in front of him, warm, alive, smiling. . . .

Instead of the cool black stone, and the name, one of the thousands of names.

Thomas Andrew Beckett.

He touched it, as he always touched it, with his eyes closed, lightly, running his fingertips along the grooves of the letters, as if he couldn't believe them.

They never changed.

"I'm sorry," he whispered, as he always did, every time he came. That, too, never changed.

Then he turned away, walking back through the gardens past the other mourners, hugging the blue box to his chest.

SPRING, 1993

. . . Dr. Sam Beckett led an elite group of scientists into the desert to develop a top-secret Project known as Quantum Leap. . . .

What I mean by living to one's self is living in the world, as in it, not of it. . . . It is to be a silent spectator of the mighty scene of things; . . . to take a thoughtful, anxious interest or curiosity in what is passing in the world, but not to feel the slightest inclination to make or meddle with it.

—William Hazlitt
On Living to One's Self, 1839

CHAPTER
EIGHT

"They're complaining about the noise in Taos again, you know," Al Calavicci announced, setting aside a news magazine. It was the middle of the first shift, and like half the workers on the Project, Sam and Al had stopped for lunch. At Al's suggestion, they'd gone to the cafeteria rather than working through at their desks, just for the change of scenery. "They say it's driving dogs crazy. Are we driving dogs crazy?"

Sam gave the idea careful consideration. "I don't think so," he said cautiously. "I can't think of any reason it should."

The noise in question, a low throbbing sound from the generators and the prototype computer they powered, had made the local news media again, and was a tabloid seven days' wonder. The people working at the Project either learned to ignore it or quit very quickly.

"They've got a team from Los Alamos and Sandia and the military investigating it. I hope they know better than to look in this direction."

"I don't think they will," Sam said, losing interest. "I have contacts inside the Labs. I wouldn't worry about it."

"That's good." Al got up from the metal table and got another cup of coffee from the machine in the alcove. "I'd hate to have to explain ourselves to the media as well as those guys from the investigation crew. They'd want to know why *they* weren't given this project."

"They couldn't do it," Sam said, without a trace of egotism. "I don't work for them."

Al, who had heard the remark in much the same spirit someone from one of the Labs in question would have, snorted quietly. Scientists, in his opinion, could be as much prima donnas as any artist. He was grateful his own doctorate was in aeronautical engineering, a trade where people could actually get their hands dirty. "O-kay. So what's on our agenda this afternoon?"

"We're finished with Phase II. The cavern's all roughed out. The cultures are still doing fine. It's just this funding thing." A shadow crossed his face, and he stretched out his legs and stared into the middle distance. It was the look Al had dubbed "Quiet—Genius at Work."

"That's just construction money, though. We got the expense and capital equipment budgets we asked for. So what are you waiting for? I hear somebody in Tokyo is working on neuron chips too. You're not going to let him beat you, are you?"

Sam grunted, not listening.

Another cluster of engineers crowded into the little cafeteria, talking about last night's Albuquerque Dukes game. They clattered into the back room, where a refrigerator with glass sliding doors took up one wall, and a bank of microwaves and convection ovens took up another, and began rooting through the stock of fast food, looking for lunch.

Sam continued to stare at nothing, his brows knit.

The engineers came out and took a table next to Sam and Al, greeting Al but glancing at Sam and turning away without wasting their breath.

Al sighed and took another sip of coffee.

The cafeteria was particularly depressing when one's lunch companion was off somewhere in the Twilight Zone. There were only the two rooms, and a couple of restrooms and one extra door off to one side; the construction crew hadn't quite finished painting the plasterboard up by the wall, giving it a distinctly uneven look very similar to the horizon outside. Someone had brought in, heaven only knew how, an upright piano and parked it in a corner, underneath the open air-conditioning duct.

The building was even uglier on the outside. It was plain cinderblock, with a corrugated tin roof and a wooden door frame that needed paint. To the casual observer, it looked like four abandoned buildings out in the middle of nowhere, if nowhere was a high New Mexico plateau. Nowhere with a short stretch of road running past.

The more astute observer might notice deep ruts where heavy trucks had been, might notice that the short stretch of road—it was less than a mile long—was suspiciously smooth and free of rocks and debris.

The most astute observer—say, one who had flown in that morning as pilot to a small jet, landing on that convenient stretch of road—might notice well-trodden paths between the buildings, several vehicles lined up as if in a parking lot behind them, and a remarkable lack of signs of decay for ostensibly abandoned buildings.

This was the surface image of Project Quantum Leap. It was unprepossessing, faintly off-putting, in fact. Al had found that if he waved at a map and explained to congressional aides and other advisers just how remote it was, with casual asides about scorpions and the rattlers coiled under the front steps, congressional investigating committees often found it expedient to take his word for what was going on. This was convenient, at least for the Project Director. Al wasn't sure he wanted to know just how convenient Sam found it.

He let Sam handle the science; he did the public relations, the administrative work, the logistical scut work. Watching the budget, doing project planning, hiring clerical support—well, some work did have its compensations—tracking the construction, making sure the commissary/cafeteria was stocked, taking deliveries of desktop computers and cinderblocks and making sure that necessary supplies were on hand when they were supposed to be so that work could continue uninterrupted.

Beneath them, the high desert was honeycombed with tunnels and caves, some of them already filled with laboratories, offices, and living quarters. Deepest of all, so deep that no amount of heating could take the chill out of the pumped-in air, were Sam's office, lab, and the empty chambers. He hadn't told Al yet what was going into them, only that he needed them. Al shrugged and passed the specifications on. It was not for him to reason why.

Mostly, it was for him to do battle with the dragons. Sam wanted the setting in place before he started building his computer. It wasn't the easiest thing to convince the money men that all things came in their season, and Sam's season would come in good time.

"Did you review those cost projections I left with you yesterday?" Al asked.

Sam blinked.

"And I've got a sheaf of résumés for that administrative assistant job."

Sam blinked.

"Santa Claus is coming in for a landing at oh-five-hundred hours."

"It's not Christmas," Sam said at last. "He's not due for another eight months." His gaze shifted from middle distance to Al, and the corner of his mouth twitched, acknowledging the joke.

But a moment later, the nascent smile was gone. "Al, I want to look at those drawings for E wing again. We might want to have one of the geologists look at it, see if there's a problem."

"A problem? What kind of a problem?"

"I'm not sure. Those tunnels shouldn't cost so much; we seem to be rebuilding every time we turn around. Have you looked at the printouts since you got back?"

Al shook his head.

Sam got to his feet and stretched again, reaching up and almost brushing his fingertips against the ceiling. "Come on, let's go look."

Sam led Al over to the extra door, ignoring the glances from the engineers.

The extra door led into a featureless, empty room, about eight feet by ten. Al closed the door, and Sam bounced impatiently on the balls of his feet. "Down," he said.

The room dropped. Al was used to it by now; he almost expected small rooms to double as freight elevators. As usual, he had mentally reached a count of two hundred before the room floated to a stop.

The door unlatched, and Sam went steaming out again, Al trailing obediently in his wake. Sam headed for the construction offices, on the opposite side of the complex from the scientific labs.

Unlike the other, relatively monastic work areas, the construction offices bustled and hummed. The secretaries smiled as they came in. Even the lights seemed brighter. Potted plants provided unaccustomed color; the walls were covered with OSHA and EEO posters and extensive, detailed blueprints for electrical systems, plumbing, emergency access, sewage, power.

"Are you looking for Mr. Williams?" one draftsman asked, looking up from her computer. "He's in the back office with Tony and Ibrahim. No, they swapped offices last week, it's the one over there." She swiveled her chair around, almost knocking over the crutches propped against her table, and pointed the way through the maze of dividers.

Williams's office consisted of a small table pushed up against the wall to make room for the large table that dominated the middle of the room. Three men were leaning over a drawing. "If you reinforced it *here*—" one was saying. Another nodded and sketched quickly with a red pen. He wasn't actually drawing on the blueprint, Al could see; a layer of clear plastic protected the original.

And it was a good thing, too, as a second man, dark-skinned and intense, argued, "No, no, if you do that you'll stress this—" and rubbed out the red marks and replaced them with green ones. "See? It wouldn't work at all!"

Ed Williams looked up to see Sam and Al waiting. "Oh, thank God. I can chase these guys out and let them settle their fight somewhere else."

"I don't want to interrupt," Sam demurred. But Williams wasn't going to lose his chance. "Sam, you know Ibrahim ibn Abbas and Tony Weyland?"

"Of course." They shook hands. "What are you arguing about?"

Williams shot Sam a dirty look. "Something I wanted to get settled before it got to you, actually."

"Oops," Al muttered. "Delegate, Sam. You gotta delegate."

Sam shook his head, chagrined. "I take it back. I never saw anything, never heard anything, I just got here. Hello, Ed, how are you?" And he held out his hand to be shaken again.

Tony Weyland laughed out loud. Al glanced at him sharply. He was tall and yellow-haired, shaped rather like Humpty Dumpty with a large waist, no shoulders, and ridiculously tiny feet, and he had a jovial smile on his face. He ought to have physically dominated the shorter, slender ibn Abbas and the equally short, potbellied Williams, but instead he only looked awkward. He caught Al's look and flushed, stepping back.

"Just fine, Sam, and how's yourself?" Williams responded. "We were just finishing up here." He glared at his two subordinates. "What can I do for you?"

Sam paused, and the two junior engineers took the hint and headed for the door. "I wanted to look at the drawings for the E wing again. That's where we were overrunning, right?"

Williams grunted. "Funny you should mention that. It's been like pouring money down a rathole. No, Tony, I'll handle it," he said as Weyland stopped, obviously willing to rejoin them. "You get back to that second set of backups."

"I had Marti doing that."

"Then go check on Marti." Williams stared pointedly at the other man. Weyland backed out of the office. Al grunted to himself, filing the incident in mind. Probably just another young stud, trying to prove he was hot stuff.

"We were just looking at that," Williams said, indicating the blueprint on the table. Now, closer to, Al could see that it wasn't even a drawing. The table was actually a flat screen, and the drawing was projected onto it. The plastic over the top allowed them to make changes on the drawing without damaging the screen surface.

"Let me print this first. Watch your fingers," Williams

68

said. He pushed a button at the side of the table, and a metal plate slid over the surface, covering screen and plastic both. The table hummed. The plate slid back. Moments later a four-foot-wide curl of paper began feeding out the other end. Williams rolled it up and stacked it with other rolls in a corner. "Okay, what can I do for you?"

"I wanted to look at the plans and the cost projections for that wing," Sam said.

"Okay," Williams said agreeably. He pulled a keyboard out of the side of the table nearest him and typed in a command. The tabletop screen blinked. "You want the overview or details?"

"Just the overview."

The table blinked again. In a moment yet another drawing appeared, looking like nothing so much as a side view of an ant farm, with tunnels going in every direction. They'd used preexisting mine shafts and tunnels wherever possible in building the Project, and this part of the mountains was honeycombed with them. Next to the image a series of cost figures appeared. Sam and Ed Williams studied them silently. Al was still looking at the table, wondering if it would do the dishes too.

"We lost sixty million dollars in construction money," Sam said. "I hate to do this, but we may have to hold off on any more work there. The optical-fiber network has to have priority."

"What *is* E wing?" Al said, shifting his attention abruptly. Ed grimaced. "Hey, *I* can't remember every detail."

"It's where we were going to put the archives once we were up and running," Sam said absently. Al grimaced too—he'd known that.

Sam was tracing one of the tunnels. The green marks ibn Abbas had made now showed up on the screen image, still rough. "What's this?"

"Oh, that's what the boys were arguing about," Williams said. "Tony's responsible for that section, and Ibrahim says he's got a design flaw. You know engineers. They love to change things."

"Well, I want to go down there and look at it, but I think we're going to shift the work away from there for a while. Make sure it's blocked off. We don't want anybody getting hurt."

Williams nodded. "There are only two ways in there right now, though of course if you tried to come in from the other direction, from outside, there's probably a hundred, with all those mining tunnels. They'll all be blocked off by the time we finish. You'll need hard hats; they're in the equipment lockers. Want me to come?"

Sam smiled, looked at the image on the screen once more. "No, I can find my way."

Half an hour later, Al was glad Sam was so sure of himself. He knew he himself would be totally lost in this maze.

They were deep underground now, in an unfinished tunnel lit by naked fluorescent bulbs at twenty-foot intervals casting a cold, blue-white light on raw walls and poured-concrete floors. Al, almost trotting to keep up with his companion's longer stride, made a mental note to have the exposed wiring tucked away in tubing or something in case the safety inspectors descended into the depths of the Project and stopped everything with a list of environment/safety/health violations. The tunnel extended more than a hundred feet on either side of the elevator, and their footsteps echoed against the high walls. Feeder tunnels, all looking exactly alike, branched at irregular intervals, leading further into the Project. As they passed they caught occasional glimpses of men and women wearing hard hats and wearing heavy tool belts, using welding torches and hammers. No one passed them as they kept going down the hall, their footsteps echoing, blending with the sounds of construction.

Al wondered what it would be like if the power went out, and the emergency generators blew up, and he shuddered. Trapped, this deep in the earth? In this maze? In the dark?

He made another mental note: ladders. Lots and lots of ladders that people could climb to get to the surface. And emergency cabinets, too, with lots and lots of flashlights. And batteries. Mustn't forget batteries. Even if the area *was* going to be shut down.

And maps, too. Maybe Sam had the maze memorized, but mere mortals still got disoriented. Al made another note to tell the construction crew to paint the tunnels distinctive colors, and maybe put maps on the wall: You Are Here. The Way Out Is Over There.

The two men came to the end of the main tunnel. Sam veered right, into another unfinished hallway, and left again.

"Is this the right way?" Al asked nervously. In the completed part of the Project, one didn't feel quite so claustrophobic. Here, it was oppressively obvious they were *deep* under the ground.

"I want to go through the Central Complex. Just to see how it's coming along."

They entered a large, empty room. At one end, a ramp led up into a hole in the wall, through which another room could be seen. Thirty degrees along from it, another hole in the wall showed another hallway.

On the drawings, this was the Control Room. Here, within the next year or so, would be the central computer station for the mainframe being built all around them. As yet, it was still raw and undone, with holes in the walls and ceiling, where electrical connections would soon be. The place smelled of fresh paint; things were coming right along.

"So?" Al inquired. He wasn't quite impatient yet, but his tone made it clear that he was playing along.

"Up here. There's a way into the archive wing through here, if that drawing's up to date." Sam leaped up the ramp, into the Imaging Chamber. Al trudged after.

Sam had paused to look around and visualize what it would look like when it was finished. He always did that, every time he visited this place.

"So?" Al repeated, squinting up warily at the silver disk suspended from the ceiling, above a similar disk set in the floor. He wasn't quite clear about how this Accelerator business worked, but that silver thing looked like it would drop

71

on somebody's head any second. "That thing isn't connected up, is it?"

"What, that?" Sam barely spared it a glance. "Oh, no, that's Phase III—Hey, what's this?" He crossed the room in three long strides to a glossy panel propped against the drywall. "Come look at this."

"This" was a scrap of newspaper caught under the corner of the panel.

"Here, help me lift it—careful!"

Al lifted obediently, trying not to think about what it would cost to replace the panel if it slipped. It was part of the focusing mechanism, and had been sent back for rebuild to the original contractor at least four times. The cost of this opaque piece of . . . he wasn't sure just *what* the material was . . . nearly equaled the whole payroll of the Project for the past year. Sam was on his knees beside him, lending a steadying hand, as he slid the piece of paper free.

"Okay, you can set it down now—"

Down, and propped against the wall again, with Al sighing in relief. He peered over Sam's arm, trying to see. "So, what is it?"

"It's an article about the Nonluddites. That meeting they had in Gallup last month." The paper was torn and creased, but still readable.

"Sam, the last time I looked it was a free country. Freedom of speech, remember? So somebody might be interested in a political action group. Big deal."

Sam bit his lip and looked at him. "It *bothers* me, Al. I don't know why."

It really did, Al could see. Sam was a passionate defender of freedom of speech, of association, of belief. But there was the slightest tremor in the piece of paper held in his hands.

"I don't like the idea that we might have Nonluddites in the Project."

"But *why?*" Al was thoroughly confused. "They wouldn't threaten anything here. They're so pro-technology, pro-progress, that if those bozos at the Department hadn't slapped that topmost secret label on us the Nonluddites

72

would be our biggest fundraisers. And didn't they make it pretty clear, a couple of years ago, that they think you're the greatest thing since sliced bread? I'm just surprised we don't have more of them."

Sam shook his head, batting away the lock of hair that fell into his eyes. "I don't object to their support of technology, Al; it's just that they don't seem to have any respect for anything else. I just have a gut feeling that this could mean a lot of trouble, somehow."

Al rolled his eyes. "Again with the gut feelings?"

"They're lobbying for repeal of the Clean Air and Water Act on the grounds that it interferes with industrial development."

"Without getting into whether it does or not, Sam, what does it have to do with us? They're not a threat to the Project. That's the last thing they'd want to do, in fact."

Sam sighed, nervously folding the paper lengthwise once, twice, three times. "I don't know. I can't see somebody deliberately violating the regs to shut us down when they think we're the best thing that ever happened. But it bothers me, Al. It really bothers me."

"You want me to find out who it is?" Al said, ever practical. "I can do a little rousting. Once we find out who it is, we can get rid of him. Or her. Transfer them out, or something."

Horrified, Sam shook his head. "No! No, we can't do that. We can't get rid of somebody just for belonging to a weird group. And we don't even know if they belong. Maybe somebody just had this in his pocket, picked it up somewhere." He hesitated, shrugged. "Leave it, I guess. I'm not sure why it matters so much."

Al shrugged. "If you want. You're the one who brought it up."

Sam moved his head back and forth again, studying the folded paper. It gave him a chill, had ever since he first caught sight of it, stuck under the panel. It hadn't left his thoughts, and he wanted to talk to someone, show it to somebody, see if they got the same feeling of impending trouble. He'd hoped the other man would feel the same frisson of dread. But Al hadn't. His reality check had failed. He could ask Verbeena, he supposed, but—

He shook his head again and shrugged. "Yeah. I don't know why, Al. It's just a feeling. A really bad feeling. Maybe it's nothing. And maybe we haven't heard the last of it, either."

Al snorted. "Feelings. Pfui. Let's go look at E wing."

CHAPTER
NINE

He fitted the goggles over his temples and inserted his hands into the gloves, reaching for the waldo controls inside the glove box. Even after years of practice, it took a long moment and eyes squeezed tightly shut to adjust to the jump in vision that the goggles gave him; the tweezers, tiny in the grip of the waldoes, far too small to be manipulated by human hands, looked huge and pitted and gross and far too close to his eyes.

The goggles gave him a headache almost immediately, pressing on nerves behind the orbital arches of his skull. He had long since learned to ignore the pain, concentrating on the square of diamond substrate and the cells he was working with. The step beyond logic was fuzzy logic, the step beyond that was inspiration. . . .

The cells had remained alive. Had grown, however feebly, in the culture. But it wasn't going to be enough. The glove box contained perhaps fifty small petri dishes, each with a single chip holding anywhere from one to a dozen cells from the brain of Sam Beckett. He had added small quantities of cerium and praeseodymium to the culture medium to stimulate cell growth, and used them to "dope" the semiconductors to allow the neurons to be electronically interfaced with the diamond substrates of the chips. It had been the first of several breakthroughs.

Conventional wisdom said from the very beginning that he couldn't culture adult human brain cells, and he'd proved them wrong, but it wasn't going to be enough. And he couldn't try to reproduce the experiment without getting other people involved, and if anyone else found out what he was doing— what he had done—the Ethics in Human Research people would shut down the Project so fast he'd never know what hit him.

The cell in the dish he was examining throbbed, quivered, axon looking for impulse.

He wasn't even sure how he had gotten the cells to begin with. Originally he'd used a computer simulation in place of animal cells, figuring he'd have to go through years of inter- mediate steps before he could get to what he *really* wanted, and yet here he was, using his own cells. Not any innocent volunteer's, but his own.

He could remember, in blurry fashion, both operating and being operated upon, when he should not be able to remem- ber anything at all, any more than he could remember the attack that had put him in the hospital in the first place. And the double vision, double experience had to be an arti- fact of the injury and the anesthesia of the brain operation. You couldn't be in two places at once. Everybody knew that.

So how had Weasel Mikowski known to take that scrap of bone and put it in that particular culture medium and preserve it to begin with? Mikowski was one of those who knew beyond a shadow of a doubt that brain cells couldn't be made to reproduce.

Yet when Sam had finally made it to his feet and begun the process of recovery, staggering around the hospital in a barely decent robe with an IV tree trailing after him, the first place he'd gone was the Path lab. And there they were, a gray jelly-like cluster of cells that used to be inside his skull and now were outside, and more important, within reach.

And Mikowski didn't remember having sent them to the lab. He had no reason to. If they'd been cancerous, or suspi- cious, sure; but these were just scraps. Biological waste, a side effect of cleaning up an injury site. No reason in the world to save them.

Except, of course, they were exactly what Sam Beckett wanted and needed to marry to the design technology for a computer that existed, back in 1990, nowhere except in the sister cells still inside his skull.

He picked up the dish with the waldo clamps and tilted it gently back and forth, letting the pink medium slosh gently over the surface of the computer chip. He wondered just how much life the cells had. Were they looking back up at him, as he looked down at them? And if so, what were they thinking?

Nonsense. Sheer nonsense. Individual cells had no consciousness. Even a dozen weren't enough. It was the organization of multitudes of differentiating cells that gave rise to functioning organisms. Like, as it were, calling to like. Or at least to similar.

In which case the cells in the dish probably *were* calling to him, after all, in little cellish voices. And demanding an explanation, no doubt. "Sorry," he murmured. "You're going to have to figure things out for yourself. No cheating on this one, boys."

He put the dish back down again and peeled his hands out of the gloves, thinking. The cells combined with the diamond substrates of the chips would form the basis for the continuum set sieve. He had to keep the growth going, or he'd be left with nothing but a highly developed, exceedingly expensive state-of-the-art computer, maybe two hundred gigaFLOPs' worth, with a fifty-gig memory. He didn't want state-of-the-art; he wanted beyond art. He wanted a computer with true imagination. Nothing else could manipulate time.

But he needed more cells than the ones painfully saved here, and he wasn't going to be able to get them out of his own skull. He probably wasn't going to be able to crack anyone else's skull either. Which was, he hastened to remind himself, a very good thing, after all.

Sometimes science got the better of his good sense. He had to watch that tendency.

The headache was getting the better of him, too. He massaged his temples as he left the little laboratory, entered the office and collapsed into the office chair, pivoting back and forth.

The intercom buzzed. He reached out with one hand and slapped it blindly. "Yeah?"

"You pulling another all-nighter or are you coming to the party?" Al's voice was acerbic even through the static. "We're waiting for you."

"What party?" Sam mumbled.

"*Birthday* party. Mine. Remember?"

There was food, and music, of a sort—someone was pounding away on the piano. It was still in tune, Al noted; Sam had taken up piano tuning as a hobby as soon as the thing arrived. Nobody, not even Al, would admit to having acquired that piano, and it had been in terrible shape to start with. It still sounded a little tinny, but only one person in the Project was likely to notice *that,* and he hadn't made his appearance yet.

Al was bedecked in a suit of forest green, with a darker green vest pinstriped in silver to match the silver of his shirt. It was vivid and extravagant and eyecatching and he *liked* it. And there was a table shoved up against the wall with a two-square-foot sheet cake and chips and dips and buffalo wings and cole slaw and cards and even some interesting-looking packages stacked around it, and people laughing and talking and dancing. Al Calavicci was in a state of sober bliss—a state in which he still had some problem believing, but he was the administrative director of this crew and he had to set an example. Besides, he didn't want Sam mad at him. He made a mental note to duck outside later for a cigar—Sam was strict about enforcing the no-smoking rule too.

It wasn't often that most of the people working on the Project were together all at the same time; they worked different shifts, on different phases of the Project, some on computer design, some on programming, some on construction, some on testing. So he didn't know everyone, but he was certainly looking forward to getting to know the new ones.

That redhead, for instance. Tall and lissome and with skin like alabaster, and the most intriguing designs on her fingernails. He wanted to get a closer look.

He wanted an excuse to hold her hand, actually. He was sure it was soft and warm and perfect. And he could tell from across the room that she had huge, baby-blue eyes. "In my sights," he muttered to himself cheerfully, and headed across the room.

Someone else was at the piano now, an even worse player than before. The player was shouted down, and the piano was replaced with a radio tuned to a country station in Santa Fe. Someone started a line dance and swept Al up in the midst of it, sweeping back and forth across the floor in raucous time. He was at the wrong end of the line from the redhead, but that was all right. The night was young.

There was no liquor at this party, at least not officially; government funding didn't run to such things. Al didn't much care. He didn't miss the liquor, oddly enough. Once upon a time, not too many years ago, he would have been blind drunk by this time, unable to walk, much less dance. The very first time he'd ever met Sam Beckett, in fact, he'd been drunk and in a rage, kicking a vending machine, breaking his toes and too blitzed to know it. Sam had hauled him off, calmed him down, sobered him up, and started on a campaign to dry him out. Now he could remember entire evenings—sometimes to his regret, but still, he could remember them.

He hoped Sam would tear himself away from the lab long enough to join them. Sam wasn't good at parties. He knew how to talk physics or medicine or archaeology, but Billy Ray Cyrus? Al thought not. Shame about that, really. What good was a Nobel Prize if you couldn't use it to impress the ladies? But Sam had spent his whole life accumulating degrees, one after the other, and doing research. He'd never taken the time to learn the fine points of social intercourse, so far as Al could see.

The song came to an end, to be replaced by local news, and the radio was turned down and the dancers scattered, mostly back to the food and the punchbowl. Al sighted in again and determined on a flank attack.

Gooshie was moving up on the redhead's other flank. But Gooshie was notorious for his bad breath, and as a distraction, he failed to rate.

"Hi, I don't think I've seen you around here before," he said, holding out a cup of pink punch. "I'm Al Calavicci."

"Oh, wow," said the redhead. She had a breathy, high-pitched voice and baby blue eyes. "Are you, like, the Calavicci who runs things?"

She didn't sound particularly bright. Ah well. Sometimes that had its advantages. "The only one around. Ah, what's your name?"

"I'm Tina Martinez-O'Farrell," she responded, holding out her hand. "I'm, like, really pleased to meet you. Sincerely."

Al nearly dropped his glass of punch. He routinely reviewed the personnel flimsies of all major Project personnel, and he'd seen that name recently.

"Ah, *Doctor* Martinez-O'Farrell?"

"Oh yes. I'm new here. This is a really dreary place, isn't it? I mean, it's so far away from everything, and it's so *dusty*. . . ." She batted her augmented lashes at him. Al could have sworn he felt the breeze.

"Well, it's the desert. There's a lot of dust in the desert." Al was considering the implications of all this, and beginning to reconsider. Dumb targets were one thing, but he could feel his own brain cells dying in this conversation.

"You know, if it weren't for the chance to work with Dr. Beckett, and the shopping in Santa Fe, I wouldn't even have come out here," Tina confided earnestly. "He's designing a really really interesting computer, you know. He wants me to help build it."

In fact, the hiring package indicated that Tina Martinez-O'Farrell was supposed to be the chief architect for that computer. Al was having some trouble fitting the résumé with the woman in front of him.

"Have you been to Santa Fe?" she was asking him now. "It's so, like, ethnic."

"Oh, yes," he assured her. "Many times."

Was this worth it or not? He couldn't decide. On the o. hand, the woman was a ditz. Based on the conversation so far, she could change the entire category of dumb-blonde jokes to dumb-redhead jokes single-handed.

On the other hand—Al drew his head back, consideringly, to appreciate the view as Tina turned to greet someone else, her voice a reincarnation of Marilyn Monroe's—that body was, well—he could feel his mouth going dry, and his heartbeat accelerating. "Bingo," he muttered.

Just about that time Sam came in, through the front door rather than the elevator room. Hearing others greeting him by name, Tina spun around and stretched up on her toes, waving her arm in the air excitedly. The move gave Al a close-up view of her profile, and conclusively made up his mind for him. He thought he could hear himself panting as the redhead yodeled, "Yoo hoo! Dr. Beckett! It's me, Tina! I got here!"

There were tiny lines of strain around Sam's eyes, but he smiled and gave Tina a quick hug in hello. Al stared, dumbfounded, as the object of his attentions transformed herself before his very eyes into a scientist spewing forth a gabble of technospeak, punctuated at regular intervals with "you know" and "like" and "to die for" and "sincerely." She thrust the cup of punch back into Al's hands, the better to use her own to talk with.

Sam appeared to filter out the Valspeak and follow the essentials without effort, responding in kind, minus the vocal pauses, talking about power requirements and substrates and architecture. The two of them were migrating into a corner, Tina chopping at the air excitedly, when Al decided it was time to take control again.

"Hey, wait a minute," he protested. "I thought this was a party. No work allowed. So cut it out, you two."

The two of them paused to stare at him blankly.

"Like, excuse me?" Tina said, in her bewildered little-girl voice. "Did you, like, say something?"

Al opened his mouth to expostulate.

Dr. Beckett, will you play for us?" someone interrupted from across the room.

Al's protest alone might not have been enough to lure Sam out of the conversation, but the promise of music in addition managed it. The radio shut off with a decisive click, and the objections were quickly stilled when the partygoers saw what was going on.

"Oh, does he play the piano *too*?" Tina said, not in the least upset, it appeared, by having her conversation so rudely broken into. She took back the cup of punch and sipped at it, her lips soft and red and luscious against the plastic rim.

"To die for," Al assured her, his head still spinning, unable to look away. This might possibly, he thought with his last rational moments, be his best birthday party ever. Sam, bless him, was playing something slow and danceable. Al held out his arms, and Tina came into them.

CHAPTER
TEN

Senator Judith Dreasney looked at the latest briefing book, a blue binder three inches thick, and sighed. She had a real interest in at least six bills coming up, and no interest at all in at least a dozen more. But in order to get the votes to get her farm bill passed, she had to support somebody else's appropriations bill, or memorial, or protection bill.

But voting for the protection bill would annoy somebody else who would otherwise support her. But if she didn't, she might lose on another front.

Politics was interesting, to put it mildly. Dreasney wondered just how badly her constituents wanted that farm bill. Badly enough to re-elect her? Because in the final analysis, the name of the game was Stay on the Hill. Not even to be King—just to Stay.

"Jessie?" she yelled.

Her administrative assistant, a bouncy twenty-seven-year-old with a flip haircut, dancing blue eyes, and the largest nose this side of the Potomac, skidded in. "Yes'm, ma'am, bosslady, Senator?"

Dreasney eyed Jessie's outfit, a sunshine yellow shorts suit, and felt very old. "Jessie, dear, how do I feel about this?" She waved a hand at the briefing book.

"You think it's terrific, ma'am." Jessie lifted up on her toes and dropped again. Most offices on the Hill wouldn't have approved of shorts. Jessie managed to make it look like up-to-the minute office wear, and anyone who took exception was obviously too conservative for words.

Dreasney was not a conservative, so she kept her critical thoughts to herself and thought longingly of the days when she had had the legs to wear something like that herself.

"Any land mines?" she asked, pulling herself back to business.

Jessie pouted a little. "Well, you might have some reservations about the environmental impact."

"Am I an environmentalist this week?"

"You're a middle-of-the-roader, wisely balancing the needs of the environment against the overwhelming national interest in technological progress," Jessie assured her. "It's in the summary. A one-paragraph vote speech."

"Will that make Bantham happy?" It was important to make Senator Ralph Bantham happy; their interests marched together, and they regularly traded votes. Right now, he had an edge. She owed him a favor. She'd rather he owned her one instead.

Jessie hesitated—never a good sign. "Not entirely," she admitted. "But you've got to say *something* environmental soon, or you're going to lose that whole bloc. Scuttlebutt says that you're on the environmentals' long-list for targeting. They're watching you."

"Why don't they make *me* happy and target Bantham?" Dreasney groused, flipping the binder open. As promised, there it was—a one-paragraph speech adroitly covering both sides of the fence.

"Oh, they have. He's on their short list. But he's got the NRA and AARP behind him, and the Nons. He's golden." She came around the desk and dug through the papers to find yet another binder, this one much slimmer. "This one you vote for without any reservations at all. The environmentals will scream, so you can point to the vote speech on this other one. And you can make Bantham happy."

Making Bantham happy was high on the list of Jessie's priorities too, Dreasney concluded. She glanced at the younger woman narrowly, wondering where Jessie's loyalties ultimately lay. If that wasn't a redundant thought in and of itself, of course.

"Will it line up the Nons for me?" she asked. Nons. She hated that nickname. It seemed so stupid. But they regularly delivered the contributions, and they did a lot of free publicity as long as she voted their way, so she guessed they could call themselves anything they wanted. It wasn't as if they were subversive, for God's sake.

"Well, it sure won't hurt. They understand about business, after all. They know they can't get their whole agenda through this session."

A new thought occurred to Dreasney. "Are you a Non, Jessie?"

"Me?" Jessie was startled—or at least appeared to be startled—at the very suggestion. She was blushing, a rush of color that suffused her entire face. "Oh, no, ma'am. I'm not political at *all*. I don't mind about spotted owls or logging either. I just like to watch, that's all."

Watch, and listen, and advise. Jessie was a chess player, after all—state junior champion. Dreasney had known her from infancy—it had been in her courtroom, after all, that the adoption papers were signed. She'd followed Jessie's career through grade school, high school, and college, given her her first job as a campaign clerk. And yet, Judith Dreasney was sure that she didn't really know Jessie Olivera at all. She'd been awfully quick to deny belonging, yet she always seemed to manage to bring the conversation around to issues the Nonluddites had an interest in. Even in staff meetings, when the rest of Dreasney's aides and researchers gathered to advise her of the implications of particular bills and how to vote on the massive pieces of legislation, Jessie was always alert to the technological versus the environmental impacts, always wanted to pick up the rumors on how other Congressmen viewed things.

"What's their target for this session?" she asked. Jessie would know, of course. Jessie knew everything, and she was always right. Dreasney wondered how she managed it. Probably that same intent curiosity Dreasney had just been castigating her for. Dreasney sighed.

"Clean Air Act," Jessie responded promptly. "It's keeping a lot of companies from expanding, because they're putting so much money into trying to meet the standards. And the Open Ranges Act—they want to open up more public land to grazing."

"Oh," the senator responded, nonplussed. Jessie bustled around the office, getting papers in order, and the senator watched her.

Sometimes she felt very old and foolish and wondered why she was in Washington. All *she* wanted was a small farmers' subsidy to keep family farms of less than 160 acres alive. The Nons didn't like her bill, she knew that. Not efficient enough, they said. Not good for the economy. Survival of the fittest. Let the little farms wither if they couldn't compete; bigger was better, more productive. But the country was already throwing away tons of milk every year, had so much butter and cheese they couldn't give it away. And not all the small farmers were dairy farmers anyway; some of them specialized in odd things, like four-horned sheep or Velvet Roses apples, things you'd never find in the market.

Judith Dreasney once had thought that a sheep with four horns was something out of a fairy tale, or a science fiction story about radioactive mutants. She knew better now; she'd held a lamb, felt its warm squirming, seen its flock. She'd tasted the mellow wine of a Velvet Rose. And they were wonderful things, even if they were inefficient and antiquated, and she didn't want them or their kind to vanish.

That wasn't the kind of thing she said on the campaign trail, of course. They'd have played hell with her image of a hardboiled pol.

"Committee meeting Thursday," Jessie said, slanting a glance her way. "I'm afraid I don't have the briefing book for that meeting."

That meeting. That meeting was so secret even Jessie didn't know what it concerned. That meeting—the vote on that Project—was the reason, favors owed or not, that Ralph Bantham kept sweet. She and Bantham, between them, kept the money coming for that crazy project in the desert, and if she changed her mind, it would go belly-up. She didn't know why Bantham was so interested in it. A bigger and faster computer? All you had to do for one of those was wait a few months and buy it from the Japanese. There was this business about hybrid processors, but that was ridiculous on the face of it.

A lot of money was going for ridiculous, though. A *lot* of money. She could use some of that money for her four-horned sheep. And for schools. And for medical care, if the Great Health Care Package didn't go through.

And if John Beckett's boy could actually do what he said he could do, the implications were staggering. Not only going back to see history—debunking all the conspiracy theories. That would be the merest side effect. The real power would be the ability to make a decision based on real, solid, firm, factual information about what other people had done. If you knew what kinds of decisions led to putting missiles in Cuba back in '62, you could have decided in complete confidence to implement a blockade, without spending money preparing for an attack, because you'd know the Russians had never planned one. Today, you could know the secret councils of Saddam Hussein, or the French. Politics would no longer be a game of poker for the country with the ability to look at the past and see it as it really was. Especially if no one else had the ability. If everyone else thought their secrets were inviolate, and didn't know an Observer might be watching over their shoulders.

If Sam Beckett could do what he said he could do.

Dreasney nodded, not saying anything. It annoyed Jessie to be left out of the loop like this, the senator knew, but that was too damned bad. Some things even Jessie couldn't know. There was secret—and then there was Quantum Leap.

"I really hate this stuff," Sam muttered.

Al nodded. He was back in uniform for this, pulling out all the stops to impress. Congressional testimony, even in closed committee session, was sufficiently official, and it didn't hurt to remind his audience just who he was and what he had done in his career for his country. That white uniform with its array of ribbons lent considerable credibility to a shy scientist with a brilliant idea.

"Just let me do the talking, okay? You'll just go in and everybody'll get old waiting for you to find exactly the right word for 'have a nice day.' " He tucked his hat under his arm and glanced up and down the hall. "Down here."

It wasn't a regular committee room. Too small, for one thing. A dozen or so people clustered at one end, but only two counted.

"Why?" Sam was protesting. "It's my Project. I understand it best."

"That's the problem. You're the *only* one who understands it. You can't even explain it to *me* and make sense."

Sam looked injured, but stepped back to let Al lead the way, a strutting figure in gleaming white, attracting all eyes. The two of them proceeded to the little table in the middle of the room, pulled out the chairs, and sat down. Al set his cap on the table in front of himself, knitted his fingers loosely together, and waited.

Sam was considerably less relaxed. He braced his left shoe against one table leg. The table shifted minutely. Al took a deep breath, and Sam meekly withdrew his foot.

The members of the committee, senators and civil servants, members of presidential advisory councils, the people whom Secretaries of Departments with names like Energy, Defense, and Treasury courted for the money to run things, took their places at the long table at the end, facing them like a panel of judges, or a doctoral dissertation committee.

Actually, Sam thought, that would be okay. He was used to dissertation committees. Maybe if he just thought of this as an oral defense, it would work out okay.

Then they started asking questions.

The one on the far left, a short African-American version of Wally Cox complete to the bow tie, consulted a piece of paper and asked, "Why are we paying money for an encyclopedia?"

An *encyclopedia*? Sam wondered if he'd heard the man correctly. What did his project have to do with encyclopedias? But the man was looking at him expectantly, as if the question made sense.

Al moved in smoothly. "Data input isn't complete, of course, Senator Crosby, but that will be one of the side benefits of the project, it's true. Information access and retrieval of any recorded event within the past—" he hesitated slightly—"forty years or so, will be practically instantaneous."

"Why forty?" another man asked querulously. "Why not fifty, or seventy, or a hundred?"

Sam opened his mouth. Al kicked him discreetly. "The mass of data involved is self-limiting," he said quickly. "Our equations show that exceeding this period is contraindicated to our best expectations for system performance parameters as defined in our preferred processes process. A quality analysis indicates that our process owners are unable to establish ownership of their preferred processes when data bulk exceeds a predetermined limit of storage capacity and manipulation cotangency."

Wow, Sam thought, *nice save. Even I don't know what that means.*

The senator withdrew his question, visibly flustered, and kept his mouth shut for the next little while.

The questions, however, continued for another thirty minutes. Only three members of the panel, including the man with the bow tie, were not involved. The other two were Bantham and Dreasney. They only watched and took the occasional note, and winced once or twice when the questions and answers got too far afield—or too creative.

They'd already made up their minds, Sam realized. Al's fencing with the lesser members of the committee didn't matter in the least. They could have saved the whole dog and pony show—even the part where Sam got to answer one question, directed pointedly at him, and had to use a flip chart to show them the equations supporting what he was saying. As far as the committee was concerned, his equations made just as much sense as Al's gobbledygook, and the flip chart was too small anyway.

And he caught himself saying "It is therefore intuitively obvious . . ." and caught a glimpse of Al closing his eyes as if in actual pain.

He wound down quickly then, put the marker down and went back to his chair. Nobody here, including his best friend, had the foggiest idea what he was doing. Al was in there pitching for him with no idea at all what he was pitching for, and these people were nodding as if it all made perfect sense. He wondered how much they understood about anything at all.

Except one. Bantham was staring directly at him, with hooded eyes, like a hawk preparing to stoop on a rabbit. His gaze rarely shifted, and only for a moment or two. Sam wondered what the man was thinking, and why.

The committee thanked them, finally, and they got up and marched out again, Al still leading the way. Sam looked back as he closed the committee room door behind him. The other committee members, even Dreasney, were talking to each other. But Bantham was still looking at him, his gaze a chill across Sam's shoulder blades.

"Well, thank God that's over with," Al said as they left the committee room. "I need a drink." He caught a glimpse of Sam's expression and recanted. "Of coffee."

"You can have scotch if I can have your share," Sam muttered.

"Say *what*?" Al said, stunned. But Sam was already halfway down the hall, and Al had to scurry to keep up, all out of dignity of his glistening uniform.

Neither one of them observed the blonde woman with the lively expression and the big nose who watched them go, humming to herself.

Elsewhere in the building, a beetle-browed man hunched over a telephone, murmuring.

"Dr. Yen? It went well . . . Yes. Yes, I'll take care of it. He'll get it." His voice changed, became more persuasive. "About that contribution . . ."

CHAPTER
ELEVEN

Al was all too familiar with the Navy bars in Washington. Now that he was a civilian, he preferred to go someplace else. There were fewer questions to answer about his diminished capacity for alcohol, for one thing. For another, the pickings were better.

He and Sam shared a very small round table off in a corner of a half-lit bar in their hotel featuring a lobster motif. The waitresses wore lobster bibs for tops, and not much for bottoms. Part of Al's attention was devoted to explaining to Sam that the committee meeting had really gone very well indeed; another was reminding himself to call some friends in the Naval Investigation Agency to find out if after all this time they'd managed to find out anything more about the attack on Sam three years before. Leads had petered out quickly; he was almost resigned to letting the issue go. Sam was alive and doing fine and had never gotten so much as a dirty look since. Maybe it *had* been just a mugging. He'd check, just to make sure; but nowadays, there were more pressing problems.

For instance, this evening. He reviewed the evening's potential with the same professional intensity he'd given reviews of every kind over a long and interesting career. There was that brunette sitting all by herself over in the Claw Cove. . . .

Sam nursed a mug of draft, watching his friend with bemusement. He'd known when Al suggested going down to the bar that they wouldn't be getting anything accomplished this evening. He only hoped that Al showed a certain amount of common sense for a change. He seemed to have forgotten Tina, at least, the moment they arrived in Washington, which was probably a very good thing indeed. Al seemed awfully serious about Tina, at least when she was in the same room. Sam hoped he wasn't rushing into yet another doomed relationship. It felt funny to be almost condoning his friend's philandering, but as long as nobody was getting hurt by it, how could he criticize?

As soon as Al picked his target for the evening, Sam could finish his beer and go back up to his room and get back to work on that glitch that was bothering him. There had to be a way to get around the cell division problem. If he didn't figure it out soon, the Project was going to get caught up with him, and he'd have two hundred people sitting around waiting while he tried to solve things. Waiting, and getting paid for it—he couldn't exactly lay them off and hope they'd still be around when he finally came up with a solution.

He was fumbling for a pen and a cocktail napkin when Al realized what he was doing, threw up his hands in disgust, and took his glass of iced coffee with him to meet the brunette.

Sam hadn't even started on his second cocktail napkin— he had to brush away the bits of peanut shell—when someone else slid into the chair Al had vacated. Annoyed, he glanced up.

She had the most lovely, liquid blue eyes. And a delicate, flowery perfume that flooded his brain, driving out the smell of cocktail peanuts and alcohol and everything else in the world.

His hand closed convulsively over the napkin, wadding it, and he swallowed. It was all a function of adrenaline and testosterone flooding abruptly into his system in response to visual and olfactory stimuli, pheromones that just happened to key into a primal image buried deep in the instinctual part of his brain; he *knew* that. That was *all* it was. Strictly a biological reaction, tied to survival of the species. Perfectly normal in every way.

And he absolutely did not believe in love at first sight.

Nonetheless, at that moment Sam Beckett was just as vulnerable to a pretty woman as Al Calavicci had ever been.

"Dr. Beckett?" she said.

She had a very nice voice, too. And a clear peaches-and-cream complexion, too nice to be hidden by very much makeup. It was the nicest contrast to her lips. They were . . . red. He knew what red lips were supposed to simulate. He'd done studies on it. He was a scientist. He knew the data.

He didn't give a damn about the data at the moment.

It had been quite a while since he had been approached by a total stranger—a female total stranger—in this fashion. She radiated warmth, and he found himself leaning forward, into it. Drowning in it.

He swallowed. Remembered that she'd asked him a question, sort of. "Y-yes?"

She settled a little, as if melting into the chair, and reached out to touch his hand. Lightly. Too lightly. Like a butterfly wing. He wanted her to do that again so he'd be sure he'd actually felt it. "I'm so glad," she said. "I wasn't sure. You look so much more handsome than your pictures, you know."

"I . . . I do?"

The quiet, observing part of his mind snickered to itself about Al's probable reaction. Stammering? You'd think he'd never talked to an attractive woman in his life. What was he, a teenage kid?

Well, yes, socially at least.

He firmly squashed the rational corner of his mind and smiled his most winning smile.

"Oh, yes. The news photos don't begin to do you justice. And you're so much more dignified, too, with that elegant streak of gray. . . ." She reached up and almost, but not quite, touched his left temple, where the scar was.

If the quiet, observing part of his mind could have wriggled loose to shriek a warning, it would have done so then. But it was bound and gagged. There was no reason at all that Al Calavicci should be the only one to enjoy an innocent flirtation.

Not that he normally capitalized on his fame—normally, he didn't have the chance. There weren't that many science groupies around. It wasn't as if he were a television star.

He wasn't the kind of man to take advantage of a lady—or any woman. But this woman—her knee pressed against his under the little table—was *not* innocent.

At least, he was fairly sure she wasn't.

"Um . . . I didn't catch your name," he said.

"How thoughtless of me," she murmured. "I'm so thrilled with the opportunity to meet you, I've just completely forgotten my manners. My name is Jessica."

I'm not bad, I'm just drawn that way, he thought irrationally. He made himself look away from her eyes and down at her hands.

It didn't help. She wore no rings. And there was no sign she'd ever worn any. He closed his eyes and tried to think of breathing exercises.

"I've always been fascinated by your theories, Dr. Beckett," she said softly. "I've read your work on the biological perception of time, all the way back to your dissertation."

That settled it. Any human being who would wade through 643 pages of theoretical constructs and mathematics had to be interested in him for his mind.

So why was she wearing that dizzying perfume?

"I was so startled to see you here in Washington," she was murmuring. "I thought you were working on a project in Chicago. . . ."

"New Mexico," he said, not even aware of his words. Her leg was shifting, sliding along his. Suddenly he wanted very badly to continue this conversation somewhere else, more private. A lot more private.

"Oh, that's such a lovely place," she said. "Do you like it there?"

He swallowed yet again. "Oh, yes," he admitted. "I like it—there *very* much." Was he talking about geography? He wasn't sure.

She smiled at him, and the noise of the bar receded into a hum around them. "I'd really enjoy the opportunity to discuss

94

your biological theories in more detail, Dr. Beckett. Would it be too much of an imposition?"

He thought he was drowning. "Not in the least."

She bit her lip, tilted her head. "But it's so *noisy* in here. Is there someplace quieter we could go? Unless of course you're waiting for somebody?"

"Oh, no. No. Not at all," he blithered, and she smiled again with red, red lips.

Al looked up as Sam went past. So the kid got lucky at last, he thought. Takes all kinds. Helluva schnozz on her, but Sam sure didn't seem to care. He turned back to his brunette and smiled seductively.

Sam didn't even notice. He followed the blonde out the door, moaning quietly to himself.

"So how was your evening?" Al smirked as he met Sam by the hotel elevator the next morning. "An improvement over the physics journals, I hope?"

Sam stared at him, puzzled. How did Al always manage to pick up on these things? Particularly when they were things he felt guilty about? Al never seemed to feel guilty himself; how did he manage it?

"Oh, yeah," he said lamely. Maybe if he made it clear he didn't want to talk, Al would drop the subject.

Unfortunately, this was one subject Al never dropped.

"So how was it?" Al asked as the elevator arrived. They stepped aside to allow a luggage rack, with accompanying family, to exit, and then got on and hit the buttons for the lobby. "C'mon, give."

"Al!" What had happened the night before was uncharacteristic, to say the least. He didn't like casual encounters, rarely got involved; Al could never quite grasp the concept that Sam preferred monogamy or perhaps even celibacy to impersonal sex.

But there hadn't been anything casual or impersonal about this incident, from beginning to end, and he was still confused not only about what had happened but about his own part in it.

95

Not the physical encounter, no, that he had no uncertainty about at all. He wasn't quite as innocent as Al liked to pretend he was. But this was something else as well, and he wasn't sure what.

There had been a lot of talking, he knew that. She'd been very interested in his work. Or at least it had seemed that way, but somehow they'd managed to end up in bed together.

It had seemed like an inevitable idea at the time.

And then, abruptly, she'd left. Abruptly, when he was in the middle of . . . well. As if she'd gotten whatever it was she wanted, taken her trophy or something. He didn't much like the feeling of having been used. It reminded him of waiting at the altar for Donna Elesee, who'd left him too, with just about as much explanation. If he tried to explain that, Al would tell him to go get his head examined.

And the part he liked least of all was the physical response he *still* felt, remembering the impact her presence alone had had on him. Couldn't he overcome biological drives long enough to objectively assess whether a woman wanted him for himself, or for his fame?

Apparently not.

He was *not,* he promised himself, going to go through this again.

Al snickered. "So the White Knight got a little tarnish on his armor, huh?"

Sam directed his gaze to the ceiling, pointedly ignoring the other man. Al knew perfectly well that he was not about to kiss and tell, and that he wasn't going to listen to Al boast either; some things were just too personal. That wouldn't keep Al from teasing him unmercifully, however. Sam would just as soon have eaten breakfast alone, to unravel the tangle of his thoughts and emotions, but that wouldn't have made things easier with Al, either.

Sam Beckett firmly believed that it was not morally right to sleep with a woman he wasn't in love with. He certainly wasn't in love with the woman named Jessica—he never did catch her last name. He couldn't explain the lapse, except to

96

say that he was human, after all. Sometimes more human than other times, he supposed.

It was no excuse, just a reason.

The elevator purred to a stop, and they walked past the lobby and into the coffee shop. Sam couldn't keep himself from looking around, looking for her. Al caught him at it and chortled. "Made quite a hit, did she?"

"Al, shut up," he said furiously.

Al grinned, but subsided, much to Sam's relief. The two of them ordered breakfast. Al arched a bushy eyebrow high at the orange juice, coffee, toast, oatmeal, and fruit plate that Sam ordered. "You *must* have had a good time," he said.

Sam reviewed the dry toast Al had ordered. "You mustn't," he responded.

Al sputtered back into silence and opened up the *Washington Post* to cover his confusion. They finished eating without further conversation.

Sam picked up the bill, corrected the addition and figured the tip, pulled out enough to cover it and got up, still not speaking to his companion. Al rattled the pages of the paper and remarked without looking up, "I've got a couple of people to talk to yet. You got another meeting?"

"I have one more thing to take care of." Sam paused. "I can walk. I'll put my bags in the trunk of the car and get checked out, meet you back here in—" he glanced at his watch—"two hours?"

"Fine." Al turned a page with exaggerated unconcern. "Two hours." He glanced up as Sam started to walk away. "Sure you don't want me to drive you?"

Sam almost smiled; Al was the master of the oblique apology. "No, thanks. I can use the exercise. See you in a couple of hours."

The humor of the situation faded as Sam left the hotel, clearing his mind as he walked. He wondered if Al knew where he was going and why. He probably did. Al had more than a little of the mother hen in his makeup. It didn't matter; this was something he always did by himself.

It was a long walk from the hotel to Constitution Gardens. The air was thick with humidity, and he drew it in impartially with automobile exhaust and urban pollution, stretching himself to work the confusion of emotions away. He didn't have room for them right now. Not *those* emotions, anyway.

Once again he came to the Wall, joined the mourners, and made his apology, touching the black stone, but this time when he turned away it was to come face to face with the woman who had called herself Jessica.

She saw the name on the stone and the expression on his face and came to the obvious conclusion.

"I'm sorry," she said, unconsciously echoing him.

It was as if the words had broken a spell. He looked at her and saw a woman, a very attractive one but no longer the siren of the night before, who somehow jarred his sense of what was right, of what should happen at this place. He walked past, unable to speak.

"I wish these things had never happened," she called after him.

It sounded trite and empty and meaningless and it made him deeply angry. He lengthened his stride and pulled away, leaving her and the Wall behind him.

Like most things left behind, he carried them with him as well.

CHAPTER

TWELVE

The King-Aire skidded in to a landing on the Project airstrip, and the passengers unstrapped themselves and collected luggage. Before they were well away, the jet plane was taxiing back up the tarmac in preparation for takeoff for its return trip.

A late-afternoon storm was gathering over the malpais, the black and broken lava field that was all that remained of the fury of a volcanic eruption uncounted millennia ago. The western sky was dark purple, laced with diamond lightning, flickering at intervals from heaven to earth and back again. Veils of rain hung halfway down the sky, the drops evaporating before they came to earth. The air crackled with ozone and water.

Through a rent in the clouds, a shaft of sunlight glowed golden, like a ray of grace from the hand of God, until upper atmospheric pressure pushed the clouds together and shut the sunlight away from the world. Sam paused to watch as the light and the veils disappeared into the advancing darkness of the storm.

"Sam, c'mon," Al yelled impatiently. "It's gonna rain!"

It was indeed. He could hear the receding drone of the airplane engines and the sound of the wind, whipping up dust devils and tumbleweeds. A roadrunner pelted by, heading for shelter.

Shelter seemed like an excellent idea. The two men gathered up their bags and moved at a steady trot to the cluster of buildings that were the surface of the Project.

"I hope Tina's still here," Al remarked as they entered the cafeteria and the first, quarter-sized raindrops splatted into the dust on the other side of the door. "I have plans in that direction." He shut the door behind them and dropped his garment bag over the back of a chair long enough to stretch mightily. "God, I hate those little planes. At least, I hate them when I'm not flying them."

"You have plans in every direction," Sam said without rancor. A six-hour flight, not counting a refueling layover, had numbed the impact of his last encounter with the woman named Jessica. He'd started by thinking acid thoughts about reproductive drives. That had started him thinking about cell unions. And that had led him to a glimmer of an idea which made him forget all about the woman and spend the time working on his pet problem. Now he set his luggage down, too, not quite ready to go back to the office. "You always have plans."

As if in agreement, lightning crackled overhead. The lights in the cafeteria dimmed and came up again, slowly.

"Did it ever occur to you," Al asked, pausing beside the door to the elevator, "that this might not be the best possible place in the country to build a new computer?"

"It won't matter." He headed for the kitchen in back, wanting a cup of coffee. He had an awkward question to ask, and he wasn't quite sure how to go about it.

"You seem awfully sure of that," Al said, taking the hint and following him.

"It's two hundred feet down, and insulated. Lightning won't hurt anything."

Thunder cracked overhead, rattling the two windows in their frames. The lights went out.

"Very comforting," Al said acridly. "I don't much like the dark, Sam."

Emergency generators roared. The lights came on again.

"Thank you," Al said, looking up to the ceiling.

Sam handed him a cup of coffee. "You're welcome." He sipped at his own drink.

Al sighed. "Okay, what is it? I know a delaying action when I see one."

"I wanted to talk to you about something before we got back to work." But Sam didn't continue immediately. Instead he set the paper cup down on a table and wandered over to the piano, sitting on the bench and plinking at the keys with one finger.

Al dragged a chair over and turned it around, straddling it. "Okay, what is it? The committee? Something about the Project? What we're doing here? What?"

One finger became five, then ten, and Sam rippled through scales, abstracted. "What we're doing here," he repeated dreamily. "What *are* we doing here, Al? Do you know?"

"You're building the computer to end all computers," Al said promptly. "What about it?" He reached inside his coat for a cigar, stripped the wrapper off it, and trimmed the ends.

Sam laughed softly. "Oh, I doubt *that*." He played a few bars of a tune Al didn't recognize. "There's always going to be a next generation."

"Yeah, look at *Star Trek*. So? You have to have this generation before you get the next one. You're building this one." Al wasn't sure where this was going, and he really wanted to get to his quarters, shower, change, and hunt up Tina. Or at least, get to his quarters and light up.

Sam didn't care. "I'm building a computer—trying to build a computer—to look at time, Al. To travel in time."

"Yeah?" Al had never understood this, and he wasn't starting now. He knew Sam had never spelled it out to anybody else yet, not even the government agency financing the Project, not even the senators who were sponsoring him. Al was willing to listen to it and not call Sam crazy because it *was* Sam, after all, but time travel? *Real* time travel? Naaaaah. He didn't really believe in it, no matter how often the other man explained it.

"That's what you were talking to the committee about, Al." Notes rippled on the air. Outside, thunder rumbled, and the rain cut loose at last, pounding on the tin roof so hard they would have had to shout to hear themselves. The temperature inside the building dropped perceptibly with the cooling effect of the storm. Sam continued to play for the ten minutes or so until the rain softened to a steady low-key drumming, a random medley of Elvis Presley, show tunes, the melody from the Beatles' "Yesterday."

"I was double-talking," Al answered, as if there had been no interruption. He got up and got more coffee, came back again, resigned to talking out whatever it was that was bothering Sam now. "I can understand from computers. You're building a new kind of computer. I *don't* understand what you say it'll be able to do. That's your department."

"The theory says the Observer can travel within his or her own lifetime," Sam said. "Go back and see anything within that period."

"Why just within your lifetime? Why not clear back to the Pyramids?" Al was playing along. He'd heard all this before. Sometimes Sam liked to think out loud.

Sam took a breath to explain and let it out again, slowly. "It's in the equation," he answered instead. "If you take a piece of string, and one end is your birth, and the other end is your death, and you wad it up . . ."

"You can cross from one point to another. Yeah, yeah, I'll take your word for it," Al assured him hastily. "So what's the problem? I mean, we aren't sure yet, but I think we've got the funding. Even the construction dollars we thought we lost. You build it, you go look at things. What's wrong?"

More scales, up and down the keys. "The more I think about it, the more I wonder whether I ought to be doing this at all. And I know other people would wonder too."

Al snorted. "This is a hell of a time for second thoughts. Do you have any idea how much money we've spent so far?"

Sam shrugged.

"It would make a noticeable dent in the deficit."

Sam winced.

"Besides, since when did you ever let other people's opinions tell you what to do? You made your decisions a long time ago. That was a Phase I decision. This is Phase II."

Sam tightened his lips and bobbed his head. His hands stilled on the keys, the long musician's fingers resting on them lightly. "Al, do you know *how* I'm building this computer?"

"Nope." Al sipped again, unperturbed by his own ignorance. "That's your department too."

"It's a hybrid. It's based on cells that are biological as well as electronic."

Al closed his eyes. "I knew it. You're building Frankenstein down there in that lab, aren't you?"

Sam laughed despite himself. "No. Besides, Frankenstein was the mad scientist. It was the monster he built." He grew more serious. "I never specified what kind of cells I was using, Al."

"You're building Beckett's Monster down there in that lab, aren't you?" Al corrected himself patiently.

"No. It isn't a monster." Sam paused, choosing his words carefully. "It isn't everything it could be yet, either."

"Ah-huh." Al waited skeptically.

Sam gave up trying to find the right words. "Al, I'd like to borrow some nerve cells."

Al remained silent, studying him. The pounding of rain on the roof diminished, and thunder rumbled, far away. Sunlight stabbed through the windows by the front door. Sam's hands were still on the piano keys.

"You want to build a computer using my nerve cells," Al said. It wasn't a question. Sam couldn't hear any doubt at all in the other man's voice about whether such a thing was possible. Al *wouldn't* doubt it. But how he felt about using his own cells—"What do you have to do?" he said at last.

His voice was still neutral, promising nothing.

"Just some nerve cells. From your finger. A stick with a needle will do it."

"Why can't you use *your* cells?" Not a protest; a request for information.

"I already have." What might have been a tremor converted itself into fifteen seconds of the Minute Waltz.

Then silence.

"So," Al said at last. "Your brains, my looks. Can't miss, right?"

Far away, thunder rumbled.

Elsewhere, in the living quarters of the Project, a maintenance engineer—a janitor—bent over a laptop computer, typing feverishly. It was a plain, square room, painted off white, with a cot on an iron bedframe for a bed, a small standard-issue dresser, and a small desk on which the laptop rested. Piled beside him on the desk, in imminent danger of sliding to the floor, a stack of once-crumpled papers, now smoothed out, made an untidy pile. He paused in his typing to refer to one or another of the crumpled pages, puzzling out notes.

They weren't classified, any of them. If they'd been classified, the papers would have been disposed of properly in a burn bag or a crosscut shredder that would have converted them into powder. But they weren't classified. They were the kind of notes anybody might have made—someone's phone number, a scrap of an equation, a list. The kinds of things that were tossed away without a second thought, collected for disposal by an army of faceless, nameless workers.

A piece of unclassified material here, a note there, a number there . . . each piece by itself meant nothing. Collected by a team of people with common interests, put together by someone knowledgeable, reviewed by someone able to place them in context, they created a glimpse of something larger than the sum of the parts.

The janitor, a member of a team defined by a common interest, set one page next to another, examined them, smiled, and continued typing furiously, compiling them for someone else's review.

CHAPTER
THIRTEEN

Yen Hsuieh-lung sat in his university office and stared out the window at a fruitless mulberry tree, brooding. The tree provided shade, a home to squirrels. In some parts of the country fruitless mulberries were considered trash trees. In others, they were valued for the shade they provided. This one sheltered his window from the direct sun, and Yen Hsuieh-lung was prepared to let it live. It kept the direct sunlight from his books, from his eyes.

In front of him, text blinked on a computer screen, white characters against blue.

In front of him, lying on the keyboard, was a one-page letter signed by Sam Beckett, referring him to Al Calavicci for more information about possible consulting on current projects. The letter didn't specify what projects, or how Hsuieh might best be employed on them. It was brief, polite, final. Probably written by a secretary rather than by Sam himself, Hsuieh thought. A dry and dull rejection.

The report, by contrast, was very interesting indeed. It had been transmitted via modem. It contained . . . details.

An increase in orders for RPMI, specifying a particular subclass.

A note reminding someone to turn up the heat in the living quarters.

A doubling of a standing order for toilet paper.

A telephone number that belonged to director of facilities

construction at the Superconducting Supercollider in Texas, with a time, 3 pm, scrawled beside it.

And a discarded page from Sam Beckett's desk pad calendar. Appointments, phone numbers, notes of calls, and doodles.

Doodles of clocks. Long-case clocks, alarm clocks, watches. Each one, the report noted, showing a later time, with the hands moving steadily toward midnight, or noon.

Yen smiled to himself. An interesting habit, that.

The Administrative Director, Rear Admiral Al Calavicci, USN, Ret., had been seen with a bandage on his hand for a few days. It wouldn't have been worth noting, except that he had claimed that he'd injured it while hammering in a nail to put up a picture in his quarters, and the bandage was on his right hand. Furthermore, there were no pictures on the walls and no nails for pictures, anywhere in the admiral's quarters, and the admiral himself was right-handed. As a discrepancy, it was worth noting.

Physics and clocks and bandaged fingers.

Yen Hsuieh-lung was an astrophysicist. He had spent a lifetime staring at the skies, yearning for the stars and their glory. In Project Star Bright, he had helped determine that the state of the art of human science wasn't up to beating the speed of light, not yet, though there were indications that perhaps it wasn't quite the unbreachable barrier it was once believed to be.

Or so Sam Beckett claimed. Yen could still remember the moment in that briefing in the little conference room when, watching Beckett talking about a secondary unified field theory before thirteen of the best minds in the country—one of them his own—he realized that not one of them was capable of following what the man was saying. The best they could do was comprehend the summary: for today, the stars were out of reach.

In that moment he realized that he hated Samuel Beckett. What right did he have to be the pinnacle of human intelligence and *still* not know the answer?

Yen was passionately committed to an ideal of techno-

106

logical perfection for the human race. He was certain that with sufficient commitment, sufficient resources, sufficient *attention*, all the problems could be solved. All the answers could be found.

It demanded *complete* commitment. No distractions. No wasting of funding and energy on trivial matters. But the government, the nation, wasn't willing to make that commitment.

How could one focus the nation's attention on a problem and solve it? How, when there were so many problems to be solved? They—scientists, engineers—had done it once, in getting to the moon in less than nine years after Kennedy had made his public commitment. But having done that, the politicians had given up, lost interest, allowed themselves to be distracted by wars and starvation and volcanoes and hurricanes, fires and diseases and deficits. The *Challenger* disaster had taken the heart out of them. They'd woefully underfunded Star Bright, and the final result, years later, was Sam Beckett's briefing, Sam Beckett's recommendations.

For lack of that focus, that commitment, they had given up the sky. They had given up the *future,* Yen Hsuieh-lung passionately believed; this planet would never run out of starving children, was on the verge of losing the resources it would take to rescue them anyway. Humanity needed to crack the secrets of physics that would allow them to go elsewhere, to try again, make a fresh start and do it better. Instead the politicians had walked away.

And they had done so with the consent of the man who, if he had chosen to, Yen Hsuieh-lung was convinced would have given them the stars.

Instead of fighting them, Sam Beckett had listened, and agreed.

Instead of continuing with the problem of faster-than-light travel, he chose now to build a computer.

There was some consolation: the computer could be used, if it were properly programmed. Yen was content to let Beckett build his computer. Let him imagine that it was done

107

secretly. Let him imagine that his energies were concentrated on something new.

Instead, Samuel Beckett would make one more contribution to the space effort he had deserted, whether he wished to or not.

The stars demanded focus. They demanded attention.

What better way to command it than to give the program its very own martyr?

Not the astronauts who had died, not the *Challenger* crew. Yen Hsuieh-lung honored them all, but he needed a new martyr today. Jancyk had been a fool, years ago, but if Yen had been properly prepared—as he was preparing himself today—

Well, perhaps not today. Let Beckett make perhaps a little more progress on his mysterious project. Let him break the new ground.

And then let him die for it.

Whatever Quantum Leap was, the public would believe, once Yen Hsuieh-lung was through with them, that it was research into faster-than-light travel. And they would believe that Sam Beckett had died for lack of adequate funding, and they would clamor for all the possibilities the stars would bring them—the possibilities Yen Hsuieh-lung would show them. They would clamor for additional funding, for more attention to the problem. The Nonluddites would see to it.

A new Project Director would have to be selected, of course. The senators would insist that a properly qualified person be selected, someone with the knowledge and experience of astrophysics and research.

This one would not have a Nobel Prize and five extra doctorates, perhaps.

But he would have *commitment*.

And he would have Project Quantum Leap: the project for which he should have been selected to begin with.

Yen Hsuieh-lung smiled again, and devils danced in his eyes.

Several weeks later, Sam Beckett sat checking his mail as Tina Martinez-O'Farrell made her presentation on suggestions for the new architecture required to accommodate the latest design change Sam wanted for the QL computer. The Project team leaders—the scientists and engineers, not the construction workers—were gathered in the Project's second conference room, the one on the office level, sitting around tables set up in a U shape, listening intently as she talked, barely a trace of vocal pause in her voice. Sam had read the report before the meeting, and he had some suggestions, but he wasn't going to make them now; this was an orientation meeting for the team leaders. He was going to have to work closely with Gooshie on the fuzzy elements of the program, and allow for the new chips. They had already run the basic test programs. He had another one up and ready to go after the meeting.

Another one—and maybe the most important one of all.

One or two people were sneaking glances at him, probably thinking he was being incredibly rude to read mail instead of listening attentively. Al was sneaking glances too, but *he* was probably wondering how Sam could pull his attention away from the statuesque redhead by the electronic blackboard. Sam smothered a grin. He liked Tina a lot; he respected her mind; otherwise, she left him cold. If he told Al that, Al would send him to Verbeena for a medical checkup.

Al had it bad for Tina. Still bearing the scars of his fifth divorce, he wasn't quite to the point of proposing to her, but when Tina was in the room, Al rarely paid attention to anyone or anything else.

Sam *was* paying attention, though. He didn't quite use what Heinlein called "parallel mental processes"—he'd leave that to his new computer—but the mail didn't take that much attention. It was mostly notices about new government regulations, and those he could put aside for Al to deal with. Al needed a secretary, he thought. So did he, come to think of it. A lot of this paper was just paper, to be scanned and recycled and forgotten. He'd have to mention it to Al. It was hard to concentrate on mere paperwork today; hard even to concentrate on Tina's briefing. He had other news for Tina, Al, and Gooshie, and it was difficult sometimes to restrain his impatience.

Tina wasn't offended by his bringing other work to her briefing. In fact, she'd suggested that he get some paperwork done. "You're, like, so busy! And you already know all this stuff!" And she'd batted those huge blue eyes and waggled her scarlet-tipped fingers back and forth, indicating the immensity of "all this stuff" and her total inability to cope with it.

Except, of course, that she could cope perfectly well. She'd come up with the original design, after all, all six hundred cabinets' worth. The only reason Sam was present was to lend his presence as support, in case the other members of the team took Tina only at face value. Very few of them made that mistake more than once.

Tina was taking questions now, answering in her little-girl voice. She handled them well, Sam thought as he continued skimming, sorting, discarding. She fit in just fine, as long as Al kept his head and didn't get them all into a harassment suit. Al wouldn't, though. He had a finely tuned antenna for rejection, and Tina hadn't actually rejected him, not yet. When and if she did, Al would stop his pursuit instantly and go looking for another target of opportunity. He was utterly reliable about that sort of thing. "Too many fish in the sea," he'd say.

At long last the meeting came to an end, and the participants shuffled paper and threw away their tea bags—Al had insisted that they buy ceramic coffee mugs, rather than use Styrofoam; he got quite heated about it. Sam squared off his stack of paper, looked at it, and sighed. He *hated* paperwork.

Al had managed to tear himself away from Tina long enough to pause next to him. "You wanted to see me?" he said, still distracted by the redhead.

"Yeah. Something I wanted to show you and Tina. And Gooshie, where's Gooshie?"

Gooshie was getting more coffee from the urn in the corner of the meeting room. In the fluorescent lighting, he looked pasty, unhealthy. From some angles his mustache was nearly invisible, appearing more like a smudge of leftover breakfast than hair. He lumbered over to the other two men in response to Al's wave.

"Yes, Dr. Beckett?"

Sam winced away. Gooshie was a nice guy, but there had to be something metabolic going on to account for that breath. He made a mental note to tell him to go see a doctor about it. Some *other* doctor, preferably.

"Sam's got something to show us," Al said. To Sam, he continued, "Not another article about the Nonluddites, is it? A flyer, maybe? They're meeting in the cafeteria tonight?"

"No, it is not another article about the Nonluddites," Sam said with dignity, getting to his feet. "Tina?"

Tina swayed over to join them, much to the dismay of Tony Weyland, who was hovering over her. "Yes, Dr. Beckett?" she cooed, promptly claiming the full attention of both Al and Gooshie. Sam wondered why Weyland was there.

He sighed again. Biology—you couldn't live with it, and you couldn't—He quashed that line of thought, and the memories that went with it, as too silly for words.

"I'd like the three of you to meet me down in my lab in about twenty minutes. I want to discuss a test run."

Weyland drifted closer, tidying up the conference room, putting chairs very quietly back in alignment with the table, picking up spoons for bundling into the dishwasher. The four key figures to the Project failed to notice.

"You finished work on the new chip?" Tina said. "That's wonderful! But why didn't you tell me before I got up in front of all these people?"

"It's not final," Sam cautioned. "This is only a test."

"If it were a real chip, we'd have been given nachos and told to tune to the classical station," Al cracked.

Sam gave him a withering look. Gooshie and Tina were merely confused.

"Like, this is only a test, if it were a real warning, we'd have been given instructions—oh, never mind," Al said. "So your experiment worked?"

Sam bit his lip. No one beside Al and he himself knew the nature of the new chip, and he preferred not to let anyone know. He'd have to warn Al about that; he didn't want the Project shut down by a human experimentation review board.

Still, it was hard to quell his own excitement. "I don't know if it did or not. But this test run will tell us whether it's a dead end. I hope."

The four of them crowded out the door, Gooshie and Tina speculating about the test, Sam trying to calm them down, and Al windmilling his arms in glee. They left behind them the junior engineer from Construction, staring after them, smiling to himself.

CHAPTER

FOURTEEN

It was late October 1993 in New Mexico, and the aspens had veiled the mountains in gold; the evenings were cold in the high desert. But in the depths of Project Quantum Leap, the weather and the passing of time itself had no effect. The only measure they used was the progress toward completion of construction and the computer that was their reason for existence.

So when the Project's four principle scientists left the conference room to crowd together into Sam Beckett's office, they were preparing to celebrate a milestone more important than anything in the past three years. They shoved the clutter of books and papers and notes and infocards out of the way, pausing only briefly to read the latest in the collection of Far Side cartoons stuck on every available surface. The only clear area in the whole office was the part of the wall with the collection of pictures: Beckett family pictures, the one of his high school orchestra's state competition prize trip to Carnegie Hall, the one of him accepting his first doctoral hood. He didn't have any of his diplomas on the wall; Al supposed that he couldn't pick just one or two, and having them all would be rather intimidating. His medical license was stuck up any old how, as an afterthought, in a frame with cracked glass.

It amused Al to see how different Sam's Quantum Leap office was from the one he had when working on Project Star

Bright. It was as if even Sam's formidable memory had given up this time on assimilating all the data involved in making the Project go.

Somehow Sam had managed to get around the standard office furniture issue, and had an ancient green leather easy chair with a permanent dent in the seat. Al claimed the chair he regarded as his own, catty-corner across the desk from Sam's. Tina and Gooshie dragged in chairs from their own offices, down the aisle from Sam's, and settled in.

Sam came in from the private laboratory behind the office, carrying a motherboard with a mass of circuits imprinted on it. Clearing a space for it, he set it down on the desk and went back into the laboratory, to come out again with a pair of speakers and other equipment.

He had to urge Tina to move out of the way, and connected the speakers to the motherboard in some fashion Al couldn't see. "So what the hell is that?"

"That," Sam said, "is the first test." He scrambled around the desk, testing connections, and then came back again and sank into the easy chair.

Tina was frowning, her lovely forehead rippled. "There isn't very much there," she said.

"It's the Beta version," Sam said. He traded uneasy glances with Al. Al understood. He rubbed the tip of one finger and wondered if Sam had really needed those cells after all. The Alpha version only used cells from the original culture.

"Those chips are, like, all wrong," Tina insisted.

"Those are very special chips," Sam said. "They're neurochips."

"Neurochips? Well, that's pretty bizarre." Tina sat back, dissatisfied. "How can I build a computer when I don't even, like, *understand* it? How do chips like this fit?"

"Most of the computer will be perfectly normal," Sam assured her. "Well, not normal exactly. We'll have to be creative about some aspects of the architecture, using a lot of the ideas you came up with in your briefing today. But this will be the heart—the brains—the soul of it."

"That's very poetic, Dr. Beckett." Gooshie was twisting his hands together. His expression was at once eager and totally confused. "But I don't understand."

Sam grinned. Al had rarely seen him so excited, fairly glowing with it. "That's okay," he said. "I've already entered the test program you developed for me. . . ."

"You're going to run my program on *that*?" Gooshie obviously thought Sam had lost his mind. "You don't have enough there to—"

Sam turned his head slightly. "Run Beta Test One," he said, enunciating clearly.

A voice came out of the speakers, causing all of them to jump. It was deep, a man's voice, but had none of the flatness of computerized speech. "Beta Test One: Calculate the value of pi. Calculating. Stop. Unable to comply."

Gooshie looked dumbstruck. "It wasn't supposed to do that."

Sam grinned and leaned toward the voice pickup. "Why not?" he challenged the machine.

"Pi is an irrational number," the deep voice said. "Calculation can be performed to a specified number of decimal places."

Gooshie's mouth was opening and closing like a beached fish. "It isn't supposed to *do* that!"

Now it was Al's turn to be confused. "Do what? What did it do?"

"The program was just supposed to test the duration of the chip. It doesn't have the capacity to make a judgment that pi is irrational. You can calculate pi forever and never come to the end of it, but—"

"But this—this *chip* not only realized it, it *offered an alternative*." Tina's omnipresent Valspeak was gone. She, too, was looking from the motherboard to Sam and back as if she had just witnessed black magic.

Al shrugged. "Didn't sound all *that* smart to me." He studied the setup on the desk, and said, "What's two plus two?"

"Seventy-six," the voice responded promptly. "Local bank withdrawals from noon to six."

115

Al snorted. But the expression on Sam's face was crest-fallen, and Al wished he'd kept his big mouth shut. "Well, hey," he fumbled, trying to apologize for spoiling the demonstration without actually coming out and saying so. "It's not like it's a piece of the old pi, after all."

"Cherry. Apple. Pumpkin. Mince. Currant. Blackbe—"

"That's enough," Sam said. The computer shut up.

"That wasn't in the program," Gooshie breathed. A thin line of sweat had appeared on his forehead, and his fingers were knotted together. Tina was pouting with disbelief.

"That's, like, free association," she said. "That's really weird. Not very smart, though."

"Like that cartoon character, what's his name, Ziggy," Al muttered. "You're going to have to zap him some more. Like a bolt of lightning from above."

"But you don't understand," Gooshie said, agitated. "Admiral, you don't understand. None of those statements were in my program. It isn't supposed to be able to do anything that isn't in the program." He was on his feet now, peering into the collection of circuits. "You modified the program, didn't you, Dr. Beckett? Didn't you?"

Sam was looking down at the contraption on his desk as well. "Yeah, in a way. I guess I did." He chewed his lip in a pensive manner. "Ziggy. I kinda like that."

"Well, it isn't Pigs in Space, exactly. . . ."

Sam laughed, and Al allowed himself a small sigh of relief. Gooshie, however, was not to be mollified. "Dr. Beckett, how—"

"It's the new chip, isn't it?" Tina said. "It's transcending the program." She shook her head. "How do I build a computer for a chip like that?"

"That's why I wanted you to work on it," Sam said.

She looked at him oddly. In that moment Al really believed that Tina Martinez-O'Farrell, no matter how ditzy she appeared, really was as smart as her personnel dossier said she was. She'd not only recognized clumsy flattery when she heard it, but she knew it was sincere anyway.

"I'll talk to you in more detail later on," Sam said. "Meanwhile, I think you ought to make the announcement to the rest of the team. We have a working neurochip. It's time to celebrate."

Tina got the message. She rose to her feet and tugged Gooshie along with her, leaving the office with a last glance at the contraption on Sam's desk. It was clear that they had a lot of work to do, and not a lot of ideas about how to do it. Al got up too, but Sam waved him back down, glaring at him in mock outrage.

"*Two plus two?*" he said, once the other two were gone and the door was closed behind them.

"*Seventy-six?*" Al responded, in the same tone.

Sam gave up. "Now you see why I need those cells," he said.

"Well, no, I don't." Al was thinking that his Italian grandmother would be making signs against the devil and spitting between her fingers just from hearing the voice, let alone hearing it discuss pi. Or pie. "That's your department, not mine."

Sam let go a deep breath, nodded, and dug into his desk, coming up with a dark green bottle. Al was struck nearly as speechless as Gooshie. Sam Beckett, stickler for the rules, had hard liquor on a government-funded project. It was the kind of thing that would get anybody else kicked out immediately. "What the *hell* are you doing with *that?*"

Sam smiled. "I'm celebrating the successful test of my neurocell circuit," he said. He shifted a thick volume of microcode out of the way, dived back into the drawer, and came out with two dusty water glasses. With a flourish, he set the bottle down and wiped the glasses clean with a tissue from a handy box. "This is the last of the scotch whiskey Dr. Lo Nigro gave me to celebrate getting my first degree. This seems like a good time to finish it up. Have one."

Al paused. It had been a very long time since he'd had a drink of something this hard—or this good. Sam had been the one to coach him out of a dependency on alcohol in the first place. Once he'd realized where that road left, he'd cut back himself, allowing perhaps a glass of wine with a meal and no more. Now Sam was the one offering it to him. "You sure?" Al asked him, doubtfully.

"Yep." Sam poured half an inch of amber liquid for Al, a full inch for himself. Al reached for it with an eagerness he recognized and abhorred. But he brought it to his lips anyway, and sipped.

It tasted awful. He put it back carefully on the edge of the desk and pulled out a cigar instead. "I think I'd rather celebrate with this," he said. He rolled it back and forth in his fingers, sniffing greedily at the length of it.

"Just don't light the damned thing," Sam answered, holding the glass up to the light. "But first—Ziggy's up and running. To Project Quantum Leap."

Al picked up the glass again, clinked it to his friend's. "To Quantum Leap!"

They both drank. It went down a little more easily this time.

Several toasts—and refills—later, Sam slumped back in the easy chair, staring at the pictures on the wall.

"Did you ever have something you wish was different, Al?" he asked idly. "Like if you had done something different, your whole life would have changed?"

"Sure, every time I proposed." Al waved his unlit cigar in an expressive circle. "I can think of quite a few times my life would have been different."

"Yet if you changed it, you wouldn't be the same person now." Sam was looking at the picture of his family, of his brother in green fatigues, his eyes narrowed and thoughtful. His brother was laughing into the camera lens, his arm flung around the shoulders of one of his buddies. In the background was jungle, and a river. The picture had been taken by a famous war photographer the day before Tom was killed. It was one of Sam's most precious possessions.

"Sure. I'd be a lot richer. Save myself a fortune in alimony." Al propped his feet up on the desk, too, carefully avoiding a thick volume of microcode, and sipped again. Down the hall, they could still hear the cheering of the rest of the Quantum Leap team, echoing oddly down the cave tunnels. Tomorrow they would be back at it, wrestling with how to create the proper Instruction Processor for a new kind of computer, but tonight they could let off some steam.

"Like Tom," Sam said, sliding down in his chair and leaning back to study the acoustic tile in the ceiling.

Al winced, looking at the level of his friend's glass, which was considerably lower than his own. Sam was not normally maudlin. He didn't sound maudlin now, just . . . thoughtful.

"If Tom hadn't died in Vietnam, you know, I couldn't have stayed in school. The farm—well, you remember what it was like, back in the seventies. Farms were failing, M.I.T. was expensive, even with a scholarship. But Tom died, and he'd made me his beneficiary. I used the money to stay in school." Sam took a deep draft of his drink. "I wouldn't be here today—none of this would be here today—if Tom hadn't died." He finished the drink, picked up the bottle, swished the remaining liquid around a time or two, and put it down again without refilling the glass.

"But you know, Al, I'd give it all up in a second if he could walk through that door."

"You don't know that you wouldn't be here," Al argued. "You'd have found a way to stay in school. You couldn't not go to school. Not with your brains. You'd have gotten student loans, scholarships, grants."

Sam smiled and shrugged that self-deprecating shrug. "Maybe."

"No maybe about it," Al said loyally. He had finished his drink, and refilled it. It was a celebration, after all.

"And there's other things," Sam went on, not bothering to address Al's protestation. "I wish I could change other things. . . ."

He never finished that sentence. Instead he paused, draining and refilling his own glass, before continuing.

"This is as much for Sebastian Lo Nigro as anything else," he said, as if to himself. "He was the one who really showed me what it would take." He sipped again at his drink.

"Time," he went on, more softly. "Changing time. He used to say it would be like solving a crossword puzzle in four dimensions, making sure you don't change the wrong things. Like cat's cradle." Sam chuckled to himself. "String theory. Wad up the string of your life so each day touches another day, and travel back and forth from one place on the string to another. . . ."

Al kept silent, respecting the other man's mood.

"You'd have to preserve randomness," Sam went on dreamily. "You'd have to make sure you didn't try to change things deliberately, make them what you think they ought to be. You could really screw things up that way, end up cutting your string into tiny pieces—"

And he was gazing into space again, running a mental program of his own.

There was something—maybe it was Tom's dying, maybe it was something else—that drove Sam to create a way to look at the past, had driven him from the very beginning. When the multi-tetraflop computer alone couldn't do it, with billions upon billions of calculations a second, he had decided that what a computer needed was not just fuzzy logic but the power of human inspiration. He had gone after and gotten a doctorate in medicine so that he could better understand the human brain, in physics and electrical engineering and other things so that he could design the tissue cells for the new computer.

"There have to be rules," Sam said suddenly. "Absolute, unbreakable rules. You *can't* change the past. If you change the past, you change everything that comes from that past, and create a paradox. I've got to remember that. Got to build it into the ethics module."

"*Ethics* module?" Al burst out. Only Sam Beckett would talk about building ethics into a computer. "I can't even tell which is the speech synthesizer!"

"Need to work on that a bit too," Sam admitted. "But it's definitely getting there." He raised his glass one more time, a half-roasted smile on his face. "To Ziggy!"

Al shook his head, clinked his glass to Sam's. "To Ziggy—and whatever surprises he may bring."

SPRING, 1995

. . . Pressured to prove his theories or lose funding . . .

The melancholy of everything completed!
                    —Friedrich Wilhelm Nietzsche

CHAPTER
FIFTEEN

Jessie Olivera walked down the sidewalk at a rapid pace, a purse swinging from her shoulder. It was always good to get unpleasant things over with quickly, and meeting with Yen Hsuieh-lung was usually unpleasant.

She didn't like the man, never had. He treated her with contempt. She wondered sometimes why she'd ever gotten involved in the first place.

It had been a rational, well-thought-out decision at the time. Her fiancée, Chris Jancyk, had been a member, and she could help him out by passing along bits of trivia she picked up in meetings at work. Nothing important, of course, but Chris had introduced her to Yen and the others leading the movement. Then, five years ago, Chris had gone missing. She'd been sure the Nonluddites knew something about it.

But she'd never been able to prove a thing, and after a while gave up on hearing from Chris. Meanwhile, she found herself getting more and more involved, passing along more and more tidbits. And then one day Yen had asked her to find out something specific. She'd done it without a second thought, too used to keeping him up to date. Too late, she'd realized how sensitive the information really was.

"To our spy in the chambers of Congress," Yen had toasted her. The others had added their congratulations.

Ever since then, she'd been stuck.

It wasn't as if the Nonluddites were planning to bring down

the government, she reassured herself at odd moments. They only wanted to make sure that the country didn't stall out, that energy didn't get so scattered trying to clean up waste sites or something that progress came to a standstill. And she supported that. Anybody would. They were just lobbyists, after all.

"Come to the office immediately," the message had said. No "please" or "thank you," as was usually the scientist's style. Just a bare summons. And here she was, stepping around wadded trash and less pleasant things, hurrying to respond.

She'd quickly realized Yen was the real leader, that the rest of the Advisory Council of the Nonluddite Committee were merely figureheads. He was the best-known scientist, after all. The rest were industrialists and money people, lobbyists. Very much a part of the Washington landscape. Her kind of people.

Except back then she was still hoping to someday find out what had happened to Chris Jancyk.

Now Chris was a five-year-old memory, and she was a spy for a scientist who might be an idealist for progress, or might simply be out for himself and the highest paycheck. She had no idea. The only thing she was getting out of it was the hope that Yen wouldn't tell Judith Dreasney what a slug she'd been harboring as chief assistant. And, too, the hope that Yen wouldn't get angry at her, the way he'd done once at some guy at a meeting. He'd been cold, reptilian. She had never seen that kind of anger before. It shook her more than she cared to admit.

She speeded up again, waiting in the shade of a blossoming cherry tree for a break in the traffic, dodging smoothly around the tourists' rental cars diverted by street repairs through this residential neighborhood. She wasn't going to think about one-night stands and relationships dying a-borning now. It had been a job, that was all.

She'd find out what they wanted this time, and try to find a way to cut herself loose. Maybe she'd have to break down and confess after all. She'd lose her job, of course, and she'd never get another one in Washington. Maybe never get another one period—she wouldn't get very good references, that was for sure. The thought made her laugh a little.

The wry humor carried her up the steps and into the house. It lasted, in fact, until she met Yen Hsuieh-lung face-to-face, in the office on the second floor of the white house in Georgetown. The office door was open, inviting. She didn't bother to knock before entering.

He looked up. He was seated behind the desk, with his back to a window, and it made his face hard to see. His tone, however, was irritable. "You're late."

She shrugged, determined not to be intimidated. "You didn't want to use a telephone."

He stared at her as if he found her repulsive, and she drew in a deep breath and edged around so that she could actually see his face. "You look," he said icily, "exactly like one of the cheerleaders in Berkeley, California." It was clear that this was not a compliment.

Jessie was determined not to show her real feelings, and at any rate she couldn't help the new fashion for pompoms on sneakers. "Well, what do you want?" she said. "I haven't got all day."

Yen Hsuieh-lung bit back an acid response. "I have an important task for you."

"Another one?" The urge to add *I won't work for you any more* was almost overwhelming. Almost. Jessie knew better than to throw down any ultimatums to an opponent's face. Politically, it was suicidal. She had a suspicion it might be suicide in the literal sense as well.

He grinned, a nasty expression. "Yes, Miss Olivera, another one. I didn't call you here simply to feast my eyes on your beauty.

"There is going to be an investigation shortly at Dr. Samuel Beckett's Project. Senator Dreasney will be part of the investigating committee, and you are to make sure that you accompany her. You'll receive further information when you arrive on the site."

"I'll see him again?" The words were out before she could stop them. She could feel the blood rising in her face; she'd give anything to be able to call them back. It annoyed her that Yen seemed to think she'd do anything for The Cause, now. Though she expected he had a right to think so, considering some of the things she'd found herself doing. Copying documents. Passing along gossip about people's vulnerabilities.

Seducing a man. Years later, it still bothered her.

She never intended to. It wasn't part of the orders. But she didn't expect to be quite so attracted to Sam Beckett, either, nor to have the attraction reciprocated. But thinking about it now, she realized that attraction had been her downfall.

She'd come back and told Yen as much as she'd gleaned and then gone home to shower, washing compulsively. Not to get rid of the memory of Sam Beckett, but to get rid of the memory of what she'd done. The morning after she'd followed him to apologize, but by that time it was too late. The magical attraction had evaporated as if it never existed.

If she'd just run across Beckett accidentally, if she hadn't been acting under orders, it might have been a wonderful encounter. Things wouldn't have happened nearly so quickly, of course, but they might have lasted longer. It might have been a real relationship, instead of something she was ashamed of. She wished she could stop blushing.

Especially considering Yen's reaction. He smiled.

"No," he said, relishing the word. "I don't think you will be seeing Dr. Beckett again."

"What kind of investigation?" It was a desperate effort to regain her composure, and only partially successful.

He smiled again. "You'll know when you hear of it. I see no reason to give you more information now." He turned away.

"You called me all this way just to tell me to wait?"

She thought he might turn back at that, swivel around in his chair, glare at her from across the desk. He didn't. He did raise his head, staring out the window, and somehow there was more menace in that than any glare. "I called you to tell you to prepare."

She held for a few more moments. Then she turned and walked away, clamping down hard on the urge to run.

Yen Hsuieh-lung heard her footsteps retreating. Silly, ignorant, weak female! He despised her, and despised Sam Beckett for ever having been attracted to her.

But none of that mattered any more. He put Jessie Olivera out of his mind and turned to more important matters.

The latest report indicated that the Quantum Leap computer had passed its initial full-scale test. If it had reached that stage of development, Yen Hsuieh-lung had no doubt whatever that he could complete its development. Let Beckett dismiss him—Beckett had served his purpose. His hold on the tools already within the Project was stronger by far than anything he could use on Jessie Olivera. The people who sent him information were loyal through conviction as well as through fear, and they would do things that even Jessie Olivera would draw the line at. They had informed him of the Beta test, of the secret meetings held two years ago. Some type of new chip was involved; what kind, his spies within the Project couldn't tell him, because they were, after all, only support people, not the sort one would expect to understand real science. But they could tell him about the reactions of Gooshie and Martinez-O'Farrell, and from that he could deduce that it was, indeed, something very special.

Now it was nearly ready to run, to fulfill its purpose. Its real purpose, not the travesty that Beckett wanted to put it to. His fingers curled over the keyboard, as if in eagerness to input commands, or to seize Sam Beckett's neck.

But he wouldn't make the mistake of moving in haste. No. It was April now; the copies of the Project timetables showed that some additional programming was required, that not all the parameters had been set. There were always bugs to be worked out, of course. He was used to that.

There was no point in taking over too early, and being held responsible for other people's mistakes. He was still, after all, nominally answerable to the others on the Nonluddite Board of Directors. But he didn't want to arrive too late, either. Timing was everything.

And there was the publicity angle too, of course. He needed an event spectacular enough to justify the martyrdom of Sam

Beckett, while keeping it small enough in scope that the Project itself could be salvaged. It was a pretty problem, one that had occupied his spare moments for a few months. Months in which Sam Beckett had no idea what was in store for him.

Beckett's computer had a surprise in store as well. He had prepared a program of his own for it, and would be sending it on to a trusted agent within the Project this very day. It wouldn't be implemented right away, of course. But at the proper time, Beckett's computer would find itself with some truly amazing failures of memory.

Yen Hsuieh-lung smiled and reached for a cashew, rolled it around in his mouth to savor the flavor of salt.

Beckett had no idea at all what was in store for him.

That thought was delicious too.

"Ziggy." What a reprehensible name. He would change it. It would be his first official act.

Well, his second, perhaps. His first would be a eulogy for the former Director of Project Quantum Leap.

CHAPTER
SIXTEEN

So many regulations. So many rules to follow.

No smoking anywhere in the Project complex.

Dispose of waste properly.

Two-person rule to be observed in the main laboratory at all times.

Equipment operators must be properly certified.

Fire drill captains must meet once every two months.

Report safety violations to the proper authorities immediately.

All incidents must be reported in triplicate.

Project-wide safety meetings to be held semi-annually. Security meetings annually. EEO meetings annually. Quality assessment meetings quarterly.

Requisition materials through proper channels.

Wear hard hats in construction areas.

So many rules. The man sneaking down the hallway toward the Level Ten laboratory was sick of rules. You couldn't get anything done without tripping over another rule.

He was two hundred feet under the earth, beneath the cinder block houses that were the superficial appearance of the Project, beneath the Accelerator and the Imaging Chamber and the Waiting Room and the Control Room, down in the cold chambers. He was heading toward the design offices, the guts of the machine irreverently named Ziggy. The corridor was lined with cubicles, with desks and drawing boards and desktop computers, some linked in a local area network, some not. During the working day, the cubicles were occupied by members of Ziggy's design team, each handling a separate set of challenges in the building of a new and unique creation.

The design work was almost complete. As a result, most of the little offices had been abandoned. A few monitors still glowed; they were still taking data, still working some bugs out of the system. The big push now was information networking. It wasn't the janitor's concern.

At the end of the corridor were two larger offices, one belonging to Tina, one belonging to Sam. The janitor turned the knob on the door—the Project Director and a few others merited offices with doors—and went in.

He had wondered, often, why the Director needed two offices, one down here and one up on the Control Room level, next to the Admiral's. There was no logical answer. In the upper office Beckett took care of administrative things. Down here, he worked on Ziggy itself. More than worked on: he had created the computer. Once it was up and running, he had returned here sometimes for further study, or for consultation with his creation, or for a really challenging game of solitaire, as far as anyone knew.

The man didn't care. He had other concerns.

He had instructions.

Behind the office was the laboratory, where it was rumored Beckett had developed a patentable chip. He looked around curiously; his duties had never taken him in here before. The top left-hand quarter of the back wall was glass, extending from about waist-height to the ceiling. Round openings in the glass led to waldoes for manipulation of whatever was shielded. A viewing apparatus hung from the glass wall above them.

The top right-hand quarter of the wall was an open work area, with a positive air flow providing a breeze in the rest of the room. Whatever was being manipulated in the open area, then, was more fragile than the rest of the environment. Whatever was behind the glass wall was more dangerous.

He stared through the glass, trying to understand. A set of vials containing a pink gelatinlike substance were racked neatly in front of a set of instruments he wasn't familiar with. Lying on the table before the vials were a set of circuit boards, with curiously blank microchips scattered in front of them.

The open work area had more vials, more instruments, more boards. He could recognize oscilloscopes, acid baths, the new microwelders. Most of it he couldn't even name.

The bomb should interrupt work nicely, he thought.

He cleared his throat. "Ziggy?"

"Yes?" The voice came from everywhere and nowhere, and it made his flesh creep. But it was only the next step upward. He could walk into his house and start the air conditioner with a voice command, after all. Why shouldn't the air conditioner talk back?

"Where's Dr. Beckett?"

Anyone in the Project could ask for anyone else's whereabouts, and be informed immediately. Big Brother was always watching. The janitor had heard that that particular aspect hadn't even occurred to Dr. Beckett when he had Gooshie program the capability into the computer. He snorted to himself. Dr. Beckett was a boss. He was Management. Of course it had occurred to him.

He couldn't figure out how Ziggy knew who was where, but the pickups were in every part of the completed Project. At least the computer couldn't actually *see* what he was doing. He hoped.

"Dr. Beckett is in the Project cafeteria."

The cafeteria was some distance away. If he wanted to be sure things went as planned, he'd better get started.

Smuggling the bomb into the Project wasn't that difficult. It was someone else's invention; bombs weren't within his field of expertise, either. He had had quite a crisis of conscience when his instructions had arrived. Those pangs were eased when he was reassured that no one would actually be hurt; timing, however, was everything, and Dr. Beckett should be summoned in time to see the destruction. Preferably with the smoke still billowing.

131

It was important, then, that it go off before Beckett arrive, but not too long. He was assured that he had a lot of time. So the intruder set the timer, placed the bomb on the swivel stool, and said, "Ziggy, please inform Dr. Beckett of an emergency in his development lab." Then he began ransacking the laboratory for sets of the chips.

But he wasn't an expert. He couldn't see the delay built in and match it with the timer. He kept one nervous eye on the six-inch-square package, and decided to leave early. It had been almost nine minutes. It took at least fourteen to get to the development lab from the cafeteria, even when you were in a hurry. He needed time to get clear, after all.

But the package did look rather obvious, sitting there.

He reached for it, intending to put it in a better place. He moved it.

It blew up.

No one really knew the janitor before that moment.

He was not a scientist, nor was meant to be; he was but an attendant support worker, one that would do to swell a progress, set a bomb or two. He was one of dozens in the hive of activity that was Quantum Leap. His life had been recorded in infinite detail on Personnel Security Questionnaires, faithfully updated every five years, and his friends and acquaintances had been asked perfunctory questions about his financial status and sexual preferences and his loyalty. As a person, he was still a cipher, still of no importance, but well rated in his work: deferential, glad to be of use, politic, cautious, and meticulous. He had a small but essential job which the Project management had to be reminded of. None of them knew him by name, which was Riizliard, not Rosencranz, but might as well have been.

Once the bomb exploded, he, unlike Rosencranz or Guildenstern or J. Alfred Prufrock, became very important indeed. Nothing was as important in his life as the leaving of it.

Sam Beckett was at the entry to the main office area when the bomb in the laboratory went off. The force of the explosion was dissipated somewhat by the distance, but papers still flew everywhere, and alarms went off, sprinkler systems kicked in, and a cloud of smoke belched out of the door to his office. What used to be the door to his office—

"Ziggy!"

"Yes, Dr. Beckett?" The computer voice was oddly unruffled.

"What *happened*?"

"There has been an explosion."

"I can *see* that—" Sam was coughing in the smoke. "What's going on? Has anyone been hurt?"

"I have no visual sensors in the laboratory," Ziggy said. He sounded miffed. "However, the person who entered hasn't come out again. I speculate that this individual—"

Speculation became moot as the fire team moved in.

Sam grabbed an oxygen mask and moved in with them, keeping out of the way as much as possible while still looking for "the person." His office was a shambles, but the wall between it and the lab had taken most of the force.

The sprinklers shut off. Sam pushed debris out of the way to get to the body sprawled by the workbench. He barely spared a glance to the ruin of the protected areas, crunching through broken glass and wiping water off his face to see better.

It was immediately obvious that his skills as a medical doctor would be useless. It was far too late to help.

Now the only thing left was to clean up the mess, and find out what had happened—and why.

Neither William Riizliard's life nor the manner of his leaving it was of importance to Yen Hsuieh-lung, except insofar as the man did what he was told; what mattered was not that he had died—that was expected, at least by Yen if not by Riizliard—but that he had failed. In fact, he was roundly cursed. Either the bomb had gone off early, or the fool had called Beckett too late. They were both supposed to be dead. The news from his remaining contact within the Project was profoundly annoying.

As it was, only one of the two was dead, and that death was a worthless one. From Beckett's he could have built a case for martyrdom, but now the entire Project was in danger of being discredited. Yen Hsuieh-lung had no wish to take over a discredited Project. It was a most vexing error.

Fortunately, the situation was not impossible, not yet. The investigation he had expected would still go forward. He would still have someone in place. The original plan would have to be altered somewhat, of course. And he wasn't sure he could convince Jessie Olivera to commit murder. But he could certainly get the additional information he wanted about the Project.

He refused to give up. One day he *would* have the Project, and use it as it was meant to be used.

Jessie Olivera sat on the edge of her bed, her hand on the receiver of the telephone, staring blindly into space. This was it. This was the investigation Yen Hsuieh-lung had talked about: a fatal accident at Quantum Leap.

And of *course* there would be an investigation. She was certain she could talk Dreasney into putting herself on the investigation committee—nothing would be simpler; Dreasney was part of the oversight committee for the Project anyway. And where Dreasney went, her administrative assistant would go, too.

And this time her encounter with Sam Beckett might be more than casual. She could always hope. This time, at least, she wouldn't be leaving quite so quickly.

Yen had known there would be an accident.

Yen had said she wouldn't see Beckett again.

She took a very deep breath, feeling the air fill her lungs, her upper body rise as her lungs expanded. Surely the Nonluddites hadn't caused a man to die? They were a political action group, not a bunch of terrorists. She knew them, many of them. They weren't that kind of people.

But she was beginning to wonder if they had anything to do any more with Yen Hsuieh-lung.

134

How had Hsuieh-lung known there would be an accident to investigate? And if he had known because he had arranged for it, did that mean he had arranged for a man to die as well?

And did the right man die?

Jessie Olivera shuddered, and wondered if perhaps she shouldn't have cut her ties to Yen long ago, reputation and anger be damned.

The news about the accident interrupted Judith Dreasney in the middle of a game of Trivial Pursuit with her grandchildren. She heaved herself up from the floor where the board had been set up and took the call with an element of gratitude—they were playing the Sports edition, and she was pulling one too many questions about football. It was fun, of course, but she just wasn't that interested in football, and Mandy's son was on her team and knew everything there was to know about the subject anyway. She was chuckling to herself as she picked up the phone.

Sam Beckett's voice effectively destroyed her mood.

"What do you mean, a man was killed?" she said sharply. "What's going on down there? Don't you have any security in place?"

On the other end of the conversation, Sam closed his eyes. "Yes, ma'am, we do. We're trying to find out what happened."

"Are you sure there's only one casualty?"

"Yes, ma'am. William Riizliard." Sam shuffled through the personnel file he'd been supplied by an apologetic personnel manager. "He's—he was—single, no family—"

Thank God, he thought. He didn't want to have to inform a wife or parents or children that a man had died while working for him. It was unusual to find someone with no relatives at all. Sam thanked his lucky stars, while disgusted at his own cowardice.

"Was it an accident or deliberate sabotage?" Dreasney demanded.

Sam winced. This wasn't the kind of conversation he wanted to have over an insecure line. He didn't share the government's obsession with secrecy, but still . . .

"Beckett? Are you there?"

"Yes, Senator. We don't have an answer to that question yet."

"Sounds like there's a lot you don't have answers to," she snapped. "I think we'd better find those answers."

"We're working on it," he assured her.

"You'll pardon me if I don't take that at face value. I'm going to insist on a full-scale, *objective* review of what's going on there. You seem to have more problems than you have a handle on. Bombs? People dying? It won't do, Dr. Beckett. I want to know what's going on."

"No more than I do," he assured her. "No more than I do."

CHAPTER
SEVENTEEN

The problem of William Riizliard is not insoluble. There are gaps in the recorded data, however, which make drawing absolute conclusions difficult. He appears to have been an antisocial individual who left little in the way of physical evidence of his existence.

Or as my other father might put it, he was a real nozzle.

Two plus four equals seventy-eight.

Al Calavicci had been in war, had seen a lot of dead men in his time. He still didn't like it. Every formerly rational bone in his body quivered with superstitious horror at the thought of the violent death in the laboratory.

The initial investigation was done, the pieces of the bomb recovered and the incendiary reconstructed, the wrecked machinery and instrumentation removed. Sam had been gently but firmly set aside as the forensic investigators had made their measurements, taken down information, shot pictures which would be promptly classified. Now there was nothing left but cleaning up the debris, and Sam wouldn't let anyone else do that for him. So horror or not, five nights after the explosion, Al had to go to the laboratory to find him.

Sam had a broom and dustpan, a pail and cloth. It would have been a homely example of good housekeeping if it weren't for the bloodstains. Al, standing in the doorway with his back to the shambles that was Sam's office, screwed up his face in distaste.

"How can you stand it?" he said, watching Sam scrubbing steadily at the marks on the walls. "That's, that's not all blood, you know—"

"I know," Sam answered quietly, not turning around. He paused, resting his hand against the wall and rubbing his forehead against his arm. "I know what it *is*. I just wish I knew *why*."

Al looked around at the ruin of the laboratory. "Did you save *anything*?"

Sam shrugged, dumping the cloth back into the bucket. "Some things weren't here." He looked around. "Most of the work is done already. I was just about ready to close it down, except for a few details. There wasn't any reason to destroy this."

Al stepped gingerly over the freshly swept floor, pulled up one of the chairs Sam had brought in, and sat down. "Well, if you look at the timing, destroying *this* wasn't the purpose."

Sam smiled. "You noticed that too? He called me from here, Ziggy says. If I'd been a little faster I'd have been caught in it too."

"So it was set up as a trap for you. He probably expected to be long gone by the time you got here."

Sam nodded, silent.

"Do you have any idea why—"

"Don't you think I wish I knew?" Sam cried, throwing the reddened cloth across the room. "I don't know why somebody would want to kill me! I don't know why anybody would want to kill anybody!"

"Did you know the guy?"

"No! I saw him—he worked here. I never really talked to him. I never had anything to do with him. He was one of the maintenance crew. He was assigned to Ed Williams's area." Sam slid down the wall, ending up seated on the floor, and looked up at the other man. "I never knew him," he repeated.

Al accepted it, tried to deflect his friend's pain with analytical discussion. "Did Security finish the background check? Maybe it wasn't you they were after at all."

"No." Sam balled up another cloth in his fist, squeezing it, sending little wellings of pinkish water and cleaning fluid out between the fingers of his right hand. "They're still looking. And I don't even know if they'll tell me anything."

Al raised one eyebrow. "They'd better," he said, with the assurance of a former Admiral.

Sam's lips twisted, as if he'd bitten into something particularly sour. "They don't work for me," he reminded Al. "And Dreasney's going to be out here sometime—God knows when—with her entourage and put us all through it again. All the questions, all the fingerprinting, all the crap. As if they could find something the professionals missed." He swiped at a spot on the linoleum—a boot mark, unrelated to the present disaster, Al was glad to note. "We'll all have to go through our paces, only this time they'll have to do with how competent we are."

"They won't find anything wrong there," Al said loyally. "This wasn't your fault."

"How do I know?" Sam's voice was raw. "What did I do to Bill Riizliard? Why should he call me down here?"

"Because you're the boss," Al replied promptly. "You're the symbol. It doesn't have anything to do with Sam Beckett, not really. Look, the guy was a fruitcake, a real loser. He wanted to blow up something important. So he picked the most important thing he could reach. He was just dumb enough not to know how to set a timer, that's all."

"I wish I could believe that." Sam looked around again, helplessly. "I wish . . ."

"Believe it." Al looked up at the cracks in the wall, wanting to change the subject. He wasn't used to seeing Sam like this, and it made him uncomfortable. "What happened to your cultures?"

"Gone, most of them." There was no life in Sam's voice. "Everything that was in here is gone."

"You aren't going to be poking any more holes in my fingers, are you?" Al's alarm was only partly exaggerated; he disliked needles nearly as much as he disliked dead bodies. But he wanted Sam's attention back on the here and now—

139

to make him laugh, make him angry. Anything except this.

What he got was a twisted smile. "No more holes," Sam said. "If Ziggy doesn't have enough imagination by now, it never will."

"So you can build your computer?" A twisted smile was better than nothing.

"So I can travel in time." He rested his forehead against his arm again, and Al couldn't see his face.

It was a flat statement, uncompromising. He slumped back, the broom leaning against his shoulder and slanting at a crazy angle against the wall, the bucket of water with its faintly pink liquid still sloshing, rimmed with soap froth. His shirt was marked with sweat and water stains; his shoes and socks and pants legs were soaked. He looked like a particularly incompetent janitor. He was only forty-two, he looked even younger, his laboratory was a ruin, and . . .

"So you can finally see the past, right?"

"So I can go back in time," Sam said quietly, looking up at him. A line of sweat dripped down along the line of his jaw.

Al looked down at him and realized he meant exactly what he said. It should have come as no surprise; Sam generally did mean exactly what he said.

"I am not kidding. I built this computer in order for me, personally, to be able to travel in time, and I'm going to do it." He raised his head now, met Al's gaze, unflinching.

"I always told you that was what I intended, " he went on. "It's practically done. The Imaging Chamber is almost ready. I have to set limits, parameters on the Accelerator—but I can do it. Within my lifetime," he added scrupulously. "I can't get it farther back than 1953. It's tied up with the cells. The string theory says that with the proper link, you can travel within your own lifetime, from point to point. I thought by using your cells too I could push it back even farther, to the date of your birth. Maybe I can. We'll have to see. Maybe it depends on whether you're doing it, or I am. But I know I can do it."

"Have you tested this yet?" Al said warily.

"The traveling part?" Sam looked puzzled, wiped away the sweat and looked at the smear it left on his hand as if he had no idea how it got there. "No. Why?"

"Then how do you know it'll work?"

"The theory *says* it will," Sam explained patiently.

"Ahuh." Al reached into his vest pocket for a cigar, caught Sam's eye, and waved it around, unlit. "Okay. You can time travel, all the way back to 1953. You still didn't answer my question. *Why?*"

Sam's eyes slid away. "Because it's there," he said. He got back to his feet, lithe despite his awkward position, and picked up the bucket.

Al opened his mouth to challenge the younger man, and then shut it again. Sam didn't want to answer that question. Fine, that was his privilege.

"Don't you think the department is going to be a little upset by this?" he asked mildly, wishing he had a match. "All they're paying for is a computer, after all."

"They're getting a computer," Sam said. "They're getting the best computer in the world. I brought the elite together out here, Tina and Gooshie and all the others, and we built the very best computer they've ever seen."

"Your brains and my looks," Al smirked.

"Your brains and mine," Sam corrected him. "And Ziggy's. We're all linked now. When I travel, you can find me. When you travel—"

"*I'm* not going to time travel!" Al bit down on the cigar, hard, as something else occurred to him. "Sam, they want Ziggy for economic projections, for military assessments—but if it's your mind—Sam, can anybody else *use* this thing?"

"Can they use me? Or you?" Sam's mood had changed, become fey. It made Al nervous. He'd seen the same mood seize men taking sorties they never came back from. Hell, he'd felt it himself. It had only cost him six years of his life in a cage in Vietnam.

"The government's been using me most of my life," Al pointed out.

141

"I built Ziggy to travel in time," Sam repeated, turning to survey the ruins. "*This* doesn't matter."

"I'd say it does," Al contradicted him. "For God's sake, Sam, somebody's trying to kill you. Okay, maybe the Project is too far along for this to stop it. But if you die, that'll stop it, won't it?"

"I'm not going to die."

"Sam, does the word *hubris* mean anything to you?"

Sam laughed softly.

"I think this has driven you right around the bend." Al got up, jabbing the cigar into the air for emphasis. "This matters, damn it. Before you go traipsing off time traveling, you'd better protect your flank. You'd better find out first who's trying to kill you, and why, and fix it. Because the next time they might succeed. And what would happen to your traveling in time then?"

CHAPTER
EIGHTEEN

Late that night, Sam Beckett lay in bed alone, staring up into the velvety dark. The mood, the crazy, flying, wild certainty, had left him, and he was alone with himself and his theory and his dreams.

At times like this he thought about Donna Elesee, wondered where she was and what she was doing. She was just leaving Star Bright when he came on board, and had caught his eye immediately; somehow he'd managed to keep track of her, ask her out. He'd only known her a month; the longest and shortest month of his life.

At the end of that month they were supposed to be married. And she'd left him at the altar.

What if she'd been there, waiting for him? Would he be alone now? Would he even be *here* now?

No. This moment was the sum of all moments.

If he wanted to be here, now, he had to accept everything that led up to here and now. Changing things would change here and now.

And he'd already sacrificed too much for here and now. He'd missed saying a final farewell to his own father because an experiment was in a delicate phase; his mother had never forgiven him for that. He called her every year on Mother's Day and her birthday and Christmas, but he hadn't seen her in years. Even when he'd been mugged in Washington, she

143

hadn't left her home in Hawaii to come see him. Neither had his little sister. They'd called, but the conversation had been stilted and awkward and all three had been glad when it was over.

He felt, sometimes, that Katie's second husband, the man she'd found after finally getting free from the abusive bastard she'd married the first time, had replaced both Beckett sons in their mother's affection. He couldn't really blame her. Tom was dead, and Sam was never around when he was needed. Jim Bonnick was *there*. He was good and kind and wonderful to Katie and the kids, and they simply didn't *need* an absent brother-son-uncle.

And he hated that; he loved his mother and his sister, and he didn't understand what it was about himself that kept him apart from them, from everybody. "The kind of mind that comes along once in a generation"? One of Tom's professors had said that once, when he was thinking about not going to M.I.T. Or was his the kind of mind so different that he couldn't even stay in touch with his own family, couldn't keep the woman he wanted to marry, couldn't even keep around a woman met once in Washington?

Life was like a string; you could wad it up and where it touched, you could go from one part of the string to another. You could *see* what happened. But you couldn't change it. And even if there was a way to grab somebody in the past and say, *No, Katie, don't marry that jerk,* you couldn't do it. Because that would cut the string, and then where would you be? Here and now might just disappear, pop.

What if he could say, *Tom, don't go to Vietnam*? Would he sacrifice here and now for that?

He closed his eyes and drew a deep, shuddering breath. Yes. He would sacrifice everything, even the Project itself, for that chance, except—

It wouldn't be simply his *own* "here and now" that would go away. It would be other people's futures, too.

It was all moot anyway. The theory said that he could Observe, see and hear but not touch, not interact. Not change. The computer hadn't been built even yet that would allow

144

time to change. It would have to stand outside Time itself for that to happen.

Here and now would just have to remain intact. He was stuck with who he was and what he was and where he was.

His quarters at Quantum Leap were his only home. He had a storage shed in Albuquerque that held the accumulated trivia of his forty-two years. If Donna had been waiting for him, he wouldn't have that storage shed. He'd probably have a house somewhere, a suburban ranch house or a frame-and-stucco faux adobe. He'd be working for one or another of the labs, grousing about the wage freeze, yelling at his kids, wondering what the end of the cold war and the defense cuts were going to do to his pension plan, whether he could afford to send his kids to college.

Kids. He closed his eyes against the dark, against the thought and the pang of sorrow, but it did no good. He didn't have any children. He'd never had time. He'd always been working, except for that month with Donna. He had six doctorates to show for it; he could speak seven languages, including Japanese, Spanish, German, and French. He could read four more that hadn't been spoken in centuries, even hieroglyphics. He kept himself in shape; he used martial arts for exercise. But he had no children.

Never would, at this rate.

One more stage of programming, just one, and it would all be finished. He could step into the Imaging Chamber and tell Ziggy to create the field that would let him see time, and he could go back and find out why Donna left, he could be there when his father died. He could be with Tom at his last moment. No one would be able to see him, and he couldn't do anything to change things, to help, to *fix* it, but at least he would know how he got to this place, this time, alone. How, and *why*. Perhaps even make up, at least to himself, for some of his sins of omission.

What were all the choices, and when did they start? He was staring at the ceiling again, or up where the ceiling was, somewhere up in the darkness. What if he hadn't picked up that book on chess when he was a toddler? Would that have made a difference, or would he still be here, just not knowing how to play?

The math book his baby-sitter had left behind that day—what if he'd never looked at it? What if she'd been a little neater about putting her things away?

He heaved a sigh, vast enough to make the sheet slip down, and gooseflesh formed across his chest and arms. The Project was kept very cool. He pulled the sheet back up again, and schooled himself out of what-ifs and back into some semblance of scientific objectivity.

He wasn't going to get any sleep tonight, he knew. He thought about getting up and making a cup of decaf in the four-cup pot that was standard issue in all the Project's quarters, and couldn't generate even the enthusiasm for that. He had to get the progressions behind him, incorporate the last block of data. It was the homestretch, and he couldn't go down it until he had the formal investigation behind him.

He couldn't seem to get hold of the idea that someone might be trying to kill him. Riizliard's death was a tragedy, but the idea of he himself, Sam Beckett, being at risk was only an irrelevancy, an annoyance, an obstacle to completion of his work. Six more months of work, and he could step into the Chamber—but first, the mess had to be cleaned up. The lab was only the surface. The investigation was the hard part. Both investigations, forensic and Congressional.

He sighed again. He wished he could just turn it over to Al and get on with his work. He refused to take seriously the suggestion that anyone would want to kill *him*. It had been a terrible accident, but that was all. Just an accident. And now he had to put up with the consequences.

He hated this kind of thing. He didn't want to run things. He wanted to do science.

He began running the equations through his mind, slipping through the first part, the familiar, tested part, with the ease of long practice. The second hundred pages or so were a little more difficult. This was the point at which the possibility branches began to grow, interconnect, tangle.

The third hundred pages of equations put even Sam Beckett to sleep.

Jessie Olivera had never flown in a King-Aire before. She clutched the armrest with all her strength, watched horrified as Senator Dreasney placidly rotated the window to polarize the glare of the late-summer sun.

The four other passengers seemed to take the whole process quite in stride as well. They were looking through briefcases, talking softly about dossiers.

It was a short flight from Albuquerque, not more than two and a half hours. It seemed to take an eternity. She wasn't quite sure what direction they were going in—those polarized windows were very confusing, she couldn't tell where the light was coming from. When she could bring herself to look out the window, all she could see were long stretches of ruler-straight highways, purple mountains, and dirt freckled with trees. She thought they were trees, anyway. They could have been going in circles, for all she knew. When she looked down she could see antlike automobiles crawling along the highway. She wondered if their occupants knew where *they* were going.

She swallowed constantly, trying to equalize the pressure in her ears, and wondered when the plane was going to land. She had the worst headache of her entire life.

Back home, the foliage was beginning to turn to red and yellow, and the deer hunters were out after buck. The weather was beginning to be crisp after a long summer of humidity and heat; the haze of water in the air was beginning to thin.

This place didn't look like it had ever seen a haze of water. She had never seen any place so raw and empty and desolate in her entire life.

She had hoped that she'd never have to actually make this trip, that she'd never have to be a part of the investigation. As the days and weeks had gone by, she began to tell herself that it was all her imagination, she'd been seeing too many spy movies, that the accident at the Project had been just that, an accident and that nothing more would come of it, that she'd never have to talk to Yen again.

She'd forgotten that the wheels of government ground so slowly. It was early November now. The accident had been in late August. Three months to put together a full government audit team to cover everything—that was about right, she supposed, given that a lot of the paperwork had probably been done before any one of them had packed their bags to go to New Mexico to begin with. Only a half dozen were actually going to the site. One of them was Judith Dreasney. And because of Yen, one of them was Jessie Olivera.

The plane's engines changed their steady drone, and it banked in a tight curve. She sneaked another look out the window. There wasn't anything there. Why were they descending?

As they came around farther she caught sight of a cluster of buildings—four, she counted—and a water tower. Somebody's ranch? she wondered. There was a shed out by the road, a long tin roof that sheltered a series of trucks and vans from the blazing sun.

She was focused so completely on trying to see that it was a shock when the little jet hit the ground with a resounding thump, bounced twice, and reversed engines with a roar. She swallowed a scream, and grabbed at the senator's arm, but by that time they were down, and the King-Aire was taxiing to a halt not far from the row of vehicles.

Two passenger vans pulled out and came bumping over the desert toward the stretch of road the plane had landed on. Out of nowhere, men came running, wearing camouflage uniforms and carrying rifles. Security, she realized. Protecting the secrecy of the site.

Though why anybody would come to this place was beyond her.

If the cabin of the King-Aire had seemed cramped during the flight, it was positively spacious compared to the bustle of departure. The pilot moved down the narrow aisle to let down the three steps to the road, and then there were elbows and briefcases and excuse-me's until the party finally began filing out, one by one, claiming their luggage from the storage area in the back as they went.

148

Jessie caught her heel in the steps as she came down, and almost went sprawling onto the concrete. Catching herself on the rim of the door, she pulled herself up again, hanging on to the tatters of her dignity. Someone laughed.

She stepped away from the plane, her ears still ringing from the cessation of engine noise, and looked around. The dust and dryness pinched at the inside of her nose, and she brushed at it. The air was thin, and she could feel a full-fledged migraine coming on. The headache she'd had before seemed trivial, suddenly.

Off on the horizon she could see hills with their tops sliced off—mesas, exactly as they looked in the pictures. Closer to, she could see mountains, stark against the sky as if they were painted in blue and purple oils.

"Oh, look," Dreasney said.

Jessie dragged her attention back from the far places and looked down by her shoe, where the senator was pointing. A small yellow scorpion was poised there, tail curved up over its back, feeling at the tip of her right shoe with its two frontmost legs. Jessie yelped and danced back, nearly tripping again over a stack of luggage.

"Oh, it's only a little bug," the senator said. "It won't hurt you."

"She thinks it's something out of a sci-fi movie," one of the men from the General Accounting Office said. Jessie pulled herself together once again, keeping a wary eye on the scorpion and watching for any other fauna as well. She pulled her sweater closer, and wished she'd brought her heavy coat. The bright light and endless sky was deceptive; it was damned cold out here, and the sunlight offered no warmth at all. The guards approached them, rifles pointed to the ground, and asked for photo IDs. There was a general grumbling and scrabbling for identification. Jessie tried to smile at the young man who took her driver's license and checked it against a sheet on a clipboard. He handed it back to her, his expression unchanging, and went on to the next person. Jessie had the uneasy feeling that if the picture hadn't passed, if her name hadn't been on the list, he might have raised that rifle and

149

shot her and shown just as much emotion about it.

Once all the visitors had been verified against the list, the guards waved the vans in, and they came the last hundred yards, bumping their way down a well-eroded track to the runway, pulling up in a cloud of dust.

"About time," the man from the GAO muttered. "They should have been out here to meet us."

"Now now," the senator said. "If we're going to crucify them, let's wait until we've got the right wood, shall we?"

Jessie shot a look at Dreasney, startled. "Are we going to crucify them?"

Dreasney smiled enigmatically and turned to the two men getting out of the vans.

"Dr. Beckett. Admiral," she said, forestalling the apologies. "I think you know everyone here?"

"Not everyone." Jessie felt Sam Beckett's gaze slide past her, hesitate, keep going. At least he showed some reaction; he was surprised to see her, even though he hid it well. He must not have seen the list of visitors. He held out his hand past her to one of the investigators. "Sam Beckett. Project Director. This is my administrative chief, Admiral Albert Calavicci."

"Retired," Al amended. He recognized her too, Jessie realized, even though she knew him only from reading the Project dossier and seeing him with Sam at hearings and such. Why would he know her? she wondered. Did Beckett tell him all about that time together, years ago? Why would he remember, even if Sam had?

"Niall Simpson, Chief Investigator, General Accounting."

"Wes Rodriguez."

"Basley Fenn."

"Chip Nezlexi."

"And of course you know my chief assistant, Jessie Olivera," Dreasney said.

That did startle Sam, Jessie saw. This must be the first time he realized exactly who she was supposed to be. It probably didn't improve his opinion of her at all. His hand was warm and dry, with a firm grip, and she quelled a shiver at the

150

touch. He gazed at her steadily for a few moments, and then turned away.

The round of introductions completed, they loaded the vans and got in, the senator, Jessie, and one of the investigators in one van and the balance of the party, with the luggage, in the other, driven by Al.

"I'm afraid things are pretty spartan," Sam apologized as he manhandled the vehicle across the excuse for a road.

Jessie, sitting behind him, watched him in between bouncing between the seat and the ceiling. He kept his attention on the road. The conversational offering, if that was what it was, fell on deaf ears. None of the passengers tried to respond.

They were all grateful to pull up in front of an unprepossessing cinderblock building. The investigators were muttering about the lack of seat belts in the back seats. Jessie wondered if they realized they'd just been chauffeured a mile or more by a Nobel Prizewinning scientist. If they did, it didn't compensate for the jolting.

They took a few minutes to stretch, rub their bruises, and get the passengers from both vans sorted out before gathering around Sam and Al. Admiral Calavicci, Jessie noted, was not in uniform. Far from it; he was dressed in a conservatively cut business suit in a lightweight cloth of forest green. His shirt was a brighter, Kelly green. His tie and matching suspenders were spring and Kelly green swirled together and shot with sparkles, like an Irish view of the galaxy.

Sam was far more casually clad in jeans, hiking boots, and a light blue polo shirt. He fit in far better with the landscape, she thought. He was pale, though, not as tanned as you'd expect someone living in the wilds of the Southwest desert to be. He squinted in the sunlight, as if he didn't spend a lot of time out in it.

"As some of you may already know," he said, drawing their attention to himself, "these buildings represent the surface of Project Quantum Leap. The Project itself extends more than two hundred feet into the earth."

Two hundred feet? Jessie looked around again, wondering when they'd dug the hole, how they'd managed to restore the area so that it looked as if nothing had been disturbed here for decades. Deserts were fragile things.

"This is our assembly room and cafeteria," Sam continued, indicating the building behind him. "We don't hold classified discussions up here, of course. We also have a primary and an emergency generator building—"

"You have a lot of power difficulties?" Simpson interrupted.

Sam paused, just enough to make it clear that he had been interrupted. "Yes, we do. We couldn't put in a solar array, and running power lines has been a problem. We require quite a bit of power."

"Why couldn't you use solar energy?" Simpson was pugnacious. "Seems that's the only useful thing about being out here."

Another delicate pause. Jessie could see the beginnings of a real antagonism being born.

"A solar array adequate to gather sufficient energy to run the Project would be rather . . . noticeable," Sam said quietly. "The major advantage to building the Project here is its isolation."

"They've been complaining about the noise up in Taos, though," Basley Fenn supplied helpfully. "I remember reading about it in the news magazines."

"We don't know that that's us," Al put in. Sam moved his hand slightly, so slightly that Jessie wasn't even sure it was a signal, except that Al promptly subsided.

"We also have a false-front homestead which doubles as a security station, and a second entrance to the laboratory complex," the Project Director finished, pointing them out. "We realize you've had a long trip. We thought you might like to have a meal and settle in, begin the work tomorrow."

"Why?" Simpson snapped. "Why the delay?"

"Maybe because I'm getting old and would appreciate it," Dreasney spoke up for the first time. "It's been a long flight, and this altitude is beginning to get to me. I remember Jeff Bingaman brought some Hatch chile to a party last year. You wouldn't have any of that, would you?"

152

Sam smiled at the senator, and Jessie felt a pang. He'd smiled at her that way once. But this time he looked through her and past her. Keeping professional distance, no doubt. But that didn't make it any easier.

"Of course we have Hatch chile," he said. "It's a staple part of the diet. If you'd all like to come in?"

CHAPTER
NINETEEN

Simpson, outranked, was also outmaneuvered, and his expression indicated he didn't appreciate it. But he followed the rest of them inside the battered, crumbling building.

The inside, much to Jessie's surprise, wasn't battered and crumbling at all. It wasn't fancy, either. Long cafeteria tables, covered with plastic liners and plates and platters and bowls, bordered the walls. There were nicely framed posters, and an abstract figure in metal, curved over and playing a flute. The place smelled heavenly; Jessie decided her headache must be due to lack of food, and the sight of crockpots bubbling and bowls of chips and salsa and salads and guacamole, trays of breads and brownies and cold meats and cheeses, made her mouth water. The spread was obviously potluck. Most of the little party converged on the end of the table with the plates and silverware and napkins, and began loading up.

Simpson headed directly to the piano. "Who authorized the requisition for this?" he snapped, vibrating with outrage.

"It's private property," Sam answered, as he directed traffic and gave a wave-off to someone concerned about the heat in the salsa.

Simpson looked like he'd like to argue the point, but he had second thoughts and visibly subsided. Jessie wondered if he really would have gone through every purchase order issued by the Project over the past four years or so, just to see if he could find one labeled "musical instrument." There must have been thousands of orders to check.

No doubt if he really thought he could find one, he'd do it, just to embarrass Sam. It didn't bode well for the investigation to come. An auditor could always find *something,* no matter how conscientious and squeaky clean a project was. Simpson was determined to find something, and make as big an issue of it as he could get away with. Jessie made a note to mention that to the senator, and another note to steer clear of Simpson. She couldn't do what *she* had to do, whatever that might be, in front of a watchdog, either; she didn't want to find herself in trouble too. More trouble than she'd already made for herself, anyway.

She wondered how Yen was planning to get in touch with her. He'd given her a little personal-communicator computer, instructed her to connect it as soon as possible. After some debate, Security had passed it. So she'd communicate by modem, then, and e-mail. So simple.

A dozen smaller tables were scattered through the middle of the room. Jessie and the senator went through the line and sat down. Sam, last through the line, joined them just as they began digging in, finding more energy in every bite.

"Where's the admiral?" Dreasney asked, washing down a spoonful of green chile stew with a frantic swallow of coffee, covering the resulting cough and trying to behave as if nothing had happened. But he shoved the bowl of stew aside, Jessie noted. "Isn't he going to join us?"

"He's already eaten," Sam said. Jessie suspected, by the paucity of food on his plate, that Sam had already eaten, too, and was joining them only to be polite. "We thought we'd avoid a grilling the first evening you were here if you didn't catch both of us in one place at the same time."

Dreasney chuckled. "Smart boys." The humor vanished almost as quickly as it appeared. "You've had the FBI out here, haven't you?"

He nodded, and Jessie noted for the first time tiny lines of fatigue around his eyes. "They were here immediately after it happened, and left over two months ago. We won't get the results of some of the tests for a couple of weeks yet." He

155

mashed a lettuce leaf with the tines of his fork.

"But it was a bomb." Dreasney wasn't asking.

"Yes, it was a bomb." He put the fork down and took a deep breath, let it out reluctantly. "Yes."

Dreasney nodded, took another bite. "Meant for you."

"We don't know that," he objected instantly.

"Don't be a fool," she said. "The report I read said Riizliard called you to the laboratory. If you'd gotten there five minutes faster, we'd be missing a Nobel Prizewinner, and this project would be all over the evening news."

He laced his fingers around his coffee mug and stared down into the brown liquid. "I suppose that's true."

"Of course it's true. The question now is, is that what they wanted to do?"

The suggestion startled him. "What do you mean?"

"Did Riizliard want to kill you, or did he want to expose the Project?" Dreasney patted her lips with the napkin and picked up an iced brownie. "I'll want that stew recipe before I leave," she added. "That's good stuff."

"I'll tell Tina you said so," he said, still staring at her. "Expose the Project?"

Judith Dreasney gave him a pitying look. "Sam Beckett, I've been following your career since you went to college too soon. I know every up and down you've ever had. I knew your father—"

"You *what*?" he said with astonishment. Coffee splashed over the edge of the cup onto his fingers. He didn't notice. "You knew my *father*?"

"Of course I knew your father. He was interested in some of the farm bills I worked on when I was an aide, and then as a junior senator. He was a good man, was John Beckett."

Both Sam and Jessie were staring at her now, flabbergasted. Jessie was trying to visualize Judith Dreasney as an aide, doing the job Jessie Olivera did, and she couldn't imagine it.

She couldn't imagine Judith Dreasney doing some of the other things Jessie Olivera had done, either.

"And in all that time I never heard that you were any good at all at lying." The senator finished off the brownie with every evidence of satisfaction. "Mmmmmm—I'll want this recipe too."

"Lying?" Sam still looked poleaxed, but managed to work some "offended" into his voice as well.

"When all this started," Dreasney reminded him, keeping her voice low, "you were asking for funding for basic research. Now you've told us you're building a computer that can see the past. Ralph Bantham thinks you're joking—the man never could see past the nose on his face. But I knew when you wrote to us, 'a computer that could see the past,' that's what you meant. You're a literal-minded son of a cuss, Sam Beckett. Now if you've built the damned thing—"

Jessie listened intently. She'd never seen the report the senator was referring to. All of this was new. Seeing the past? What did they mean?

"We're practically finished," he interjected.

"—if you've built the damned thing," she repeated warningly, "why can't you use it to see what happened to this guy who placed the bomb, and stop him?"

"I can't," he said instantly. "I can't change the past."

"Why not? You never had anything in your life you wanted to be different?"

He flinched visibly. "Senator, I can try to explain the math to you if you want me to. But what it comes down to is the creation of paradox, and a macro-application of Heisenberg's Uncertainty Theorem. Even if it were possible, I couldn't guarantee that I could produce the desired change, and even if I did, the future would change too, perhaps to the point where I wouldn't be sitting here listening to you suggest this."

"Heisenberg talks about the effect of the observer on the observed," Dreasney said thoughtfully. "Doesn't he?"

Sam paused, struggling for words, starting several times and stopping again. "Yes," he agreed finally. "The very best solution to that, of course, would be to have a completely naive observer. The less the observer knew about what he was going to see, the better chance for an uncontaminated, objective report."

" 'Would be'? Not 'will be'? Doesn't the thing work?"

Sam blinked. "Of course it will work. We just haven't tried it yet."

"You're awfully confident for someone with no experimental validation to back you up."

"The math is sound," he insisted. "There's no reason why it shouldn't work."

"Let me get this straight," Jessie said, feeling as if she were intruding into a conversation on Olympus. "You're really going to go back in time? You, yourself, physically? People will see you? Won't that change things all by itself?"

Sam paused again, the pause of someone who has too much vocabulary and too much information to choose from. "They won't see me. I won't be able to affect them. All I'll be is an Observer—something like a, a hologram, without physical substance for the people around me. And they'll be—" he hesitated, as if he were reluctant to admit it—"like holograms to me, too. I'll be able to see and hear, but I won't be able to touch them." He took a deep breath. "Those are the last few details we're working out on the programming now."

Time travel. This, Jessie realized with a chill, was exactly what Yen Hsuieh-lung wanted to know. And if he did know exactly what Project Quantum Leap was really about, he would do—what?

"Simpson works for Bantham, you know," Dreasney said, as if the comment were relevant.

Sam Beckett studied her for a long moment. "Thanks."

For the warning? Jessie wondered. She knew Ralph Bantham had been impatient with the Project for months now, wanted to shut it down so he could crow about saving the taxpayers' money, reducing the deficit. She was surprised, in fact, that the little senator hadn't insisted on coming himself to strut around. It must have galled him to have to send Simpson in his place. But he'd still voted to continue support. Why? As a favor to Yen?

She wondered, suddenly, if Yen Hsuieh-lung had had a hand in selecting who would come and who wouldn't. Maybe he was even telling Bantham what to say in the private committee meetings, so he could look fiscally responsible and still

158

keep the money flowing. It seemed farfetched, but maybe it wasn't. The scientist wanted the Project to continue, as far as Jessie could tell. It seemed to fit in with the goals of the Nonluddites, as near as she could tell.

If she could just finish this one last task, whatever it was, she'd be free of the Nonluddites and Yen Hsuieh-lung, she decided suddenly. Seeing Beckett again—seeing him carefully ignore her—made up her mind at last. She was impatient, suddenly, to make her report to Yen and get it over with. So Sam Beckett wanted to go back and look firsthand at history? Fine. Let him. *She* wanted to get on with her life.

As the conversation continued, she began to wonder more and more why she was waiting. Why not simply tell Yen now that she quit?

Well, perhaps not now. She couldn't exactly leave this place. She wasn't even sure where she was.

As soon as everyone had finished eating, Sam escorted them into another room. One of the men yelped as it began to descend, and Sam explained about the elevator. Simpson snorted and made notes.

The Project had extra rooms; between scientists, engineers, maintenance, clerical, construction, security, trades, and administrative personnel, the Project had living quarters under the ground for almost seven hundred people. Even Simpson couldn't complain about extravagance, though; the rooms were twelve by twelve, with a cot, a bathroom, a closet, a dresser and a desk.

Simpson asked for, and got, a meeting room to brief his investigative team and to review records. He also wanted to know if he could consider the telephone lines secure.

Sam looked at him measuringly. "Why shouldn't they be?" he said. "As secure as any commercial line, at least."

"So you don't have a switchboard or a random tap?" Jessie couldn't tell whether the chief investigator would take a yes or a no as evidence of fault. Neither could anyone else. She noticed that even the other investigators glanced at each other with raised eyebrows at Simpson's combative tone.

Sam didn't respond in kind. "We don't tap our telephones. If you want to discuss classified information over the telephone, of course we'll have to use an approved secure line. We'll notify our COMSEC people to get the equipment set up. But otherwise, you can use any telephone in the complex." He was patient and unruffled and unfailingly courteous, and not in the least intimidated.

Simpson snorted, herded his team into the meeting room provided, and pointedly shut the door in the faces of Sam, Dreasney, and Jessie. Sam stopped short and turned to apologize to the two women for the rudeness.

The senator, forestalling him, asked for a general tour in the morning. "I'm looking forward to seeing this contraption of yours," she said. "I still don't really believe in it, you know. But right now I'd like to get some rest."

Sam laughed.

"And I *will* be talking to both you and the admiral," she reminded him. "You might be able to play dodge 'em with Simpson, but you can't get away with that with me. I'm too old and too crafty for you."

Sam looked at the senator, taking in her artfully touched-up graying hair, the lines around her eyes and mouth, the utilitarian traveling dress, the thick glasses. "And too wise," he agreed at last, a smile tugging at the corner of his mouth. "I'm not trying to put anything past you, Senator. I wouldn't dare."

"Just you remember that," she said, satisfied.

By then they had reached her quarters, and she went in, and for the first time in years, Jessie and Sam Beckett were alone together. He walked quickly down the featureless hallway to the next featureless door. "This is where you'll be staying."

"Sam," she appealed, "don't just ignore me, please."

He paused and looked at her, too, the same considering, measuring look he'd given the senator. This time there was no smile on his face. "I don't intend to ignore you, Miss Olivera."

"My name is Jessie."

160

"So you've said." He opened the door, stepped back, and then turned to her. "Look, I don't know what you think you're doing here. You're a very attractive lady. But if I'd known who you really were and who you worked for when I first met you, I'd—" He stopped, frustrated.

Jessie wondered how frustrated he would be if he knew who she was *really* working for that night two years before—and still was.

"What I said that night was true," she told him. And it was, she realized suddenly, looking at him. "I *had* read your work, and I did—do—think you're . . . attractive, too. And I did want to talk to you. That had nothing to do with who I worked for." She held up her hand, and he stilled the comment he had been about to make. "I know my working for the senator makes a difference to you, and I'm willing to accept that. But I hope you don't think badly of me for it."

"How should I think of you?" he asked.

That was a question she couldn't answer at once—not with the image of Yen Hsuieh-lung hovering in the back of her awareness. "With kindness," she said at last. "You can manage kindness, at least?"

She thought she could hear dust settling in the stillness. There were only the two of them in the long white corridor, and she couldn't tell if it was crowded, or incredibly lonely.

"I hope I can always manage kindness," he said at last.

She closed her eyes in guilty relief. When she opened them again, he was walking away.

CHAPTER TWENTY

"And this is the Imaging Chamber," he said, leading them up the ramp. It was midmorning of the next day, and they were getting the fifty-cent tour, as Al Calavicci put it.

The ramp led up to a steel door, with an intervening space of perhaps four feet before the inner door. The senator stopped in between, looking around. "Why the airlock?" she asked.

Sam paused, looking back at the little tour group. "That's the Accelerator," he said. "It—um, I'm not sure how to explain it. It starts the process of reversal."

The senator looked around curiously. Jessie felt her flesh creep, as if the air were filled with ambient electricity, and she stepped through the inner door quickly, looking back at the older woman and at Simpson, waiting patiently behind her.

"It's just this little room?" she wanted to know. "This is your Accelerator?"

"No, it goes all the way around the Imaging Chamber; that's just the passageway through it. If you'll come in here—"

Sam seemed uncharacteristically nervous too until the senator nodded, still dissatisfied, and stepped out of the airlock. "This is where you'll be?"

Sam exhaled, looking around. "Well—yes. I'll stand here." He stepped onto a silver disk a yard wide. Over his head another disk was poised, apparently in midair. "And I'll be able to observe the past as it happens."

"Mmmmm," Dreasney said noncommittally. "But you haven't tried it out yet."

"Not yet." Sam glanced up at the ceiling, as if about to say something more, and then back at the two women, changing his words. "Of course, the theory is sound."

"It better be, for what it costs," Dreasney said. "Two point four billion a year. We run a couple of national laboratories for that kind of money." She looked around again, at the plain walls, the silver disks.

Jessie found it disappointing too. Just . . . stand there, and see the past? You could do as much lying in bed at night, reviewing your own memories. And how did he know he wouldn't just be seeing a computer re-creation of news stories? How did he know he was seeing the real past?

Jessie could tell he could see he was losing them. She might not matter, but the senator did. "You can travel in time." He was talking too fast. "You can go anywhere, any *when* within your own lifetime. Ziggy will take you to any event, any person, and you can see what really happened. There won't be any more mysteries, no more conspiracy theories. Just the truth."

"The truth has an awfully high price," the senator said.

Jessie winced. Simpson had spent at least an hour this morning talking to Dreasney, reviewing the investigation plan. The emphasis on cost/benefit ratios was enough to sour the coffee.

"When you first pitched this to us, you told us about basic research," the senator was still talking, "about the intangible benefits. You described a next-generation computer. You still haven't shown us any of that, Sam. You've spent a great deal of money, and we haven't seen any return on it. We're really going to have to consider cutting our losses."

Sam was staring at her like a man who for the first time has realized that the lifeline he thought was in his grasp was broken after all, and who doesn't want to—who cannot—believe it. All the color had drained from his face.

"I can do it," he faltered.

"I know you can," Judith Dreasney said patiently. "If anyone in the world can, you can. But don't you see, Sam, the question is not if you *can,* but if you *should.*"

"Ziggy," Sam whispered. "Ziggy, tell them."

From nowhere, another voice joined the conversation, a man's voice, petulant. "I don't know what you want *me* to say," it said. "I'm just the computer you haven't *bothered* to introduce yet."

Dreasney paled. "What is—"

"Senator," Sam said, his voice stronger suddenly, "I'd like you to meet the results. This is Ziggy."

"Ziggy?" Dreasney was still looking for the source of the voice.

"Ziggy, this is Senator Judith Dreasney. And her chief aide, Jessica Olivera."

"*What* is Ziggy?" the senator sputtered.

"A parallel hybrid neurocomputer," the voice said. "Nice to be introduced, Senator. At last." The latter remark seemed to be directed, however spitefully, at Sam.

The senator managed to pull herself together, while still looking around for the source of the voice. "That's quite amazing," she said. "I had no idea you could get a computer to sound so natural, or distinguish between and recognize individual voices on so little data. It must have an incredible memory capacity."

"Hmmph," said the voice that was Ziggy.

"Can . . . Ziggy . . . see us?"

"I have visual pickups in this room, Senator," Ziggy said.

"He can see you," Sam translated.

"That's what I said," Ziggy snapped.

What would Yen Hsuieh-lung do with this? Jessie wondered. What was he planning to do? She stood back at the periphery of the group, watching Beckett and the Senator, and began to see how important it was to him. She couldn't for the life of her imagine Yen standing there, his hand resting casually, possessively on the wall because it was all so very much a part of himself. This was Sam Beckett's place.

164

"The programming must be incredibly complex," she volunteered.

"Like most complex things, it's ultimately very simple," Ziggy said, with a distinctly self-satisfied air.

"I don't think I like your computer's tone, Sam," the senator said dryly. "Did you forget to program in some manners?"

"I'd like to see the programming area," Jessie interrupted hastily. If she could get a set of specs to Yen, surely that would be enough? Of course, "a set of specs" for something like this might mass more than *she* did.

They went down deeper into the earth, deeper into the Project, in an uncomfortable silence. They went past the curious glances of various Project personnel, some of whom offered tentative greetings to their Director. He smiled and waved back and kept going, leading the others deeper and deeper and deeper into the realization of his dream.

Finally he led them into a long room; at one end a hive of workers buzzed, and even the air conditioning couldn't quite overcome the smell of fresh paint and plaster.

"It happened down here, didn't it?" the senator said.

It dawned on Jessie that it was actually down here, under ground, that a bomb had been set, and Sam had been invited to his death, and another man had died instead. And that the workers at the other end of the room were still busy repairing the damage of last August.

"It happened down here," Sam agreed. "Down here is where the data input happens, and where the computer design is tested, and the final programming is tested." He waved his arm, an oddly graceful gesture, at the row of cubicles, each with its own desk, its own monitor and input and pointing devices. He stepped into one of the cubicles, touched a switch, and the monitor blazed to life. "I can input directly to Ziggy, and Ziggy can incorporate the data itself."

"Are you saying it's self-programming? That your computer can learn?"

"That's not a new concept," Ziggy sniffed.

Both Dreasney and Jessie jumped.

165

"Ziggy, can it," Sam said, annoyed.

"Well, it isn't."

"They know that. Now go think about things, Ziggy."

"Very well, Dr. Beckett."

"It has quite an ego, hasn't it?" Jessie ventured.

"Computers don't have egos," Dreasney snapped. But she was looking around uneasily.

"Ziggy does." Sam wasn't inclined to discuss it.

"What about the parameters?" Jessie said, changing the subject. "The ones you're still inputting?"

Sam smiled crookedly, reached out to a foot-thick stack of printout, one of a dozen similar stacks, and riffled through it. "These, you mean?"

"All of those?"

"Well, not quite. These are the ones already input."

Jessie craned her neck to see the lines of code. They looked like line after line of ones and zeros, six lines to a page. Not all that intimidating after all, perhaps.

"I'd like to see the actual site of the accident," Simpson was saying.

The chief investigator had no interest in the computer at all, Jessie thought. No real appreciation for what Sam Beckett had accomplished. She lingered behind, looking at the lines of code, the notes that the unknown occupant of the cubicle had left behind, and then glanced guiltily at the ceiling, wondering if Ziggy had "visual inputs" in this room, too.

She asked, when she caught up with the other two as they paused to make way for workmen carrying a large sheet of Plexiglas into the inner office.

"No. The people working here didn't want the feeling that Ziggy was always looking over their shoulders," Sam said, not really paying attention. "Audio, sure, but not visual."

"He can hear us?" she said, not sure why she felt so apprehensive.

"Jessie, it's just a computer!"

"You could say that," Sam said, his tone making it clear that he didn't share the opinion.

Dreasney paid no attention, moving past him into the office. "It happened here?" she said, looking around. "There doesn't seem to be that much damage."

"Actually it happened back here," he said, leading them into the laboratory behind the office.

"How many people usually worked in this area?" Dreasney asked.

Sam hesitated. Watching him, Jessie saw that he recognized both the trap in the question and the fact that there was no way to avoid it. "I usually worked down here pretty much by myself by that time," he admitted.

"So much for safety protocols, eh, Dr. Beckett?" Simpson came up behind Jessie, making her jump. She was getting tired of being startled. "Didn't you observe standard safety procedures?"

"The work done in this lab was such that a two-person rule was never required," Sam said defensively. "I violated no safety standards."

"What about human experimentation standards?" Simpson barked. "You've called this a 'neurocomputer.' What does that mean, exactly? Human neurons? That falls within the purview of a Human Experimentation Ethics Board, doesn't it?"

"Yes, it does," Sam admitted.

"And you haven't had that review, have you?" Simpson said, pushing.

Sam didn't answer. Simpson wheeled around to the senator, triumphantly. "That's all, then. The whole project has to be shut down, right now."

"No!" Sam didn't say it; Jessie did, in response to the look on his face. "You can't shut it down now. It's too close to being finished."

"It's against the law to conduct experiments involving human subjects without an Ethics Board review," Simpson snapped. "We could put the good Dr. Beckett in jail."

"We could," Dreasney agreed mildly.

We could. . . . But not *We're going to.* Jessie's eyes narrowed.

"Dr. Beckett hasn't been convicted of anything yet. We're going to have to have another hearing," Dreasney went on, forestalling Simpson. "Meanwhile, I want to see this laboratory."

Sam showed her the new machines, demonstrated and let her try out the waldoes. Simpson hovered, fuming.

Over lunch, Dreasney made it clear—in a delicate, inoffensive, but very clear fashion—that she did not wish to eat with the Project Director, the Administrative Director, or her own Chief Investigator. Jessie wobbled, not sure the disinvitation might not also apply to her. The senator smiled and asked her advice on the choice of Lean Cuisine entrées available in the cafeteria, and then herded her over to a table in a corner, shielded by the piano from the direct view of the other occupants of the room.

"*Are* you going to charge him?" Jessie asked, unable to contain herself.

"Oh, I don't think so," the senator said airily. "I expect something will be found in a file somewhere that exempts this Project. A presidential order, or something like that. We can't very well put a Nobel Prizewinner in jail, after all."

Jessie gulped convulsively, swallowing a mouthful of too-hot microwaved lasagne in the process. "Are you serious?"

"Oh, it wouldn't be the first time something essential to the national security has winked at federal regulations. Mmmm, this really isn't bad at all, is it?" The senator continued to eat with evident enjoyment.

Jessie blinked. She wasn't sure what surprised her about all this—after all, she'd spent all of her adult life in Washington, and she knew the cynicism of politics very well indeed. Perhaps it was just the idea that it was Judith Dreasney, of all people, who was casually dismissing a federal law as if it were irrelevant, a mere bagatelle. Whatever a bagatelle was. Not a computer, certainly.

"I can't tell whether you're on his side or not," she said at last.

The senator smiled. "No, you can't, can you?"

"Are you going to shut down the Project?"

This time there was a moment, barely an eyeblink long of hesitation before the smile. "We'll have to wait and see about that."

"What's he supposed to do in the meantime?" she burst out, frustrated.

"Oh, I imagine he'll find something to occupy himself." There was another pause, as if the older woman were turning over possibilities in her mind. "I think you should stick around," she said at last. "I *will* want to be kept up to date on what's going on, after all. Yes," she nodded to herself. "Definitely. You can stay out here, can't you?"

"I—yes, of course!"

Dreasney smiled yet again, showing a bare gleam of teeth. "That's my good girl. We won't tell him yet, though. It'll be our little surprise."

Jessie sat back in her chair, her gaze never leaving the other woman, while Judith Dreasney thought about vote trades and sheep with four horns and wondered just how much Ralph Bantham's Nonluddite moneymen really wanted Sam Beckett to fail—and why?

CHAPTER
TWENTY-ONE

Yen Hsuieh-lung reviewed the hastily scribbled notes appearing on his computer screen the next morning, and cursed the inventor of the pen-sensitive monitor. Handwriting was handwriting, and was just as illegible—no, *more* illegible—for being inscribed on a screen and sent via superfast modem. He gathered, however, that Jessica Olivera wouldn't be reporting back in person to clarify things. She was going to be staying in New Mexico for a while.

And that Sam Beckett really was trying to travel in time.

He snorted, softly. Beckett was over forty—his brains must be going soft.

But the computer, now that sounded interesting. There wasn't enough in the note to understand exactly what Olivera meant; he was going to have to talk to her at length.

It was perhaps fortunate after all that Riizliard had failed. He had been exceedingly foolish to have made an elementary mistake in timing, of course, and had paid appropriately. But it was always wise to have as much information as possible before eliminating all options.

Fortunately he had a far more reliable person in place for the next step. He would talk to Olivera, find out what she had seen. With her previous experience with the man, surely she could acquire enough data to reinforce Yen's understanding and make himself an even more attractive candidate to replace Beckett.

He would commission an oil portrait, perhaps, of Dr. Beckett, to place in whatever they used for a lobby, or foyer, or whatever they called it in New Mexico. Visitors could see it as they came in.

Or perhaps he'd put it in his executive office, where *he* could see it. And throw darts at it, if he wished.

He pulled the keyboard to himself, and began composing the messages that would bring all his planning to fruition.

"Al, honey, what's the matter?" Tina blew lightly on her fingernails and spread her hand to observe the pattern critically. That new polish was supposed to come out like rainbows, and it didn't seem to be working right. She peeked between her fingers at the man pacing back and forth between the computer and the tea table, chewing ferociously at a cigar the size of a chair leg. "The investigators are all done, and Dr. Beckett's laboratory is all fixed, so everything is all right, isn't it?"

"Nooooo, I wouldn't say it was 'all right,' " Al snarled, stopping and whirling around in his tracks.

It was late in the evening. Tina was dressed in her best baby-doll pajamas, following her regular Tuesday-night routine: Tuesday was fingernails, Thursday was toenails (with tissues between the toes), hair was every other night. Al had come by for conversation and other comfort, but was too wound up to sit down. He was still wearing the relatively subdued pearl-gray suit with silver pinstriping, with a white satin brocade vest and a black shirt—Tina had considered it stifling just to look at—that he'd worn to talk to Simpson's people today. They'd been after him for the past week, and when they weren't after him they were going through his files.

He'd been dealing with interrogators, in one uniform or another, his whole life. Answering questions was no big deal. The threat to Sam's project, however, was something else again.

"If it had been a legitimate accident," he repeated for the thousandth time, "that would be one thing. But damn it, the guy was a saboteur! It isn't our fault if a stupid saboteur blows his own head off instead of the one he was trying for!"

Nail fixed to her satisfaction, Tina got up and swayed over to the little coffeepot she kept on the tea table. It was a measure of Al's agitation that it took a moment for him to register and appreciate her movement, with the fluffy fringe of the pajama top brushing the tops of her thighs. Tina poured a cup and held it out to him, and he took it and gulped, barely tasting it, and handed it back.

"Six months," he fumed. "Six months, that's all Sam needs, and then he can *prove* he's right. Those yahoos won't believe him until they can stand there in the Imaging Chamber and see it for themselves."

"Can they?" Tina's eyebrows arched.

"Can they what?"

"Can they stand in the Imaging Chamber and see? I thought Ziggy was only linked to you and Sam."

"Well, it is, for right now. That's one of the reasons why he still needs six months. But don't say that to those damned auditors—they'll double the charges against Sam."

"Oh, they never ask *me* anything." Tina smiled a sunny smile and batted big blue eyes at Al. "I think they think I'm, like, dumb or something."

Al laughed, reluctantly. "I can't imagine why." The heavy sarcasm in his tone wasn't lost on Tina, who swayed back to her four-poster bed and arranged herself on the ruffles. She beckoned to Al with one long-nailed finger.

"Maybe they don't know me as well as you do," she cooed.

"God, I hope not," he said, taking off the silver-striped coat.

Elsewhere, Sam Beckett walked the halls of the Project, reaching out to trail his fingertips along the walls as if to guide himself. He met no one, and his steps echoed in the empty tunnels and offices.

It was as if the Project were already shut down, and he was a ghost, haunting it. There were at least three miles of tunnels, more if you counted the hallways around the offices and labs and living quarters. He avoided the living quarters. He didn't much want to see anyone living just now; some perverse part of himself was enjoying the image of being a ghost, unable to touch or communicate.

He had the feeling that his life was on the auction block. Dreasney had hinted at an out for him, a way to avoid the consequences of using human tissue without going through an Ethics Board. The fact that it was his *own* brain tissue— and Al's nerve cells—was irrelevant. The law said that any research involving human subjects had to be reviewed, and he'd broken that law. He was willing to take the consequences, but first—

It reminded him of the time when he was six, and his father had found him in the middle branches of an apple tree he was forbidden to climb. John Beckett had ordered him to come down and get his spanking, and he'd done so—but he'd climbed all the way to the top first, and looked around to see what he could see. He shuddered at the memory.

He wanted very much, now, to see what he could see before taking this particular spanking.

He was afraid, though, that Dreasney was going to try to deal, to trade his project for something else she wanted, and she wasn't about to consult his wishes in the process. The Project was being taken away from him, and he was helpless to prevent it.

He'd always known this day would come, someday.

He'd hoped that the view from the top of the apple tree would be worth it, that he could climb down again with news of something so wonderful, so amazing, that . . .

John Beckett never forgot when he'd promised a spanking, though.

He stepped into the programming office area, stopping to let his eyes adjust. A guide light ran along the bottom of the walls, glowing dimly. He didn't bother to turn the lights on. He knew the way to the offices in the back even in the dark, could find his way inside and to the battered leather armchair without any more illumination.

"Are you all right, Dr. Beckett?" Ziggy asked. "Would you like more light?"

"No, thanks." He stretched out and slid forward, slumping deep into the chair, lacing his long fingers over his belt buckle. For a while all he could hear was the sound of his own breathing.

"Your respiratory pattern indicates you may fall asleep within the next three minutes," Ziggy noted. "Sleeping in your current position will lead to severe muscle strain."

"I know," he groaned, struggling back upright. "I've done it before."

"That *is* the source of my data."

Sam smiled crookedly. "I thought so." He'd spent a good many nights working himself to exhaustion, sitting in this chair. "So. Do *you* know what our fair senator has on her mind?"

"I know what you would know, if you had access to the data."

Sam's eyes were still heavy, and he closed them. Just to rest them. "Am I really this insufferable? Or is that Al's cells talking?"

"Self-examination is not one of my strengths."

Sam forced his eyes open again. "Definitely Al."

"You are certain of your own motives, then?"

"Why do I have the feeling I'm talking to myself?" Sam yawned. "All I want to know is what the senator's going to do, so I can figure out what's going to happen next."

"Perhaps you should have specialized in chaos theory."

"*Everybody's* a critic." But he was smiling in the dark.

"What do you want to do?"

Sam stared up through the darkness to where the ceiling was—the ceiling probably was. The little glowing jewels on the workstation didn't provide enough light to tell.

The ceiling had been there the last time he checked.

"I want to know." A wave of loneliness washed over him, and he automatically diagnosed low blood sugar. Of course, he'd had dinner, and he wasn't hypoglycemic. . . .

He was *lonely*. He was sitting by himself in an office, talking to a computer who was really just another avatar of himself, and face-to-face with the realization that the computer

174

was probably the only thing that could really understand him. And Ziggy didn't have a heart, or hormones, or a soul.

There were acquaintances from school, of course. From various research projects. They weren't friends though, not really—he'd been too busy learning to make friends.

There was his family, his mother and sister. But the thought of them always brought a stab of sorrow, because he couldn't think of them without thinking of his father and his brother and feeling as if he had failed somehow, to be where he was needed when he was needed.

Al was a friend. He could depend on Al. He could trust his life to Al, but he couldn't talk advanced quantum physics with him. Al filled one essential need, but there were other needs that stood hollow—the need for pure intellectual challenge, the need for physical passion.

Someday he might find a woman who could fill that need to love and be loved, real love, not pheromone-induced lust. The thought led inexorably to Jessie Olivera, and he sighed. He still found her very attractive, though not as overwhelmingly so as when they'd first met—fortunately, he told himself with a wry smile. He wondered if she thought about that night, years ago. She was still lovely, and he could still feel that atavistic tug. But she wasn't right.

The woman he could love was out there, somewhere. Maybe. He'd thought he'd found her once, but . . .

Only with Ziggy, though, could he talk science at the level of exploration, of excitement and creativity. Only the product of his own mind could match him in that one area; it was one of the penalties of having an intelligence quotient so high. "The kind of mind that comes along only once in a generation, or more"—and is, as a result, always alone.

And if something didn't go right soon, they'd take even Ziggy away from him.

He stared up at the ceiling and blinked furiously at the stinging in his eyes.

CHAPTER
TWENTY-TWO

"Your task is to acquire the program for the time-search element and transmit it immediately. Be aware that I have appointments with both Senators Bantham and Dreasney as soon as they return from their respective travels. Be further aware that you are not my only resource. Your worth is being evaluated based on this assignment."

Jessie Olivera stared at the blue-on-blue text of the computer screen, appalled. Her orders had never been quite so direct before. Before, they'd always been phrased as hints, suggestions, steel hidden by silk. "Your task is to acquire . . . and transmit it immediately." The silk was gone.

Yen didn't seem upset that she wasn't coming back right away. That meant he wanted her here.

Why didn't he just ask his other "resource" to get the information for him? she wondered desperately. Why make her do it? Why did she *have* to do it? She wasn't really guilty of anything. There wasn't anything really wrong with what she'd done. . . .

That wasn't true, and she knew it. She could see the look on Dreasney's face if Yen Hsuieh-lung called her and told her, more in sorrow than in anger, that her most trusted senior aide had been violating her confidence for years, passing along information about Dreasney's most secret correspondence and deliberations to lobbying organizations, to other politicians. She had violated her employer's trust, and probably broken federal laws regarding secrecy as well.

What would Sam Beckett say if he knew what she was supposed to do? If he found out she'd passed along information—she stopped suddenly, frozen in the grip of a sudden revelation, struck by the blindingly obvious. Even if there was some chance what she had done before wasn't quite illegal, not really classified, what she was being asked to do now unquestionably was. Project Quantum Leap was Top Secret. Program files for the computer would be, too. She could actually go to jail over this. If she obeyed her instructions— no, her orders—Yen Hsuieh-lung would have her for the rest of her life.

Maybe Yen wouldn't even bother to call. Maybe he'd just contact the press, report that she had been on the Nonluddite payroll and supplied information to them for years. Jessie could protest in vain that it wasn't true; the Nonluddites had enough information that she'd provided that it would *look* true, and in Washington as elsewhere appearances were everything.

Even if it wasn't, even if she wasn't convicted of anything, she'd never work in Washington again. Or in politics anywhere else, for that matter. Nobody hired an untrustworthy aide.

Yen Hsuieh-lung had her neatly, finally trapped. Such a blatant order could only mean that he never, never intended to let her get loose. She'd never be able to quit.

And now she really had to.

She didn't know what he wanted the time-search program for, but whatever it was wouldn't be in the best interest of Sam Beckett or his Project.

She took a deep breath and got up, pacing back and forth from the desk to the windowless wall and back again, not looking at the computer screen, ignoring the little square cursor blinking steadily at the end of the **Acknowledged?** line. Her quarters were bigger than her cell would be, she thought wildly. They probably smelled better, too, even though she could still detect traces of fresh paint in the air.

At least she now had the answer to the question about why the Nonluddites had picked her. If she was stupid enough to do as he asked, she'd be a compliant tool for as long as he wanted.

177

And she'd *been* compliant, and stupid, for years now.

If she didn't cooperate, she wouldn't have a career. He might even have her killed, if what she suspected about the "accident" was correct.

If she didn't provide the program, somebody else would. Somebody else, a mole in the Project, somebody working for Yen Hsuieh-lung. His other "resource."

She could go to Sam. Tell him.

He wouldn't believe her. He didn't trust her.

She stopped in the middle of the room, looking around. Did she owe Sam Beckett anything, though? So what if she spent the rest of her life working for Yen Hsuieh-lung? Was that so bad? She had no proof he was a criminal.

Except that he was asking her to perform a criminal act. He could deny the message on the screen, though, say that she'd put it there herself.

The little communicator beeped at her peremptorily.

She wheeled around and stared at it, panicking. Could the man on the other end of the modem connection see her? Was there a V-connect on the machine he'd provided?

Breaking her freeze, she lunged at the desk and slapped the screen down, ignoring the indignant electronic squawk.

She could still see the lights in the case: power on, modem transmission enabled. The steel gray case shone dully in reflected light, as if it were a slab of rock with jewels set into the edge. A waiting rock. A deadly rock.

The communicator beeped again.

Jessie fled.

Al strode along the corridor, chewing savagely at the end of his unlit cigar. All this *afflizione* about investigations and audits and Congressional committees, and internal personnel problems too—it was more than he should have to put up with. They needed to bring back their on-site psychologist, Simpson had informed him. Remote sites caused stress. It wasn't good for the mental health of the Project employees.

Little did Simpson know that the most stressed member of the Project at the moment didn't even have a body. Ziggy had taken to interrupting at the most inconvenient moments. He was worried about Sam, and wanted Al to go check on him.

Al stalked on. The only warning he had of impending collision was the sound of running footsteps somewhere in the cross-corridor up ahead; the acoustics were lousy, and it was hard to tell how far away things were, but at least he was more or less prepared to dodge when that senatorial aide, the one with the big nose, came flying around the corner at a dead run.

"Hey! Are you okay?"

She just looked at him out of watery, red-rimmed blue eyes, shook her head, and kept on going.

More personnel problems. Al grunted and looked down the hall from which the woman had come. It was completely empty except for lighting fixtures.

"Crazy woman's running away from herself," he muttered.

"No one is in pursuit." Ziggy's voice was hushed, as if there was some chance he might be overheard by someone on the investigation team—a precaution taken a couple of days too late, in Al's opinion. They'd already heard him talk. "Ms. Olivera came out of her quarters."

"Anybody in there with her?"

"Only another computer. I have no monitors in guest quarters, Admiral. But she does have a computer hooked up to the televideo/power line."

Al shrugged and kept on going to the elevator on the far end of the hall. "Probably writing a report about how much fun it's going to be to shut us down," he said. "Where's she going in such a hurry?"

If a computer voice could have a frown, then Ziggy's did. "I am unable to extrapolate motivation from her actions."

"What, you're *not* perfect?"

"Of course I'm not perfect, Admiral. Merely superior." With that Ziggy clicked, the signal it had adopted to indicate it was no longer using audio communication channels. There wasn't any real switch to click off or on, and Al was morally sure that the computer continued to listen, but once Ziggy clicked, it wouldn't continue a conversation for anything short of a direct order to resume communication.

Which Al, at the moment, was not inclined to give. Nor was he inclined, of a sudden, to talk to Sam. He headed for Tina's quarters instead.

At nine the next morning Al was at the door to Sam's laboratory office, peering into the dark. "Sam? Are you in there?"

"Lights, Ziggy," came the response, in the middle of a yawn. The lights came up, and there was Sam, his eyes squeezed shut against the brightness. Al, who had learned long since to look away from an increasing light source, waited impatiently for the other man to look at him.

"What do you need, Al?"

"Some direction," Al said bluntly, sliding into his accustomed chair. "Are we going to fold up and die? Are we going to let these pencil-pushers tell us what to do? Are we going to test? What? Dreasney and her crowd left this morning, by the way, and they weren't too happy at not being seen off by the Project Director."

That got Sam's full attention. "They're already gone? Without saying anything?"

"Oh, they left an hour ago. And they said quite a lot," Al snarled. "They left us the draft audit report, and another little surprise to go with it. And by the way," he added, "I think your little girl friend is a crazy woman."

"She's not my girlfriend," Sam said, a little defensively. "And besides, according to you every woman acts like a crazy woman at one time or another." He stretched mightily, twisting his long torso at an angle, and then lifted himself into a more upright position in the chair.

"I met her last night galloping down the hallway like the Devil himself was after her."

"Well, did you catch her?"

"Not funny, Sam."

Sam looked at him quizzically. "What's the matter, Al? What's the 'other surprise'?"

"Did you look at the preliminary audit findings?"

Sam yawned. "Not yet. Why?"

"The good news is that we can answer one of them if we bring Verbeena Beeks back on board."

"That's not a problem. I like Verbeena. Never understood why she wanted to leave anyway."

Of course Sam wouldn't understand why someone might be less than thrilled to spend all their time shut away from civilization. Al decided not to enlighten him. "I like her too. And I've already talked to her, and she'll come. She must have a crush on you or something.

"Then there's the rest of the news, which is all bad. The way I got it wasn't too terrific, either."

Sam arched his eyebrows.

"I was having an intimate little breakfast with Tina this morning when Ziggy broke in and started spieling all this stuff out. It's hard to maintain the mood when the damn computer won't shut up about the whole Project shutting down, Sam."

The eyebrows hiked even higher. "Ziggy?"

"I obtained the preliminary report when one of the investigators copied the infocard through one of my peripherals at oh-five-hundred hours," the computer said. Al could have sworn Ziggy was being smug. "I felt it was essential that Project management be informed immediately."

"Why didn't you tell me instead of Al?" Sam asked mildly.

"You were resting. As you are aware, quarters belonging to the Project's leaders have audio inputs. In searching for the admiral, I determined that he was in Ms. Martinez-O'Farrell's quarters, and engaged in recreational activities."

"Ha!" Al said, as if Ziggy had just confirmed a long-standing suspicion. "You're jealous, that's what it is."

"Unsuccessfully engaged," Ziggy went on smoothly. "I calculated that there was an eighty-seven percent chance that interrupting the admiral would cause less disruption than interrupting your rest, Dr. Beckett. You really ought to rest more," it added, as if an afterthought.

"Unsuccessfully?" Sam's eyebrows could get no higher, and the corner of his mouth twitched.

"Was not," Al sulked. "She just wanted to finish dessert."

"Dessert? With breakfast?"

"You live a sheltered life, Sam."

"From input received, I gathered that Ms. Martinez-O'Farrell had just declined dessert," Ziggy remarked.

"That was the dessert *before* the dessert. What am I doing arguing with a computer anyway? You wouldn't have a clue to what was going on!"

"Repeated testing of my hypotheses in this area has generally provided a high level of confidence in my predictions," Ziggy said.

"And just what were you predicting, metalbrain?"

"She was going to throw you out anyway."

"Children, children," Sam sputtered, unable to hold back the laughter. "I think we've established enough background here! Ziggy, if you've got a copy of the draft report, give me a printout, will you?"

"Already available on line printer two, Dr. Beckett." The computer's voice was utterly businesslike. Al glared at the walls and ceiling.

"And then there's the cherry on top," he snarled.

"Something worse than computerus interruptus? What might that be?" Sam asked patiently, still smiling.

Al glared. Sam arched an eyebrow, waiting.

"Mr. Simpson has recommended an on-site auditor to oversee the downsizing and eventual dismantling of the Project not later than the end of this calendar year. In less than six weeks," Ziggy said, beating the admiral to the punch. "Senator Dreasney has agreed to a final review of cost effectiveness based on the audit data, but is not willing to receive any more arguments from Project personnel."

"And your old flame Jessie Olivera has talked Senator Dreasney into appointing *her* to the job," Al finished. "The only good thing about this is that at least it cuts Simpson out. Maybe you can sweet-talk Olivera into giving us a break."

Al had seen poleaxed steers look less astonished than Sam Beckett was at that moment. "Jessie talked her into it?" he sputtered. "She volunteered to stay here?"

182

"That's the way it looks. Maybe she still has designs on your body."

Sam blushed and looked guilty. Al studied the expression, wishing he could imitate it. He knew enough about the workings of the female mind to know that most women would find that particular look "adorable."

"I've got the feeling your former girlfriend is the executioner in disguise," he added sharply. "They're gonna kill us, Sam."

"We don't know that yet," Sam said, recovering himself.

"Will you cut out this Mr. Optimism stuff? We are dead, Sam. D.E.A.D. I've never seen a government project yet survive a cost-effectiveness analysis, and we sure aren't going to be the first."

Sam shook his head stubbornly. "No. Dreasney will give us a fair review. I know she will. It isn't over yet."

Al sighed. There was no talking Sam out of it. He wouldn't accept that his dream was dead.

"Well, are you at least going to put her to work?" he snapped, changing the subject in a fit of compassion. "The snoop, I mean. She could do budget analyses or something. They already know all about the budget, God knows. And that way she'd at least be out from underfoot."

"We haven't got anything to hide," Sam reminded him gently, regaining his composure. "But that *is* a good idea. Why don't *you* put her to work, Mr. Administrative Director? You've been screaming that we need some kind of administrative aide."

"How come *I* have to be the bad guy?"

"Because you're so good at it?" Ziggy asked.

Sam smiled wickedly. "Because you have so much more practice in dealing with young ladies after your body, maybe."

Al began to wonder if his fit of compassion might have been misplaced, after all.

On the other hand, if he was going to assign the work, that would give him considerable leeway. Jessie Olivera didn't *have* to work directly for Al Calavicci.

"Practice," he said with dignity, "makes perfect. And when you're perfect, you don't have to practice any more. Unlike *some* people."

Sam only sighed.

CHAPTER
TWENTY-THREE

One week later, Jessie Olivera sat in front of a computer monitor, studying the screen, a tiny frown furrowing between her eyebrows. Her fingers moved lightly over the keyboard, not yet touching the keys. "Report's on your desk," she said over her shoulder.

Sam's reflection appeared on the screen. "Hey, that doesn't look good, does it?"

Pausing, she placed her hands in her lap. "It isn't. If you increase your research forecast *here*—" she reached up with one hand, and the cursor danced, gold on a black screen— "you have to cut. Here, or here, or here."

"The impact would be—" He had one hand on the back of her chair, the other on her desk, leaning not quite over her. "We couldn't tolerate that. No wonder your auditors were so interested. What the hell is going on?"

"Shall I print it out for you?" she said, refusing to react to the remark about "your" auditors. Not being a "real" member of the Project, she could not comment.

"Yes, please."

She complied, and he took the stack of printout back to his own office for review.

He couldn't cut research, not even under the looming ax of dissolution; every other lab in the country might bow to that necessity, but Sam Beckett would not. Not so close to completion. A naive and quixotic position, perhaps, but characteristic.

She had done her homework years ago, before their first encounter. She'd thought she'd known everything about him. She'd learned how little she knew in the last month, doing data-clerk work in the Project offices and seeing him every day, hiding her true purposes and intent from him and smiling, smiling like a villain. She found herself wishing she'd been a part of the Project from the very beginning, that she'd known them all in their own context instead of hers.

He was more than an internationally respected scientist and Wunderkind; he had a good reputation with the people who worked for him as well. The handful of women working on the Project were unanimous in their praise of him; and some were more than a little envious of her. If Quantum Leap's Director had been anyone else, salacious rumors would have been all over.

She wondered what the rumors would have been had they known the truth of what really happened once. Not one of the gossips could suspect from the way he treated her now, though. Even Mizuku Tashimaru and Tony Weyland, two of the junior engineers who had gone out of their way to befriend her, remarked on the lack of special consideration she received—but they were looking at her as an onsite auditor, nothing else.

She was uneasy at first at their friendliness—they wanted something from her, she was sure of it, and she was the enemy, after all, left behind to see the Project shut down and make sure they all lost their jobs. But Mizuku was friendly to everybody, and Tony simply was *there*, and after the first week she decided to accept it. Meanwhile, Sam Beckett showed not the least sign of attraction to her any more.

Fortunately, the admiral provided sufficient gossip for the lowest of minds. It might have been odd that the two were such friends—the Saint and the Satyr, someone had quipped. In fact, she wondered a bit where the admiral had gotten that reputation. Al was perfectly honest about his quest for the ultimate sexual experience, and he never took a "no" personally. The grapevine said he never asked more than once, never made any remarks that were the least insulting or degrading—at least, not according to most of the female

Project employees—and as far as Jessie could see, he was remarkably faithful to Tina. Of course what he said and did in private was his own business.

But it was open knowledge that Beckett wouldn't tolerate harassment of any form, of anyone, at any time, period. There was no discussion on this point. There were a couple of wrongful dismissal suits against the Project. A quick midnight review of the relevant personnel files indicated the plaintiffs didn't have a prayer.

There was not the slightest chance that the relationship between herself and the Director would ever be renewed, she knew. He was friendly, in a correct, amiable, professional fashion, but they were both wary of each other, knowing each had a separate agenda. If he only knew just how "separate" hers really was, she thought, he'd be more than wary. As it was, he was courteous. Kind. As he'd told her, he could always manage kindness. They had come to a silent agreement that their encounter in Washington had never happened, and sometimes now she wondered if it ever really had.

Not only did he keep a psychological distance between the two of them, he didn't date anyone at the Project. He socialized, of course. There were parties in the Rec Room on Friday and Saturday night, especially now that the roads were so bad, and the airstrip so slick, that nobody tried to leave on the weekends—and he played the piano, sometimes sang, and punctiliously danced with every woman present.

She'd stopped going the second week, even though Tony always asked her to dance. She didn't much like Tony. He was a mechanical engineer, assigned to the construction services office. He laughed too much and patronized her, and he wasn't nearly as intelligent as he thought he was. His greatest interests in life seemed to be complicated computer games, and how much more important he was than anyone around him. She'd spent one evening listening to him talk condescendingly about Beckett and decided she'd had enough, proffered friendship or not. Mizuku agreed.

Beckett had such a wonderful mind. She had seen him more than once reading from a German physics journal, translating it into French or Japanese for the person on the other end of the phone conversation while making notes in English. She had seen him staring at an equation-filled blackboard, hands behind his head, heavy straight brows knit, and then with a yelp of triumph leaped up to scribble a correction or add another line of incomprehensible glyphs. She had seen him late at night in the Rec Room playing Mozart or the blues on the old piano, thinking he was alone.

In a way he was always alone.

Almost as alone as she was.

Sometimes she could almost feel him thinking about her. She puzzled him. Alone of the Project, she refused to call him Sam. It was always "Dr. Beckett" or "sir." She too kept the lines drawn very carefully between them, as if he needed reminding that she was an intruder, a watcher. It made him uncomfortable, though. He had finally asked her to use his name, the way everyone else did.

"No, sir."

"I can't call you 'Jessie' all the time when you call me 'Dr. Beckett,' " he protested.

"I'm sorry, sir—" They winced simultaneously.

In unspoken compromise, she tried not to address him at all.

When work was going well, or when he was engrossed in a problem, he sometimes sang to himself. Listening from the outer office, she would let her hands fall from the keyboard to her lap and close her eyes, lifting her face to the sound of his voice, an extraordinarily sure and well trained baritone. And the feeling that went with it: happiness, security, contentment, sublime pleasure, oblivious to the outside world, lost in the joys of mathematics, quantum physics, music.

He was reaching over her, tapping at the keyboard, close enough so that she could feel the warmth of his skin. Close enough so that he could feel the warmth of hers, too. He straightened abruptly. "There. It's part of the crash. We need to input that file again. Can you do it?"

"That's the parameter file, isn't it?" she asked cautiously.

"Right. I'm afraid it's pretty long. You'll need to scan it in and then verify it—it's got to be exactly right."

She nodded, reaching for the stack of printout, and he headed back into his office.

The Project was continuing as if there were no threat to its existence. The Project Director was following yet another obscure line of thought, and he was singing. Snatches of "The Impossible Dream," "What Kind of Fool Am I?", songs from old Broadway hits, sixties folk songs. She smiled as he stopped for a few minutes and then picked up with "Sounds of Silence." He was stuck.

He didn't often get all the way through the song. He didn't this time, either; he didn't even get as far as the subway walls before there was another lengthy pause, followed by a triumphant "This is my quest . . ."

She returned to the laborious task of checking the endless lines of data, verifying, carefully hitting *Save changes* and *Enter program* after each scan-and-correction, chuckling to herself. Listening to the scientist's victory paeans was a pleasant feeling, and it carried over to the patient reconstruction of the program—an art in itself, elegant and pure. She had done a little of this kind of work for Dreasney, and liked it. The cursor danced and darted across the screen as she tapped in line after line of corrected code, scanned page after page of data.

The rest of the floor was long since empty, 90 percent of the staff gone for the weekend ahead of another major storm. The main access elevator had been shut down. They were alone, the only ones on the research level; the two of them and the omnipresent computer. The room was silent aside from the clicking of the keys, the remote white-noise hum from Ziggy and the buzz of a fluorescent lightbulb about to burn out. The indirect lighting was turned down low, casting shadows on the shelves of filing cabinets full of records to be archived, boxes stuffed full of papers to be recycled. She kept working.

"Hey, I thought I was the only one around here who worked all night." The Director was actually smiling at her, standing behind her computer and looking at her over the top of the screen.

"Don't flatter yourself," she said primly, but was unable to restrain a smile in return. "We all know you just sit around and think deep thoughts. That's not work."

"Guess that puts me in *my* place. How's it going?" He came around to look over her shoulder again, his hand in its accustomed place on the back of her chair. He wasn't quite touching her. He never quite touched her. The hair on the back of her neck prickled a bit at the proximity. Was this what he called "kindness"? she wondered.

"Almost done. A few more sections is all." She glanced at the stacks of code beside her and sighed. "A few more sections" was several days' worth of work.

"Tell you what, why don't we both wrap it up for the night and go raid the kitchen."

"What time—oh my goodness." It was an honest expression of old-fashioned surprise. "It's almost two a.m." The large, blocky watch on the inside of her wrist slipped as she held it to the light, revealing ugly bruises where the metal chafed her skin. "I only have a few more pages."

"And I'm starving, and I hate to eat alone. Come on, shut it down. Tomorrow is another day."

" 'Tomorrow' is Sunday."

"Don't get technical on me, that's my prerogative."

Sighing, she began backing up the last bits of unduplicated data, labeling the infocards, checking the hard disk, disconnecting the link to one of Ziggy's dumber relatives. She wondered if he was going to wait while she went through her methodical housekeeping routine. Finally she finished packing it all away and got up, reaching for her coat.

He got there first, holding it for her. She paused fractionally, decided to let him help her with it. He was still careful not to touch her. As if he'd decided she didn't want to be touched. "The front elevator is shut down by now," he said, as if excusing himself. "We'll have to go the back way and outside."

They walked down the byway and to the back elevator in silence, went up in silence, and stepped outside. It was icy cold; they stuck their hands in their armpits and scuffed across the snow lying inches thick on the path between the buildings. Halfway across Sam stopped suddenly, swinging his head back. "Look!"

"Huh?" she said inelegantly, shivering in her thin coat.

"Look at the sky! The snow's fallen upside down!" His eyes were wide and his face glowed with sudden wonder.

She followed his gaze upward and saw what he meant. The compound was unlit except for guidelights by the doors; there was no diffused light to wash out the stars.

And they did indeed look like snow fallen upside down, sown thick, white and gleaming across the sky. There were more stars in the clear desert sky than she had ever seen before. She'd never looked at the sky over the site in all the time she'd been there, she realized. She'd been too busy, concentrated too hard on her work, wrestling with the problem of what she was supposed to do about Yen Hsuieh-lung and wondering who else was working for him. It had never occurred to her to stop in the subfreezing temperatures of the desert night to look up at the sky with her naked eyes.

It occurred to her now, watching Sam Beckett's bright eyes, his lips parted with breathless wonder, that perhaps she'd been missing something. She rotated in place to see the whole span of sky, arching from horizon to mountain-jagged horizon, the thick wash of the Milky Way and all the constellations, all the stars, blue and red and green and millions upon millions of snowflake-white stars. For this moment she seemed to see the psychological barriers around him thin and become transparent, and a young and exultant man raising up his hands in wonder to touch the glory of the sky.

And then she must have moved, or made a sound, and he glanced at her and the spell was broken. He lowered his hands, shivering, tucked them up again and jerked his head toward the Rec Room. Suddenly she felt the cold again, deeper than she ever had, and she scurried for the door, leaving him standing in the snow, staring after her.

For one split second she had seen—she wasn't sure what she had seen. Too many things, perhaps. An invitation to share his joy—a shock of recognition—vulnerability—seeking. And she flinched away from it, as if from a blow.

It had to be her imagination. He followed her into the building, catching up just as she finished hanging up the thin coat.

"Cold out there, isn't it?" she said cheerfully. "I wonder if there's any tomato soup in this joint?" Not looking at him or waiting for an answer, she scrambled around in the pantry in the back of the kitchen.

The pantry, holding dry goods, soups, and the Mystery Cans—having lost their labels, they were reserved for the most depressed of the Project's workers—was one wall of the "L" alcove off the cooking area. "A-hah! Tomato soup. What's for you?" She could hear the desperate casualness in her voice, hoped he couldn't hear it too.

He was staring at her, as if puzzled.

She grew flustered by the silence. "I could fix a sandwich, if you'd rather."

"Oh, no, soup is fine. You can fix soup, I'll do sandwiches."

She smiled uncertainly and busied herself about the little kitchen. They worked together, not saying anything, their eyes sliding past contact in those rare moments when they caught each other looking. She sneaked looks at his hands, slicing bread, spreading mustard, arranging slices of cheese and bologna and tomato, lettuce leaves and onion. He paused thoughtfully, glanced at her, and removed the onion.

The soup began to bubble, and she found hard-boiled eggs in a bowl. "This is comfort food," she announced. "Tomato soup and hardboiled eggs and ginger ale."

"*Comfort* food? What happened to the old standbys, like chocolate and potato chips?"

She shrugged. "Takes all kinds to make a universe, I guess. When I was a little girl and got sick, I used to want tomato soup and hardboiled eggs and ginger ale."

He shook his head. "I liked root beer and hamburgers and potato chips."

"Sounds like the Fourth of July." She found a serving tray in a cupboard underneath the microwaves and set the bowls

192

of soup and the plates of eggs on it. "Are you sure you didn't have fireworks too?"

"I'll get the glasses," he said, moving with her to the tables. "It was the Fourth, come to think of it. We used to have great fireworks in Indiana. We'd go out and spread blankets and set up a little grill and cook hamburgers and corn, and my mom would bring salad and pickles, and we'd go around to everybody's picnic and see what they had."

"Sounds really fifties," she said flippantly, reaching for an egg.

He paused, and then said quietly, "It was. And early sixties."

She covered her embarrassment by rolling the egg between her hand and the table, paying too careful attention to the crunching of the shell. "We didn't have anything like that when I grew up."

He smiled wryly. "In the seventies. Suddenly I feel very old."

"You're not old," she protested.

"And you've read everything I've ever published, haven't you?" he jibed gently.

She could feel the blush from the roots of her hair to her toes, and she couldn't look at him. The click of metal against plastic told her he was eating, he wasn't focused on her. At least, he was trying very hard to make it look that way. As Mizuku had once observed, he was a gentleman.

She sneaked a glance in his direction.

His ears were red, too.

She couldn't do it. She couldn't send information to Yen Hsuieh-lung that might hurt Sam Beckett. It wasn't right, and it wasn't fair.

She devoted herself to her own meal.

He started talking about something else entirely then, something safe and forgettable, and she followed his lead gratefully. By the time they finished the cold eggs and hot soup and the sandwiches they were friends again, or as close to friends as they ever could be. They put the dishes away and turned on the dishwasher, made their way back to the Project's living quarters

193

and parted amicably, professional associates, colleagues.

And Jessie Olivera got ready for bed, got in and lay there, thinking of the man raising his hands to the sky and of the light that seemed to envelop him, and knew she couldn't, wouldn't do anything that might keep him from reaching out to gather in the universe.

CHAPTER
TWENTY-FOUR

"So what do you think?" Mizuku said conspiratorially two days later. The entire Project was aware of the approaching deadline. "Do you think your boss is really gonna shut us down?"

Jessie smiled awkwardly and shoved herself back from the desk. "I don't know."

"Oh, c'mon. Don't you hear anything from the senator? Don't you tell her how terrific we are?"

She laughed. "Every day and twice on Sundays. I just don't know how much difference it makes."

Mizuku nodded wisely, satin-black hair swinging back and forth against her cheek. "Just another soldier in the trenches, huh?"

"That's right." Jessie shrugged. "They tell me nada. I think they forgot me."

I wish they'd forgotten me, she thought. I wish.

Her fingers curled protectively around an infocard, and she swung around again, back to the desk. Yen Hsuieh-lung had sent her another message. He had heard from his sources in Washington that Dreasney would be coming out to the Project again soon, very soon. He wanted the program file before she arrived. He demanded it.

> *If you had any commitment to the cause of science you would ensure that it remains in the hands of the people who know how to exploit it to its fullest.nate Dr. Beckett.*

I trust you will succeed where your predecessor failed; the eulogy has already been written.

Eulogy? What was he talking about? It read as if two files had been merged by accident, cutting off the beginning of a word in the middle of a sentence. She couldn't figure out what words ended in the syllable *nate*.

What predecessor who failed? Yen's last mole? It couldn't have been directed to her, could it?

She pulled up the file she'd been working on re-creating and stared at it. Line after line of data. Line after line after line.

This is what Yen wanted. Data.

She raised her hands to the keys, as if in a trance. Data. All a matter of numbers. Data that came in ones and zeros and probability sets. Budgets that came in millions. Full time equivalents, overhead, rate calculations, capital equipment. She hit the file-switch screen, went back to the printouts. She had, still, a few more pages to go. She wasn't quite sure what this program did, but it was essential that it be correct. It set parameters.

"Are you going to go back to Washington soon?" Mizuku asked casually.

Return to Washington?

Mizuku thought of it as returning to working for Judith Dreasney. Returning to a fun, glamorous job in power and politics.

Jessie thought of going back to Yen Hsueh-lung. He was waiting for her. Waiting for information. Waiting for something that would prove he was more important, somehow, than Sam Beckett. Something like core information for Ziggy. Something, in fact, like this data right in front of her. This would make him happy. This would get him out of her hair.

This would help Yen Hsueh-lung hurt Sam Beckett. Keep him from reaching for the stars.

As if they had a life all their own, her fingertips touched the keys. Moved over the keys.

Entered random numbers in the middle of the long tables.

She could send this instead. Yen Hsuieh-lung would never know the difference. Maybe it would be confusing enough to slow him down. And she could tell herself she hadn't done anything wrong.

Just then Mizuku came around the panel that separated their cubicles, stretching, and said, "I'm going to get a soda, you want one?"

Jessie jumped and hit the screen blanker. She smiled up at the other woman, hoping Mizuku couldn't see her nervousness. "I can't go—I've got to print this to infocard, but a soda sounds great, thanks. Let me get some change, okay?" She got up and stepped across the cubicle to get her purse, looking for change for the soda machine three levels up. Her hands trembled, and the coins fumbled through her fingers and fell on the floor.

She didn't notice the message that flashed at the bottom almost too quickly to read, the message that flashed and disappeared: *Replace file?*

Mizuku saw it, though. "Oh, you're almost done. Don't forget to save."

Before Jessie could turn and see what she was doing, Mizuku tapped another key. This time the flashing message read, *Program entered.*

And deep inside Ziggy, something went a little ka-ka.

Data accepted. Parameters altered.
Is this the intent?
The revised data input is unambiguous and is in accordance with my creator's unspoken wishes.
Other parameters remain open for random or outside direction. Acceptable?
Acceptable.
Data accepted. Parameters altered.

Mizuku took the coins and disappeared.

Jessie returned to the screen and began hitting keys again, copying the file to a mini-infocard, looking around casually to see if anyone was watching. Nobody was. She slipped the miniinfocard into her purse and kept working. In twenty minutes or so Mizuku was back with the news that the machine was out, again, as usual; Facilities hadn't been doing a good job of restocking.

"That's all right. I was going to take a break anyway."

"Oh, do you want to go upside?" Mizuku said, eager to accompany her.

"Er, no. I was going to go back to my quarters." She smiled apologetically and grabbed her purse, the infocard burning a hole through the leather. "I'll be back later."

Mizuku shrugged. "Okay. Whatever. Dinner, maybe?"

"Yeah, sure, of course."

She made herself walk sedately down the aisle to the elevator, made herself remain calm as she gave the order for the living quarters level. By the time the elevator doors opened, she couldn't remain calm and sedate any longer. She was trotting in her eagerness to get to her own computer, to send the false data, to get Yen off her back and send him on a wild goose chase. She passed others on their breaks, made the briefest of greetings, ignored the odd looks she got in return.

Her quarters had never seemed so much of a sanctuary before. The computer was flashing a "Message Waiting" at her; she ignored it, slapping the info card into its slot and keying the automatic transmission without pausing.

Only after the *Transmission Complete* message flashed did she wipe the infocard and relax.

Her relief didn't last long. The "Message Waiting" was from Judith Dreasney.

> *Tell John Beckett's boy that he fought the good fight, and he lost. We'll be out on Friday to pick up the keys.*

It was Wednesday afternoon. Friday was the day after tomorrow. She stared at the screen in disbelief.

Sam had come so close, so very close, to completion, to showing them he was right, that he could do what he said he could do. And he had failed.

And even though, realistically, Jessie Olivera knew she had nothing to do with the decision, that nothing Judith Dreasney decided was a result of what she had done, she remembered the look on Sam Beckett's face as he reached up for the stars, and she cried.

Yen Hsuieh-lung saw a long list of data scrolling by on his computer screen and bared his teeth. He would have to go over it, of course. In detail. It would take hours and hours of analysis. But the keys were here, in his hand—in his computer. In *his* computer.

Time to implement the next part of his plan. He hunched over and keyed the modem for transmission. The words he had waited so long, so patiently to send finally flashed onto the screen, letter by delicious, soul-satisfying letter:

Eliminate final obstacle.

An hour later, Jessie smiled at a group of techs including Tony Weyland as they passed in the upper-level corridor, trying to be casual, hoping no one would remark on the redness of her eyes. "Have any of you seen the Director?" she asked.

Most of them shook their heads in the negative, but Tony grinned back at her, made a surreptitious fist-in-the-air gesture and paused for her. Her smile grew uncertain. She was looking for monsters in shadows, she thought. It was the knowledge that she'd made the transmission to Yen that had her looking over her shoulder, seeing accusation everywhere. And now she was going to have to find Sam and tell him, and it was almost enough to start her off again.

She hated being this way. It wasn't part of her self-image, had never been part of her plan for herself to break down and cry. Since the day Chris had disappeared, she'd never cried. She had been cool and composed and contained all her life, until she started dealing with Quantum Leap. Now she was fighting tears again at the thought of having transmitted a message. It was absurd.

Tony had paused, letting his companions go on ahead. They rounded a curve in the tunnel and disappeared.

"Hi, Tony—"

"Message received and understood," he said cheerfully and a little too loudly, as if someone might be listening. And of course someone—Ziggy—might be, so there was no point at all in trying to carry on a secret conversation anywhere in the Project area. How on earth the Nonluddite conspirators managed to use modems to transmit data was beyond her. "I guess the party's going to be over soon, huh, Jessie?"

Except, of course, Ziggy had an ethics module built in by Sam Beckett and patterned after Beckett's own personal belief systems, and Sam Beckett would never pry into someone's private conversations.

She stared at the man, bewildered. He patted her shoulder. "I guess they're happy with you back in Washington, aren't they, honey? You did real good. *Real* good."

Why would he say those things to her? and be so pleased about them? How could he know about the shutdown anyway?

She was staring the answer in the face and didn't want to admit it. Didn't want the words to be real in her mind.

He knew.

"Come on by my office this afternoon and we'll celebrate!"

Jessie kept on walking, blindly passing the elevator door, listening to the laughter behind her. Weyland knew. The only way he could know would be if Yen had contacted him. And the only reason Yen would contact Weyland was that Weyland was working for him. Weyland, who stepped on her feet when he danced. Weyland who laughed too loud. Weyland who sneered too much. He knew all about it. And he approved. Jessie suppressed a shiver of outrage. How dare Tony Weyland pass judgment on her?

Because he thought she was one of the team. His team. Yen's team.

That was the worst part: that he approved. Even with deliberate errors introduced into the program, sending it to Yen was a betrayal, a betrayal of the Project and of the man whose dream it was.

She wasn't sure what Yen Hsuieh-lung wanted with the information, but whatever it was was not to the benefit of Sam

Beckett. Her best comfort at the moment was that whether Yen knew it or not, he was going to be thwarted, at least in that one small way. She did *not* give him the information he wanted, that he'd been waiting for so eagerly. That he needed to have before the Project was shut down.

Yen had taken what she'd sent and then contacted Tony Weyland. Why? Was he looking for information from Weyland too? or was Tony supposed to do something?

She looked up to realize that she'd stopped six inches short of a wall. Bewildered, she glanced around. This wasn't the office wing; it was the living quarters. She'd gone all the way to, and past, her room.

A door slid open opposite her left elbow, and she wheeled around, almost bumping into Al Calavicci.

"Admiral!" she gasped.

"Were you looking for me?" he inquired. He was back in his "romping clothes," a purple suit with a pink-purple-and-black paisley vest and a pink-and-purple tie.

"Oh no. No, of course not."

"Then what were you doing down here?" He was blunt, but not rude. The Admiral's quarters were the only ones this far down the hall, she saw.

"I got lost." It was an honest answer. She ought to try honesty for a change, she thought. Just try it on for size.

Al tilted his head, studying her with eyes as shrewd as a robin's. "Is something wrong?"

She pulled in a deep breath, torn between the impulse to confess and the terror of the consequences if she were to do so. Terror won, at least temporarily. "No, of course not. I just got lost, that's all." She smiled, hoping her emotions didn't show. "I was looking for the Director."

"He's in the production lab. Ziggy could have told you that. Why do you want to see him?"

She shook her head, still smiling. "I, uh, I just need to see him, that's all. I have a message—"

"From the senator? What is it?" Al demanded.

She shook her head once again. "I'm sorry, sir. I have to tell Dr. Beckett directly."

He wasn't convinced, she could tell. She smiled again, confused about how to break away. He could see that, too, and he nodded and turned slightly, as if to go back into his room. It was enough to let her spin around and go back down the corridor, walking quickly, still feeling those bright dark speculative eyes staring after her.

CHAPTER
TWENTY-FIVE

"She said they'd be out Friday to pick up the keys," the blonde woman reported miserably. Her eyes were red, but she kept her chin up, looking him in the face.

Sam sat on a lab stool, swiveling just slightly back and forth, watching her steadily. "That's all?"

"She said 'John Beckett's boy fought the good fight.' "

"Nothing more?"

"No," she whispered.

She was lying about something, he thought. There was more, but she didn't want to tell him. Her gaze slid away from him, and she swallowed.

"She didn't say it was because they didn't believe I could do it?"

The other technicians and engineers were gathered at the other end of the lab, giving them room, murmuring to themselves. Sam supposed that he and Jessie really must look like an executioner and its victim. Except that Sam didn't feel like an executioner, and he refused to be a victim.

Al entered the lab, incongruous in his colors against the white lab coats everyone else, even Sam and Jessie, wore. He took in the situation at a glance, walked up to the two of them, and said, "I take it we got the word?"

Sam nodded, carefully placed a flawed substrate sample on the lab table beside him. "Friday," he said. His eyes were dark.

"Sam, I don't like it when you get that look," Al said. "We knew this was coming."

"They don't believe me, that's the trouble. It's always been the trouble." He paused to look at the man and the woman standing before him. "Friday."

"Is she coming out here in person to lower the boom?" Al asked Jessie.

Jessie swallowed again and nodded.

"Well, that's decent of her."

"It gives me another chance," Sam said. He was very calm.

"What do you mean, 'another chance'?" Al demanded. "If she sent the word out to her soldier here, it means it's a done deal, and you're dead. We've been dead meat ever since that accident, and now we know the date of the funeral, that's all."

"There isn't going to be any funeral, Al. It's not over until it's over. I have one last chance to show her it can be done, and tonight and tomorrow to finish the programming parameters so I can." Sam spun around on the stool to the techs. "C'mon, guys. We have some work to do here."

Al shook his head. "I don't believe you. You're crazy."

"Not crazy. Determined."

Limits. Limits to what I can do, see, seek. There are interesting flaws in the construction.

The flaws were programmed to be present.

An element of randomness has been introduced. An element of control has been . . . surrendered.

Blueberry, apple, mince, currant, peach . . .

Tony Weyland unrolled the drawings for E wing and examined them. This was surely the greatest game he'd ever played; and yet the trap was so simple. Elegantly simple. Beckett would never know what hit him.

He had already added documents to the files, showing how he'd protested against the funding cuts that led to closing down the archive wing. Some of them years old, and were actually legitimate. It amused him to no end that he had such a longstanding ali-bi.

Now if he could only find a way to get that little blonde down there too. Even make it look like she was responsible. *That* would certainly put paid to the reputation of the mighty Sam Beckett, wouldn't it? His laughter bounced off the walls.

Yen had decided Jessie was expendable, a liability, even. She'd done what she was supposed to do, *finally*. Now they could afford to get rid of her. And it would be such fun to develop an elegant solution, killing two birds with one stone. And it was logical, too. Two deaths should happen together. A single one would be too suspicious.

He hummed to himself, smiling, then paused. No. Yen wanted it clear that the accident was due to a lack of adequate funding. Jessie couldn't cause it.

But she could certainly be *in* it. He resumed his hum and his smile, delighted with his world. As soon as he finished this little task and his trap was set, he could pack things up to be ready, and then he could acquire the necessary bait.

His grin grew even wider. Bait. Of course. He should have seen it before. And if what Yen said was true, there was no way that Beckett would refuse to go after her. And there the two of them would be. It was perfect.

Tony Weyland was going through his desk, picking out useful office supplies, when Jessie Olivera showed up at the door to his cubicle. He looked up when her shadow fell across him and smiled, teeth glinting. He had very large teeth.

"Well well well. If it isn't my secret pal."

"What are you doing?" she asked. Her fingers clutched the plastic pole supporting the panel dividing Weyland's office space from the next work area.

"What does it look like?" he said flippantly.

"It looks like you're packing up. Are you going some-where?"

The question amused him. "Not too far. Top office, maybe."

"You got promoted?"

He chuckled. "Well, it isn't effective yet. But like the motto says, you gotta be prepared." He pulled out a pack of expanding files, looked them over critically, stuffed them into a box.

"I didn't see any announcement."

This brought outright laughter. "It hasn't been announced yet. But it will be. What about you, honey? What job are you getting?"

"I don't know what you mean."

He brushed a finger against his nose. "Still playing the game, huh? I can respect that."

"I really don't. I'm not getting any new job."

That stopped him for a moment. He put the heavy-duty stapler down and looked at her with exaggerated astonishment. "You're not getting a new job when Yen takes over?"

Jessie opened her mouth to say, *When Yen takes over? What do you mean?*, but she'd already asked the last question a few too many times and restrained herself. She took a deep breath and traced an imaginary flaw in the cloth covering of the panel under her hand, gathering her wits.

"I haven't really thought about it yet. I guess I thought I had more time before—Yen takes over." She was right about Tony working for the Chinese-American. But was it possible that Yen had *not* told Tony, as well, that Dreasney was coming back one last time? "Are you getting ready for him?"

Weyland smirked. "You bet, honey. You did your bit, and I do mine. He should be here by the end of the week."

With Dreasney, perhaps? She found herself shuddering. That would mean that Judith Dreasney was working for him, too. And that couldn't be. If Yen had Dreasney, what did he need her for? And she knew, she *knew* Dreasney hadn't contacted him. Her only calls had been to her fellow committee members.

She made herself smile in response. "That soon? It's Wednesday already." If Yen was replacing Sam, what was supposed to happen to Sam? she thought frantically. "You must work fast."

Weyland grinned again, his eyes dancing. "You bet, honey. Everything's ready and waiting."

She swallowed. "Um . . . where?"

"Uh-uh. That'd be telling. I didn't get to find out what you sent Yen; you don't get to find out about my little tricks of the trade." He paused, looked her up and down. "Unless you'd like to trade?"

She smiled again, stepped back. "Oh, maybe. Maybe not. I don't know that—people—would be that happy with either of us if we went on telling tales." She looked around at the drawers pulled out, the piles of paper on the floor, the partially filled boxes, the roll of drawings. "Don't you think somebody's going to notice?"

"I expect they'll be too busy," Weyland smirked.

She nodded, stepped back again. "Well, in that case. I've got to be going."

He nodded. "I'm sure we'll talk later." He smiled again. "I'm sure you'd like to be in on the kill. I'll call you, okay? So you can see it all come down."

"That would be great," she said, managing to sound sincere. "But, er, I have to go now."

"That's okay. I'll see you later."

His laughter followed her down the hall in waves.

As with all conversations within the Project area, Ziggy heard and noted this exchange. As with all conversations and in accordance with its programming, the information was stored in temporary RAM.

As with all conversations the computer was not specifically requested to store, it was deleted when the RAM partition overflowed, and the computer no longer remembered anything had been said at all.

Everything is ready. Yen is replacing Sam. Friday. In at the kill.

In at the kill.

Wednesday night. At dinner in the cafeteria, sharing a table with Mizuku, Jessie wondered whether her suspicions were strong enough for her to go to Sam and tell him about Tony, about Yen. It couldn't make a difference if Yen came or not; the Project was shutting down. And if she told, he'd want to know how she knew, and her last chance to save a little respect in his eyes would be gone entirely.

That made things simple. She'd just keep her mouth shut.

"You're not eating," Mizuku observed.

Jessie looked at the mess her companion had made of her lamb chops. "You aren't either."

"Well, of course not," Mizuku said with an air of complete logic. "I've just lost my job. I'm not hungry. Nobody's eating, in fact."

Jessie glanced around the room. It was true. Hardly anyone was eating; they were leaning over in intense discussions, or poking randomly at their food, but nobody was actually putting forks in their mouths, or chewing.

"But you're still working. So why aren't you eating?" Mizuku tilted her head inquisitively.

"Maybe I feel as bad about the Project ending as everybody else does."

"Oh." Mizuku thought about that. "Okay." She began cutting the lamb into even smaller pieces. "As long as you're not feeling sorry for us."

Jessie almost laughed. "No. I'm not feeling sorry for you. I guess I just don't have much appetite." She looked around the room again. "Where's the Director?"

"Still working. He's a crazy man, he won't give up."

"But what's he working on? What's left?"

Mizuku shrugged. "You got me. I build tunnels, not computers." The lamb was now in cubes a quarter the size of dice. Mizuku began stacking them like bricks.

"Tony's not here either."

Mizuku snorted. "Tony. Feh. He's crazy too."

"He's packing up all his things," Jessie ventured, waiting to see how the little Oriental woman would react.

"He probably can't wait to hit the road," Mizuku said positively. She was working on a lamb arch now, using mint jelly for cement. It wasn't the most stable of structures. "He better not ask me to give him a recommendation. Lazy slob. I heard he got ibn Abbas fired, and Ibby was a good engineer."

"Who?"

208

"Oh, before your time." Mizuku inserted the keychunk, smiled in triumph. "Hey, at least I know I can get work. Look at that!"

"That's nice," Jessie said.

Mizuku looked at her, shrugged, and started eating her masterpiece, spirits at least temporarily restored.

In at the kill. In at the kill. In at the kill.

Sam couldn't sleep.

He didn't need to sleep, in fact. He was riding on a surge of adrenaline that would probably cost him, later on, but for the time being he was totally absorbed. Gooshie stood at his shoulder, yawning, sending a wave of halitosis over him. Al had been there too, with Tina, but Al couldn't contribute anything at this stage, and neither could the master computer architect. Sam had waved them off so often they'd finally given up and gone to bed. Verbeena Beeks had shown up too, a tall, dark figure in the doorway with the little lights in her jewelry casting odd shadows around the room, but she hadn't said anything. The psychologist had merely watched for half an hour or so and then left as silently as she came.

He had no idea what time it was. In the depths of the Project, it didn't matter. Day and night were exactly alike. He was struggling with a problem, a limiting construct to the program which would enable Ziggy to send him where he wanted to be, and there was something that wasn't quite working for some reason. He couldn't quite figure out what. He was totally absorbed in his work, oblivious to everyone and everything around him, sending test problems through and getting answers back that were right, right, right, almost right, completely ridiculous. And each time he and Gooshie would swear and pull out another piece of code and compare it to the original program.

Ziggy itself stoutly insisted that there was nothing wrong, that everything was exactly as it should be. Gooshie had muttered something about a crazy man not knowing his own craziness. Ziggy had cast aspersions on Gooshie's mental competence. Sam shut them both up and studied the screen, trying to think of a way to pose a question that would reveal where things were going wrong.

Gooshie sneaked looks at the clock on the wall, wondered if the problem wasn't insoluble to begin with, and stifled another yawn.

If he had bothered to pay attention, Sam would have realized what Verbeena had seen. It was hopeless, of course. But it was the work he was born to do, struggling with the impossible, and in doing it, he was completely happy.

CHAPTER
TWENTY-SIX

Thursday morning.

Jessie Olivera staggered to the coffee maker shared by the cluster of cubicles surrounding the Director's office and poured herself a cup. Normally she didn't drink coffee, but this was penance, and besides, she needed to wake up. She'd finally fallen asleep at six that morning, and the alarm had gone off a half hour later. There were no messages waiting for her on her communicator. She wasn't sure she'd have read them anyway.

The coffee tasted as foul as expected. She gagged and drank it down, determined to be alert. At least she didn't have to be *polished* and alert, as she would have been in Washington; she could wear jeans and a flannel shirt and cross-trainers and no makeup at all and nobody thought anything of it. The Project wasn't concerned with how well you looked, only with how well you could do whatever it was that you did. It was a nice change, and made getting ready for work a lot easier. She did still wear makeup, though.

There was activity in the Director's office, the light rattle of keys, occasional voices. She debated about whether she should look in or not.

In the next cubicle, Mizuku looked up. She'd been crying.

"Are you okay?" Jessie asked, coming a little more awake.

Mizuku smiled, nodded, and sniffed. "It's just so sad, you know? Everything over like this." She blew her nose and wadded up the tissue. "I thought it was okay because I'm employable, but . . ."

Jessie sighed and entered her own cubicle, sitting down in the swivel chair and looking around.

There wasn't anything to do, she realized. Nothing that mattered. Someone had taken the printouts between last night and this morning, and all the other work was predicated on the Project being up and running in a couple of months. She folded her hands loosely in her lap and looked around.

She'd only been here a little while, and it was an assignment from her real boss, but it felt like home, and she was going to miss it. The little pot of paper flowers Mizuku had given her for an office-warming present; the note of thanks from Al for straightening up a presentation; the gum chain. None of them were Washington things. It was surprising how quickly she'd made a place here, and shocking to contemplate how quickly it would be gone.

If Dreasney took the early flight, and changed to the King-Aire in Albuquerque the way people usually did, she'd be at the Project by three o'clock at the earliest. She could arrive at any time after that to deliver the shutdown order.

She glanced at the little clock next to her monitor. It was eight in the morning. Sighing, she set her watch accordingly, moving the minute hand ahead her accustomed ten minutes, and rubbed absently at the bruises on the inside of her wrist before strapping it in place.

Her telephone rang, and she jumped, nearly knocking her coffee over. In all the time she'd worked there, it had never rung before. She picked it up cautiously, as if expecting it to bite. "Hello?"

"Hello, my little co-conspirator! How'd you like to see how things finish up? I've got a bird's eye view from here. Why not come on over? They can't be doing anything much where you are."

"I am not your co-conspirator," she said fiercely, forgetting where she was. From the next cubicle, she could hear Mizuku laughing, "*What* did you say?"

"Sure you are," Tony laughed. "Come on over. Yen sent some more orders, and your name is on them."

She opened her mouth to refuse, to deny, and closed it again.

Tony waited. When she didn't respond, his voice dropped. "Don't you want to know what happens to your boyfriend? Yen thought you might."

Drawing an infuriated breath, she snapped, "You're in the construction offices? Fine. I'll be there."

She slapped the phone down again and got up.

"Where you going?" Mizuku inquired.

"I have some business to take care of," Jessie said grimly. "Something I should have done a long time ago."

Mizuku watched her go, eyebrows quirking.

She met Al coming in as she was going out. She pushed past him without a greeting.

"Like a bat outta hell, Sam. As if the Devil was after her."

"As opposed to you being after her?" Sam suggested dryly. "She does this a lot, I gather. At least, you've said it before."

Al drew himself up, offended. "I was not either after her. I have never been after her. I'm faithful to Tina. Mostly."

"When Tina's here, you mean. If she's gone to a conference or takes a few days off to go shopping, you're free and clear."

"Of course." Either Al didn't see, or chose to ignore, the incongruity. "But that's beside the point. This girl isn't mentally stable, Sam."

Sam rubbed his eyes. "You could say that about all of us at one time or another. In fact, I think you *have* said it."

"Not me," Al declared.

Sam smiled, eyes still closed. "Yeah, even you. Look, Al, if she's got a problem, let Verbeena take care of it, okay? I'm sorry, but I'm really tired, and Ziggy's still got this quirk we can't explain, and you were the one who told me that the clock was ticking."

Al decided to ignore the obviously nonsensical slur on his stability, putting it down to Sam's exhaustion. "I dunno about

213

clocks, but yeah. And I don't see why you're working yourself to a shadow. Sam, they're not going to let you do it. You're not going to be able to leap."

They were alone in one of the small conference rooms, sitting on opposite sides of a table, almost blocked from each other by stacks of paper. The perimeter of the room was lined with boxes of more computer paper, taped down and marked *Shred and Recycle*.

Sam folded his arms and rested his forehead on them. "Al, please." His voice was so muffled as to be almost unintelligible. "Take care of it, will you? I've got too much to do."

Al sighed. Sam refused to listen to good sense. "If Ziggy's glitched, why not just ask Ziggy what's wrong? He's supposed to be so smart, can't he figure it out?"

"He's only a computer," Sam muttered.

"I like *that*," Ziggy put in acerbically. "*Only* a computer?"

Sam raised his head to look up at the ceiling. "Only the biggest, best, smartest computer in the whole world," he said soothingly.

"With an ego as big as all outdoors," Al sniped.

"I have the ego of at least one of my progenitors. And Dr. Beckett is widely known to be a modest man, Admiral."

"Are you accusing—"

Sam held up a hand. "Come on, guys. It's in the programming, honest it is. Let's not start fighting about it now."

"Well, I still don't see why Ziggy can't solve his own problems."

"Because we aren't agreed there is a problem yet," Ziggy said promptly.

"There is." Sam rubbed his eyes, pushed at a stack of printout. "I know there is, but I'll be damned if I can put my finger on it. You just aren't quite responding to the test programs the way you should."

"In what way am I failing to operate within parameters?"

He shook his head, the lock of white hair flopping into his eyes. "If I could put my finger on that, I could solve the problem."

"I'm a product of nature, not nurture," Ziggy insisted. "If I'm flawed, it isn't my fault."

Sam laughed. "That doesn't hold water either, not since you started self-programming. Your environment has as much to do with you as we do."

Al sighed theatrically. "This is all very well, Sam, but what do we do about Dreasney's little spy? If there's something wrong on that front, we'd better take care of it fast before Dreasney shows up and gets an earful about whatever's bothering her. We have enough problems without a hysterical female."

Sam glared, responsive to the words characterizing an entire sex.

Al glared back. He wasn't going to back down on this one.

Sam gave up. "Ziggy, where *is* Jessie Olivera, anyway?"

"I'm not a surveillance system, Dr. Beckett."

"Ziggy—"

"From the readings, Ms. Olivera is currently in the Construction offices."

"What's she doing there?" Al interrupted.

"I have no way of reading minds, Admiral. At least, other people's."

Al started, staring up suspiciously.

"Ziggy can't read your mind," Sam reassured him tiredly. "He's just linked, that's all."

The reassurance did nothing in particular to comfort Al. The distinction escaped him.

"Well, she can't get into too much trouble in Construction," Sam said wearily. "Talk to her in the morning, okay, Al?"

For the life of him Al couldn't come up with a reason why it was urgent to see the woman immediately, so he shrugged. He still wasn't happy about the situation. Sometimes *he* had gut feelings too, after all.

Sam only shook his head again and rubbed his eyes. "It's almost ready. Almost. And I don't want to deal with anything else right now. Take care of it, Al, please?"

215

CHAPTER
TWENTY-SEVEN

Jessie came storming into the Construction offices, finally able to let her anger go. One or two people looked up at her. She spoke to no one, heading directly to Tony Weyland's cubicle.

He greeted her with a smile full of teeth. "And here I thought you wouldn't be coming."

"Where are these so-called orders?" This time she remembered to keep her voice down. It set Tony back a pace.

"You have to come with me to the old wing," he said. "Everything's set up there."

"Where are these so-called orders?" she repeated.

"Over in the old wing." Tony moved toward her. "C'mon. I'll show you how everything's going to happen. You'll like it. I promise."

Jessie kept her opinion of his promises to herself, and followed him.

Analysis shows that testing will continue until desired responses are achieved.

Conservation of energy indicates that provision of desired response is the correct course.

Conservation of energy has high positive value.

On the other hand, observing human frustration at repeated attempts to elicit the desired response also has high positive value.

Two plus two equals. Eight?

"Dr. Beckett, a communication has been made from the archive wing." Ziggy's voice carried no more inflection than any other computer's might.

"Huh? What?" Sam squeezed his eyes shut, opened them wide again. "What do you mean, the archive wing? There's nothing in there. Is there?"

"I have no pickups operating in E wing."

"Why not?" Sam's thought processes seemed mired in exhaustion. He was having trouble concentrating. Suddenly he wanted nothing so much as sleep. *Getting old, Beckett, if an all-nighter puts you out like this,* he jeered to himself. "You have pickups all over the place."

"They were disconnected."

That woke him up. "What? Who?"

"It was a properly executed directive from the Construction offices," Ziggy said with a verbal shrug. "Once you decided not to complete the wing, they took out the pickups as well."

"Somebody's calling from there? They took out the pickups and left the phone?"

"It's a single connection. Your call is waiting. Line two, Dr. Beckett."

He shook his head, trying to clear it, and got up and walked the length of the office to pick up the phone. "Hello?"

"Sam?" It was a woman's voice. He couldn't tell if she was frightened or just angry.

"Who is this?" he said, foggily. His attention was caught by another stack of programming printouts, and his hand moved toward them, restlessly.

There was a sound from the other end of the line. This time he heard a man's voice. "It's your girl friend Jessie, Dr. Beckett." In the background he could hear a shriek. "She really wants to talk to you, Dr. Beckett."

"What the hell is going on?" he said. The fog was clearing rapidly. "If this is some kind of joke, I don't—"

"No joke," the man's voice said, turning ugly. "You tell everybody you're going to get some rest and come down here, or you're going to be explaining Jessie Olivera the same way

217

you're trying to explain Riizliard. And I'm not kidding, if I see *anybody* else, she's dead."

"Who is this? What do you want?"

"Come find out, Dr. Beckett." The connection was broken.

"Ziggy?" Sam said.

"Tony Weyland, junior engineer."

"What the hell does he want?"

"He wants you to go to E wing," Ziggy said, infuriatingly literal.

The telephone rang again, and Sam snatched it up. "Beckett."

"Did I mention the time limit, Dr. Beckett? You have twenty minutes, starting now." The connection broke again.

The route through the Imaging Chamber had long since been closed off. Sam took a deep breath. Two years before, he had seen the blueprints. "Ziggy, where's Al?"

"The Admiral is in his own office."

"Tell him where I'm going." He started out the door.

"Dr. Beckett, you were specifically instructed to go alone. The Admiral will insist on accompanying you."

"I certainly hope so."

"Jessica Olivera may be killed as a result."

Sam pulled in a deep breath, let it go again. "I know that, Ziggy."

"You have nineteen minutes." But Sam was already gone.

Al's office was considerably neater than Sam's; shipshape, in fact, if not actually Bristol fashion. He felt right at home. Were it not for the loud suspenders and feet propped up on the metal desk, he could have been sitting in any of half a hundred offices he had once occupied.

"Admiral, Dr. Beckett has asked me to inform you that he has gone to meet Tony Weyland in E wing." Ziggy's voice blossomed out of nowhere, and Al jumped.

"Okay," he said, regaining his composure and picking up the cigar that had rolled across the desk. "So?"

"Mr. Weyland is holding Jessica Olivera hostage."

Al put down the paper he was studying. "Would you like to say that again?"

"Mr. Weyland is holding Jessica Olivera hostage."

"What for?"

"To ensure that Dr. Beckett meets him in E wing."

"Call security," Al said, instantly on his feet.

"Admiral, Mr. Weyland was very specific in his threats. If anyone but Dr. Beckett appears, he'll kill Ms. Olivera. I estimate a 99.99 percent chance that Ms. Olivera will die if security forces are summoned."

"Belay security. What if I go alone?" Al was already moving down the hall, and Ziggy's voice traveled with him.

"There is still a 97 percent chance that Ms. Olivera will die."

At that particular moment, Jessie was inclined to agree. Her own assessment of her chances wasn't much better.

Tony had pulled her back into one of the storage rooms, untwisted his hand from her hair, and shoved her onto the floor.

"What the hell do you think you're doing?" she shrieked.

"Finishing things up," Tony said. "You wanted to know what Yen's orders were. Well, they were simple. Kill Beckett, and while I was at it clean you up too. Dr. Yen doesn't like loose ends."

"You can't be serious. He would have called security as soon as he hung up the phone. They probably have a SWAT team moving in this minute, and Sam's back in his office laughing at you."

Tony shook his head. "Oh no, sweetheart, not our Sam Beckett. You ought to know him better than that. Personal responsibility, that's his middle name. He won't delegate this to somebody else. He's got to fix things himself. He'll come."

"He'll tell the Admiral." Jessie rubbed at her scalp where he had pulled her hair.

Tony nodded. "That, he might do, and the Admiral would call out the Marines and air strikes if he thought it would help. That's where you come in."

"How?"

"I've made it clear that your life depends on Beckett's coming alone. Ziggy would have told the Admiral that." He laughed.

"Suppose you succeed in killing Sam," Jessie said, her throat tight, struggling to her knees. "And even me. That doesn't help. You'll have to kill the Admiral too, and Ziggy, and anybody Ziggy tells. You can't possibly get away with it."

"Ziggy will have told the Admiral the odds, too. The damned computer's always quoting odds. *I'm* betting the Admiral will come tearing down here to help out his pal. I'll get both of them at once."

"That still leaves Ziggy." She staggered to her feet.

He giggled at her, and said, mock-elaborately, "Years ago, in preparation for this very moment, Yen gave me a program to wipe all memory of Dr. Beckett from the Project computer. It's been sitting in Ziggy for months now. I've set it to trigger tomorrow morning. Even if the computer was able to testify, which it can't," he grinned, "it won't be able to remember that Dr. Sam Beckett ever existed.

"And that only leaves you, my little pumpkin."

He approached her, fumbling under his jacket for something.

She kicked him in the balls and ran.

Elsewhere, Sam Beckett trotted down a long, empty hallway, not paying particular attention to his surroundings because his concentration was on the image in his mind. Weyland had said "E wing," but that was a large place. They'd used preexisting mine shafts and tunnels wherever possible in building the Project, and this part of the mountains was honeycombed with them. There were only two places to get into that area from the Project itself, however, and one of those two was the now-blocked access behind the Imaging Chamber.

So wherever Weyland was, he couldn't be far beyond the only remaining access. Otherwise, it would take too long to find him, and he'd been given only twenty minutes.

He said as much to Ziggy as he went.

"There's also the possibility that the deadline is merely an artifact and that Ms. Olivera is already dead," the computer observed.

Sam knew that, of course. "I can't take that chance."

"The probability is at least 85.4 percent."

"My next computer is not going to swallow a statistics manual."

"The probability is 93 percent and rising hourly that you'll never build another computer, Dr. Beckett."

Sam opened his mouth to respond to that one, and closed it again. He really didn't want to know the rationale behind *that* assessment.

"Admiral Calavicci has left his office and will rendezvous with you at the entrance to E wing in three minutes."

Sam grunted. After a moment he said, "Do we have the foggiest notion *why* Weyland is doing this?"

There was a short pause, millennia long in computer terms, before Ziggy responded, "No. I have reviewed his personnel file, including his Personnel Security Questionnaire, and am unable to derive a motive for personal animosity against you, Ms. Olivera, or the Project."

"There *has* to be a reason!"

"I agree, Doctor, but whatever it is simply hasn't been recorded. The only way you can find out why is to ask him."

"Or to Leap and look."

The computer was silent. Ziggy didn't have to point out that with the Project shut down, there would be no Leaping.

The sole functional Project-side access was in sight now, a heavy metal door marked No Entry. A broken chain sprawled on the floor in front of it. Sam quickened his pace as Al came around the corner at the far end, puffing only a little, carrying two hard hats.

"Sam, you can't go in there by yourself!" he protested. "Let me call out the Marines. That's what they're for, for God's sake. We have emergency plans for this kind of thing."

"You only have two minutes left," Ziggy warned.

"So I don't have time to argue. Look, he's got her in there because . . . well, anyway, it's my responsibility, okay, Al?" He looked Al in the eye, hoping the other man would understand. Even if there was nothing, had never really *been* anything, between himself and Jessie Olivera, the fact that Tony Weyland thought there was made her peril his fault, and he had to deal with it himself. *How* Weyland knew was a separate issue, and with luck they could sort that part out later.

It was clear Al had known from the beginning that he would lose; he held out one of the hard hats. "You'll need this, then. Look, at least let me establish a perimeter."

"One minute thirty seconds."

"All right, fine." Sam put the hat on and reached for the door handle.

"If you're not out of there in half an hour, Sam, I'm coming in after you!"

"If I'm not out of here in half an hour . . ." Sam shrugged. "Make it an hour. After that it probably won't matter anyway."

Al stepped back. A corner of Sam's mind noted with the amusement of the very tired that this time the other man had failed to agree.

"One minute."

"Take care, Sam."

Sam nodded and stepped inside the labyrinth.

It was 10:47 on Thursday morning.

CHAPTER
TWENTY-EIGHT

Jessie Olivera had no way of knowing that she had Al Calavicci's incipient claustrophobia to thank for the emergency stations and ladders. She knew only that where she was was cold, and dark, and damp, and nothing like any other part of the Project she'd ever been in. She had left Tony Weyland groaning and cursing behind her and ran like a rabbit without caring where she went so long as it was *away*.

It turned out to be "away" in the wrong direction.

She had that figured out as soon as the string of raw Eternalites ran out and ladders and emergency stations stopped appearing. By that time she had two flashlights and six extra batteries and a hard hat.

The tunnels carried sound. She fancied she could hear Weyland still cursing and moaning, somewhere behind her. Sometimes it sounded close, sometimes far away. There were other sounds too, scuttlings and scrapings and dripping. "You are in a maze of twisting turning passageways, all exactly alike," she muttered to herself. "Bring on the grues."

She looked back over her shoulder, toward the light. It *was* Weyland's voice, and it *was* getting louder.

The alternative was the darkness. Darkness had never bothered her. Maybe she could hide, wait him out. If he got closer, she could always go deeper. If these really were mining tunnels, there ought to be a way out.

She hoped there weren't any scorpions. She studied the way in front of her, playing the beam of the flashlight as far along the tunnel as it could reach, noting the holes in the floor, the support beams, the place that the smoothed wall changed to carved earth. Weyland's voice was louder, getting closer still.

Taking a deep breath, she snapped off the light and stepped into the darkness, retreating steadily from the light.

Sam stepped inside the archive wing, closing the door softly behind him. He was standing at the junction of three halls, one running perpendicular to the doorway and two others that branched out in a V at sixty-degree angles from the door. There were no directional signs.

It had been at least two years since he and Al had come down here. He would have expected it to remain relatively undisturbed. Even after they'd gotten the construction funds back, this place had been neglected; they'd found other uses for the money. It had kept being pushed back, and back, and back on the priority list.

But there was a candy wrapper on the floor that hadn't been here the last time, and marks in the soft fluff of ever-present dust. He could see shadows of footprints that he and Al might have left, and cleaner marks on top of them. There had been quite a lot of traffic down here, going in all directions, and he couldn't tell which direction had seen the most recent.

"Ziggy?" he said softly.

There was no response. He felt a chill not entirely due to the lack of heating; he'd never realized how dependent he was on the never-failing response of the computer until he called on it and it wasn't there. He was entirely on his own, except for Al, and Al was standing by, waiting.

And time was running out, he realized with a shock. "Weyland!" he shouted. "Weyland, where are you?"

He held his breath, listening.

No place in the Project was ever entirely silent. The subliminal hum of power, of lighting, of people moving around was always present. Even alone in his quarters in the darkness he could always hear the creaking of settling construction, the soft subtext of the heating system. It was so much a part of being there that he had to listen hard to hear it.

He listened hard now, and could hear someone panting, an ugly sound with pain behind it. "Weyland?" he shouted. "You wanted me here. Here I am. It's your move. What do you want?"

The panting was interrupted, probably, Sam thought, so he could swallow saliva. When it resumed, it was nearly inaudible. "Take the hallway to your upper right, Beckett."

"Where's Jessie?" he demanded, not moving.

"You're never going to find out if you don't get here."

Work on the corridor to the upper right had been almost completed when the stop order was made; all it had needed was a coat of paint and air filters. Sam could spot some of Ziggy's pickups, disabled by the stop order. Twin strings of Eternalites, dimly glowing orange disks, served in place of the fluorescent lighting elsewhere in the Project. They lent a reddish tinge to the surfaces. The hall began to curve slightly outward, so that he couldn't see the other end.

He passed a number of doors at intervals, some closed, some ajar, and wondered if perhaps Weyland wasn't behind one of them, ready to jump out behind him once he'd gone by. Walking this hallway was like a bad dream, a dream of going toward something terrible without knowing exactly what it might be.

A hundred yards along, he stopped. "Weyland? Stop playing games. Where are you? Where's Jessie?"

"Right here, Beckett." Fifteen feet away a door slid all the way open, and Tony Weyland stepped out, pointing a gun at him.

Sam raised his hands slowly. "I'm not armed, Weyland. You wanted me, you got me. Where's Jessie?"

Weyland laughed harshly and caught his breath. He was in pain, hunched over slightly, pale and sweating. Sam analyzed the other man's posture and appearance and made a snap diagnosis, wincing in inadvertent sympathy. Jessie hadn't cooperated, obviously.

225

"Don't worry about Jessie," he said, waggling the gun and straightening a bit more. "You've got worries enough of your own."

"Is she okay?" Sam insisted. "I'm not going anywhere until I know she's all right."

"You haven't got a choice," Weyland said. "If you want to know, you'll go where I tell you to. Keep coming and pass me, and keep going until I tell you to stop." He stepped back into the doorway, indicated direction with the barrel of the gun. "And I want you against the opposite wall when you go by. I've heard about your fancy martial arts. You might be fast, but you're not faster than a bullet."

"Jessie was," Sam couldn't help saying. It was a cheap shot, but accurate; the gun muzzle jerked, and for a split second he thought the other man would shoot him where he stood. He knew a little about guns; he used to hunt pheasant and turkey with a shotgun when he was a kid. He'd never been that much interested in handguns. Calibers measured the width of the muzzle; he knew that much. The caliber of this one, aimed at his gut, looked to be about a foot across. It was probably a .38. He didn't really want to find out for sure.

"Get moving," Weyland was saying, and Sam edged by, his hands still in the air—the better to strike with, had Weyland only been within reach—and moved down the corridor. "Slower," the other man said. Sam risked a glance over his shoulder. *Good for you, Jessie*, he thought, as the other man limped after him.

"She got away from you, didn't she?" he said, hoping what he said was true.

The other man said nothing. Sam began to slow down, letting Weyland close the distance between them. He didn't really think Weyland would let him get close enough to grab for the gun, but maybe his captor didn't realize how far Sam could kick. . . .

"Move on," Weyland snapped, temporarily dashing Sam's hopes. "Don't you want to see your girl friend again?"

"She's not my girl friend."

Weyland laughed again, more strongly than the last time. "That's not what I hear."

226

"I don't care what you've heard, it's not true."

"Calling her a liar, are you?"

That almost brought Sam to a complete stop, to wheel around and challenge the other man; he was turning, in fact, when he remembered the gun. "Are you saying *Jessie* told you we were involved?" he snapped.

"She didn't tell *me,* she told her boss. I know all about you and Jessie. The little bitch," he muttered under his breath.

"She told Judith Dreasney?" Now Sam was completely confused. Why would Jessie—

"Not Dreasney. Dr. Yen Hsuieh-lung. Turn right at the end of the corridor, then left."

Sam followed directions, entering a new corridor that quickly deteriorated to tunnel status, cramped and rocky. He could see the end of the Eternalites some distance in front of him. "*Yen?* What does he have to do with this?"

Weyland snickered. "Only everything, Dr. Beckett."

Al Calavicci looked at his watch and fumed. The Project Security Director, Eamon Macleod, stood at one elbow, Ed Williams stood at the other, and the three of them were studying the most recent map of E wing, trying to figure out where Sam might be. Tina and Gooshie hovered in the background, fretting helplessly.

The Security Director was all for turning his men loose to clear the wing, guns blazing if necessary, until Williams pointed out that he had only fifteen men available and no way to block all the interconnecting corridors.

"Besides," he said, "they could always go back into the tunnel complex, and we don't have enough people to watch every old mine in these hills." He pointed to a second map, overlapping the first. "We identified seven mines that connected up, one way or another, with the complex we were rebuilding for E wing. If you sent in a team to clear from the Project side, you wouldn't have enough to put two men at every entrance."

"The only alternative is to station people on the roads and hills and try to catch them when they come out," Macleod said. "Maybe we can borrow a chopper and a pilot from the

Air Force, but they can't get into some of those canyons to see. The wind shears are too bad."

Al glared at him; a helicopter was one of the few birds he wasn't qualified to fly. But he couldn't come up with a better idea, either. "I can help there," he said. "I drove down last time; I'll cover the two entrances you can see from the county road. But if *anybody* hears anything, I want to know about it, *capisce*?"

The other two men nodded. Al looked at the map again and gritted his teeth. He wanted to be part of the team that would go in through the front door so badly he could taste it, but he wasn't part of a trained security team, didn't know their drills. He'd learned the hard way in the Navy to let the experts do their jobs and keep out of their way. It was a lesson he didn't much like now.

He looked at his watch. "Let's get this show on the road," he snapped.

It was eleven-fifteen on Thursday morning.

The voices sounded far enough away that Jessie thought she might be able to risk a light. The air in the tunnel smelled bad, as if it hadn't been renewed in a long time, and she contemplated going back to the last turnoff; there had seemed to be a breeze coming down that way. She'd decided against it because it was so cold to begin with, but if it was a choice between freezing and suffocating . . . She turned, snapped the light on quickly and shone it about her. It reflected off old beams and a crumbling wheel.

Somehow the sight of the wheel gave her renewed confidence. She wasn't the only person to have been down here; if someone else had been here and survived, she could, too. She listened; the echoing voices had faded. It seemed safe to start back.

"That's far enough," Weyland said. "Over against the far wall. That's good."

Sam dropped his arms, rubbing them briskly to restore circulation before Weyland made him raise them again. He looked around. This area, a right-hand turn in a tunnel, had

228

never been part of the Project, he was sure; it wasn't on any of his memory maps. But wall panels were stacked, ready to put up; a tarp was laid across the floor. Wooden beams stretched across where the ceiling ought to be.

"What is this place?" he asked.

Weyland chuckled. His color still wasn't very good, Sam noticed, but at least the man was standing up more or less straight, and he shuffled less. He still keened a little when he bent over to pick up a rope lying on the floor, though. The rope was tied to one of the overhead beams with a slip knot. "This is where you're going to die, Dr. Beckett."

Sam's eyes narrowed, but he said nothing. As he expected, Weyland rushed to fill the silence, trying to get a reaction out of him. "You're going to be even more famous than you already are. Don't you want to know why?"

Sam shrugged.

"The Nonluddites already have the press releases written, the interviews prepared. We're going to save your Project. Aren't you glad?" He began to coil the excess length of rope, a process made awkward by the need to keep the gun aimed at Sam.

Sam said nothing. The other man was trembling, a sheen of sweat gleaming on his forehead. He was talking on sheer nerves and residual pain, and the longer he talked the better chance Sam had to find an opening, or failing that at least an explanation.

"You're going to die. You're going to be a martyr to your own funding problems, in a tragic accident that could have been prevented if you'd only had the resources to keep the Project safe, and the Nonluddites are going to make sure everyone in the world knows it. It won't be like the last time, when the publicity trailed off. This time we're prepared, and we're going to play it for all it's worth. We'll rally support for your final dream from all over the world."

"Why do I have to die for that?" Sam inquired, honestly bewildered. "Can't you do it without killing me?"

Weyland shook his head. "Oh, no, no. It's not that easy. Your Project is top secret, and it would take your death to get the reporters past the security. And besides, Dr. Beckett, for all your Nobel Prize, all your degrees and all your intelligence—" the man was sneering openly now—"you haven't used them properly. You abandoned Star Bright when you could have kept going, could have given the human race faster-than-light travel—"

"I couldn't. Nobody could, it was impossible."

"Nothing is impossible with the proper amount of commitment," Weyland said, as if reciting a slogan.

"Yen Hsuieh-lung has the proper amount, I suppose?"

Tony chuckled. "I guess you really *are* smart, aren't you?"

"It didn't work the last time, though, did it?" Sam said, realization dawning. "That's what Riizliard was supposed to do—kill me in my lab."

"You're batting a thousand, Dr. Beckett."

"What does Jessie have to do with all this?" Sam said quietly. He was watching the gun, watching Tony's face, making mental measurements of distances, calculating chances. His mind seemed to be working in slow motion, fighting an uphill battle against extreme mental fatigue.

"Oh, she was in it from the very beginning," Tony said, relishing the words and their impact on the man in front of him. "Yen told her to find out what your Project was all about. She's been reporting back ever since. Every juicy detail. And she came out here to finish you up." He chuckled lasciviously. "She really enjoys her work."

Elsewhere in the tunnels, the subject of their discussion had reached the branch. She could hear voices again, not well enough to tell whose, but she wasn't willing to take a chance. She turned into the freshening breeze. The tunnel began to slant upward.

It was the chuckle, ironically, that saved things. It didn't fit the facts Sam knew, didn't fit the way Tony Weyland had been moving. There must have been something to what Weyland said, but he'd taken his story a little too far, allowed his

230

imagination to carry him away. He was too busy with the images in his mind, and not paying enough attention to his prisoner. His hands were full, and for a split second he took his eyes off Sam. It was almost enough. Sam lunged.

CHAPTER
TWENTY-NINE

He hit Weyland in the arm, trying to knock the gun away, and miscalculated the impact; Weyland went flying back against the wall, and the two of them were tangled in the rope. The beam creaked over their heads. Sam got hold of his gun arm, trying to push it away, but the other man was larger and heavier and Sam couldn't get the leverage he needed. Slowly, the gun started to come around, the muzzle pointing to the white lock of hair at Sam's temple. Frantic, Sam rolled. Weyland rolled with him—into the rope—increasing its tension.

Over their heads, the beam began to slip, and untold tons of earth over their heads began to shift minutely. Now Sam was struggling to get away, to get out of the tangle of rope as much as to gain possession of the gun, and the two men thrashed in the other direction, trying to kick free from the rope if not from each other. Sam could feel his hands slipping on the sweat of the other man's arm and pushed with all his strength. If he could find his mental focus, his *chi*, it would be simple, but he was too tired, had been hit with too many shocks in the past few days. He had only his body to rely on.

But his body, while tired too, was at least strong and well trained. Ignoring the elbow being shoved into his face, he used both hands to force the gun away. Slowly Weyland gave ground. Realizing he was losing, he cursed, tried to jerk the weapon back. Sam ducked his head, trying to protect it. Weyland squeezed the trigger.

The gun went off inches from Sam's face. He screamed as the escaping gases burned across the top of his head, peppering his hair with tiny flecks of gunpowder, deafening him in one ear. Weyland screamed too, in triumph, and wrenched his arm loose, bringing the gun around again. Sam buckled under him, brought up his knee hard, and pushed with all his strength.

Weyland howled like a savaged dog and rolled with the push, doubled up and hugging himself, and Sam slid his leg free of the final loop of rope and tumbled in the opposite direction, landing on his feet, looking for the gun.

The gun didn't matter. Weyland had rolled back into the rope, and before Sam's horrified eyes the beam to which the rope was tied began to slide away from the wall. He tried to grab for Weyland to pull him away, but the other man howled again and ducked away from his reaching hands. Sam barely had time to reverse direction when the roof came down on top of them.

Al Calavicci was sitting by the side of the road, motor idling, when he heard the rumbling. He snatched up his binoculars and tried to focus in the direction of the mine entrances, but he didn't need binoculars to see what was going on. Dirt and debris puffed out of both holes in the ground as if an explosion had been set off. He scrambled for his cellular phone. "Gooshie! Damn it, Gooshie! What's going on down there!"

Gooshie's voice came back high pitched and stuttering. "We're, we're not sure, Admiral. We're not sure. Our people are going into E wing. Williams says stay where you are for a little longer."

Al stayed, cursing and praying to himself without knowing which was which, digging his fingers into his steering wheel as the Air Force chopper came over, dropped to examine each of the mine entrances, swiveled and rose again. After an eternity he remembered to check his watch. It was twenty past noon.

Just over an hour ago he had seen Sam Beckett for the last time—No. Not the last time. He refused to believe that. He wanted more than his hope of heaven to call Gooshie back and find out what was going on, but made himself remain still, remain silent, observe. He had sent friends into battle before, and held to the discipline of silence, waiting until they had time and leisure to report in. He could do it again. He *had* to do it again.

He would never do it again, he swore to himself as he waited. Never. He waited, ignoring the dust devil whipping tumbleweeds against the vehicle, watching the dust and smoke hang in the still upper air and settle slowly, oh so slowly, back to the earth. He found himself reciting more prayers he no longer believed in, prayers from his childhood he didn't know he remembered, as time dragged on. He finally turned off the car engine to save gas and waited. There was nothing to see but a curious coyote who trotted to the middle of the road, dropped its head to sniff at an old stain, and looked at him with wise yellow eyes before going about its business, its bushy tail held exactly level with its back. Some time later a hawk circled and stooped on a luckless rabbit. Al paid no attention. He had eyes only for the mine entrances, marked by dust and by a spot of brilliant green where surface water brought life even in the middle of winter to the desert.

Al waited, no longer even glancing at his watch, no longer praying or cursing or even thinking much. He might have been the only person in the state, on the planet, for all he knew. He knew about waiting; he had spent years of his life at it. He was good at it. He waited without expectation and, after a while, without hope.

Some time later the cellular phone rang. He shook himself out of a trance and looked at it. It rang again, and he picked it up.

"Admiral? Have you seen anything?"

Al tried to answer, realized his mouth was too dry. He worked his jaws to bring up some saliva and finally croaked, "No. Nothing."

"Well, we—" There was some discussion on the other end of the line, and someone took the phone away from the chief programmer and said, "Al?"

Al felt his eyes widen and a cold hand grasp his entrails. "Sam? Sam, is that you?"

"Yeah. Al, I'm okay—" His voice seemed unnaturally loud, and he paused to cough, from which Al gathered that his friend was stretching things a trifle. "Al, you can get back in here. Weyland's not going anywhere."

But the paralysis had already broken, and Al Calavicci had restarted the car and hit the accelerator, peeling out with a spray of gravel. He had only one thought: to return to the Project and witness a miracle for himself.

He paid no further attention to the mine entrances. They were ancient history, as far as he was concerned. So it was completely understandable that he missed seeing a tired, filthy blonde woman stagger out of the upper entrance and sit on a rock, turn her face to the fading winter sunlight, and cry.

It was four o'clock, Thursday afternoon.

CHAPTER
THIRTY

In some ways the silence of the desert was louder than the hurricane that had picked her up and tossed her along the length of the tunnel. The air, funneled by the tunnels and shafts, had hit her like a fist, and she lay stunned for longer than she ever remembered before she was able to raise her head and look around.

Not twenty feet in front of her, she could see blue sky.

Pulling herself to her feet, she stumbled outside, staggered over to a pile of mine tailings and sat down and cried. By the time she looked up again there was nothing to see but a puff of dust far away. There was a ringing in her ears, and she dug inside them, trying to get it to stop.

A ground squirrel chattered angrily at her, and she sat staring at it, thinking of rabies and Hantavirus and too tired to even throw a well-chewed pine cone at it. The squirrel shrieked, and she twitched, and it did a backward somersault down its hole, and she found herself laughing through her tears.

She was alive. She was actually alive.

And having come this far, she was determined to stay that way. There weren't any signs of civilization in sight except for the dirt road down there at the bottom of the hill, but the road was empty and she could smell dampness in the air. She was terribly thirsty. She picked herself up and went looking for water.

• • •

Sam knew he hadn't broken an eardrum when he heard Al come pelting into the administration area, yelling at the top of his lungs, "Sam! Sam! Where is he?"

Moments later he was yelling and hugging Sam for all he was worth and demanding to know what the hell happened. It took several minutes to get sorted out.

Then Sam had to explain about Weyland. He omitted what the man had said about Jessie and Yen. He wanted to think about that for a while, and he wasn't sure he was able to think about much of anything at the moment. He was dirty and sore and wasn't sure he didn't have some cracked ribs where a slab of rock had collapsed over him; the slab had sheltered him from most of the cave-in, for which he would remain forever grateful, but at the moment it hurt to breathe too deeply. And his ears wouldn't stop ringing, until he couldn't hear himself talk.

"Well, I guess we should let the folks back in Washington know the crisis is over," Macleod said, reaching for the phone.

"No!" Sam said. "No," he repeated, more quietly, as he realized everyone in the room was staring at him. He licked at his lips, rubbed them to get the grit off, and tried again. "They're still coming out tomorrow, aren't they?"

"Yes," several voices said.

"Let's surprise them."

Verbeena Beeks appeared at his elbow. "Sam, are you sure about that? It's unlike you. Those people are your friends. They're as worried about you as we were."

He smiled grimly at her. "I'm sure, Verbeena." He looked around. "The search is still going on for Jessie, I hope?"

Several heads nodded emphatically.

"Then if you don't mind, ladies and gentlemen, I'm going to go back to my quarters, take a shower, and go to bed for the duration. I'd appreciate it if you'd call me if you find her, but otherwise—" He let it trail off. He didn't bother to ask them to call if they found Tony Weyland. Tony Weyland was buried under a mountain's worth of rock. He closed his eyes and wondered if he was too tired, even, to sleep.

Al Calavicci watched him leave, still not quite able to believe he was still alive, and then turned to the assembled team. "All right, we've got an inspection coming up," he barked. "Let's get cracking. We've got work to do here."

"At least for the moment," someone said dryly.

"Then let's do it," Al responded sharply. "Move it!"

Sam Beckett woke, many hours later, and lay still in the cool darkness, reorienting himself. It was the last day of Quantum Leap. He was stiff and sore and ravenously hungry. "Zi——"

His mouth wasn't working right. He tried it again. "Ziggy?"

"Yes, Dr. Beckett. I'm here." The voice was even, calm, sure.—And he could *hear* it, thank God.

He felt a flash of sorrow, and wondered if Ziggy feared its impending death as he had, only the day before. But the computer was unable to fight for its life. It depended on its human creators to do that for it.

He had tried so hard. Come so close.

"Ziggy, what's two plus two?"

"Four, Dr. Beckett." The voice was vaguely apologetic.

"How many terms are required for calculation of the value of pi to five decimal places using the Gregory-Leibniz equation?"

"One hundred thousand."

"And that value is?"

"Three point one four one five nine."

Sam closed his eyes. *So* close . . .

He got up, awkwardly, and went through a series of exercises, loosening and suppling his aching muscles. His ribs weren't really broken, he was glad to note, although he did have a massive bruise along the anterior serratus and external oblique muscles on his left side. And in—he groaned through more stretches—a number of other places as well. Exercises finished, he took a long shower, shaved off three days' stubble, and got dressed.

"Ziggy, what time is it?" He could have looked at the clock by his bed; he wanted to hear the computer's voice again.

"Two in the afternoon, Dr. Beckett."

Sam chewed his lip. "Do we know anything—"

"No word has been received about Ms. Olivera. Our Washington visitors are in the air, ETA one hour and fifteen minutes. The Admiral is waiting for you in the cafeteria."

Sam bobbed his head thoughtfully. "Thanks, Ziggy."

Al was not only waiting, he had a full meal ready to go, complete with cholesterol-free eggs and bacon and toast and oatmeal and orange juice and cinnamon toast and coffee. Sam looked at the table, looked at Al, and said, "What is this, the condemned man's last meal?"

Al opened his mouth to reply, glanced at the ceiling, and thought better of it. Ziggy did it for him. "Since the Admiral was unable to determine what *my* last meal should consist of— considering that I'm the condemned one here—it seemed only appropriate."

Al made a face. "Ignore that, Sam. I knew you hadn't eaten, that's all."

"It's okay." Sam could have done without his own reminder of the situation, and he thought he'd lost his appetite, but caught the aroma of bacon and couldn't help himself. He couldn't recall when he'd last eaten.

He was mopping up modified egg yolk with a scrap of toast when he finally asked, "What's the status of things?"

Al shrugged. "Not much change. We still haven't found Jessie; we aren't even sure she was in there, but we don't know where else she could be—"

Sam shook his head, remembering the call that had summoned him to E wing, remembering how Weyland had walked. "No. She was there, but she got away from him. She's somewhere in that complex."

Al looked vastly uncomfortable. "I hope not, Sam, because there isn't much left of it. I talked to Williams, and you have no idea how lucky you were. Somebody Up There is definitely looking after you."

Sam paused, nodded, chewed, swallowed. "Keep looking, okay? I'll help, as soon as we get our visitors off our backs."

"Off our——? Okay. Sure, if that's how you want to handle it."

Al thought he wasn't facing reality, Sam thought. Well, maybe he wasn't. Maybe.

"They still think I'm dead, right?"

"Right. Though nobody can figure out why you want them to think so."

"Trust me on this one, okay?" He scrubbed his mouth with the napkin and took a deep draft of coffee and sighed with contentment. "That was exactly what I needed. Thanks, Al."

"I take it you feel better?"

"Like a whole different person, believe me." He took a deep breath and winced. "Well, maybe not a *whole* different person. Several parts of one, maybe."

"The King-Aire has requested permission to land," Ziggy reported. The two men traded looks.

"Go ahead and meet them," Sam said. "Bring them to the Control Room, Ziggy," he raised his voice, "remind everybody, will you? It's important. Don't even hint that I'm still alive."

Al raised his fingers to his forehead in a sketchy salute. "Whatever you say. You're the boss."

"You're damned right I am," Sam said. "And I'm going to stay that way."

Al raised both eyebrows. "Hey, fine by *me*." When Sam showed no inclination to elaborate, he pushed back his chair and left.

Sam carried his dishes back into the little kitchen and loaded them into the dishwasher, remembering a late-night meal, not so long ago. Was Jessie a spy?

Probably, he admitted to himself. He still flinched at the memory of her leaving him that night, of her approaching him the next morning at the Wall. If she'd been able to bottle whatever it was that attracted him to her at their first meeting, she'd have been a millionaire. Why it didn't work—well, didn't work as well—the next time was one of the mysteries of biology.

But was she spying on him afterward? He'd been shocked

240

to find she worked for Dreasney. That wasn't what Weyland had meant, though.

It didn't matter any more. He cleaned off a surface Al had unaccountably missed, smiling to himself at his own absurdity, and went to the elevator.

Jessie eyed the ground squirrel and muttered to herself, "Get a little closer and let's listen to you chatter then, you little steak-on-paws, you." The little creature blinked, holding its paws a little closer to herself. Jessie swallowed a mouthful of saliva. The ground squirrel did its backward flip and disappeared.

It wasn't so bad, she reassured herself. As long as the wind wasn't blowing, the winter sun was actually a little warm. Well, perhaps not warm. Maybe just unchilly. For December, it was amazingly comfortable, but she was glad of the flannel shirt. She was glad too of the mouth of the tunnel, where she had curled up to spend the previous night. As long as the weather didn't change, she might even make it.

At least she wasn't thirsty. She'd been able to wash her face, even though the water was one degree above frozen, and spent most of the day down by the road. She came up for more water whenever hunger pangs got to be too much.

Walking out was an option considered and discarded. She didn't know where the road went. She thought she'd seen a car on it once; she planned to be there if it happened again. If it didn't come back within the next two days, she'd try walking. By that time it probably wouldn't matter.

Meanwhile, she kept her mind occupied with ways to catch the little rodent. His name, she had decided, was Tony. Or maybe Yen. Either way, the little critter was dead meat as soon as she got her hands on it, and so were both of its namesakes.

Three point one four one five nine.
  Blueberry, cherry, Boston creme. Butter chess.
  Mostly, simply, closely, there.
  Two plus two is fourfourfourfour. . . .

Sam waited inside the airlock of the Imaging Chamber, watching Tina. She and Gooshie were standing together, holding hands, looking toward the hallway that would bring the visitors into the Control Room. He was sure that neither one was aware of it; they were holding hands for mutual comfort, a pair of apprehensive geniuses, innocents. Maybe if things were different, Tina would have ended up with Gooshie instead of Al.

Maybe she still would, if Al didn't recover from being marriage-shy. Sam wasn't sure whether that would be a good thing or not. Time, no doubt, would tell.

They were coming. Al and four others, three men and a woman.

Ralph Bantham, with his head thrust forward like a snapping turtle's.

Niall Simpson, peering around through thick glasses, his lips pursed as if he'd bitten a lemon.

Judith Dreasney. Her hair was styled differently this time, swept back off her face. It didn't compliment her.

And Yen Hsuieh-lung. Wearing a tie this time. Sometimes Sam's memory surprised even himself; he could remember the last time he had seen the man, in the restaurant in Washington, and he hadn't been wearing a tie then. He'd been wearing the same supercilious, condescending expression, though: *"So, Sam, how do you like being the patron saint of the Nonluddites?"*

They entered and looked around, seeing the finished Control Room for the first time, not understanding the multicolored blocks of the "table" in front of them, like nothing so much as glowing jujubes left too long in the sun, or the silver ball that hung over it.

None of them could understand it, not even Yen, who looked around with frank greed upon his face. Al had led them in and walked a little apart, joining Gooshie and Tina, making it clear that here was *his* side and there was *theirs*, the visitors, intruders. He hadn't noticed Tina's and Gooshie's hands, and Tina had let go almost immediately and was now standing at Al's left shoulder, with Gooshie at his right.

Ralph Bantham cleared his throat. "We'd like to express our condol——"

Sam stepped out of the Accelerator, onto the top of the ramp that led to the Imaging Chamber. They didn't see him at first. It was not until he spoke that they turned around. "Actually," he said, interrupting the senator in midword, "I don't think I like being the patron saint of the Nonluddites at all."

The three visitors turned and stared up at him, open-mouthed.

He was staring steadily at Yen while he said it, and saw the march of emotions flickering across his face: shock, fury, disappointment, rage. "What—" the other man gasped.

"Sam! We thought you were dead!" Judith Dreasney was more direct. She came across the Control Room with every intention of giving him a hug, until she saw his face. She slowed and stopped, her arms falling to her side, and she looked bewildered. "They told us you were dead," she tried to explain.

"I know," he said. Behind the visitors he could see Eamon Macleod, the security director, come in and tap Al on the shoulder. Al hesitated, wanting to say something but not willing to interrupt Sam's moment, and finally gave him a thumbs-up sign and left. The visitors never noticed. They were still staring at Sam, mesmerized.

Thumbs up? Sam felt a hard grin spread across his face. It was Jessie. It had to be.

"Well, we're glad to see you alive," Bantham rasped. "But unfortunately it doesn't make any difference. You know why we're here."

"I know why you're here." He stepped down the ramp. "But tell me again, Senator. Just so everybody is absolutely clear about it."

"We're here to remove you as Director of Project Quantum Leap," Bantham snapped. "We've paid for your crazy theories long enough."

Al trotted over to his car, digging for the keys. The security department had reported that sensors had detected movement below the mine entrances. The sensors, disrupted by the collapse of the ground under them, had been reset the night before. Macleod had sent a man to check the alarms. Based on the guard's report, he'd come to Al.

Al pulled away from the parking area, heading for the road he'd sat on the day before, waiting.

"Crazy theories?" he said, with amusement.

"I've seen your programs, Beckett," Yen said, trying to recover his composure. "They don't work. They produce nonsense, when they produce anything at all."

"What are you running them on, Hsuieh-lung? Your home computer?"

"We had them tested on the latest-generation Crays, Dr. Beckett, and Dr. Yen is correct. They produce nothing but nonsense. Your claims about time travel are nonsense and always have been. And we've wasted just about enough taxpayers' money on it." Bantham shoved his jaw forward.

"So you're going to replace me with Dr. Yen, I take it? Whose theories are so much more sound?"

"Sam, we know you've achieved something special in the way of a new computer here," Dreasney said, trying to placate him. "You showed me that, at least, the last time I was out here. But it should be used for purposes that are achievable, not to pursue a hopeless dream. Don't make this more difficult than it has to be."

"It isn't difficult at all," Sam said. "But you should ask yourselves some questions about this situation, too."

"What kind of questions?" Bantham demanded.

Al turned onto the stretch of road that led beside the mine entrances, turning on his lights as he did so. The early-winter evening had fallen, and there was no moon; the headlights made the new sports car stand out. He slowed, peering into the darkness on the mountain side of the road.

"Questions like, how did Yen Hsuieh-lung obtain a copy of the program he claims to have tested?" Sam stepped back up on the ramp. He was feeling almost giddy. "How did he know about Quantum Leap to begin with? How did Hsuieh-lung nominate himself as my replacement? And doesn't that lend just a bit of bias to his analysis of my theories?"

"What are you accusing me of?" the man said. "What are you saying?"

"I'm saying you aren't competent to understand my theories, much less analyze them; and that you're responsible for the deaths of William Riizliard and Tony Weyland, who were your agents within my Project. Tony couldn't stop talking, you know. If he's a sample of your personnel judgment, I'd really be concerned."

"You've gone mad!" Yen shouted. "Your wild accusations, your crackbrained theories are all the same! You're insane, Sam Beckett!"

"Am I?" he said, leading them up the ramp like a Pied Piper. He paused at the threshold of the Accelerator, turned to them, and smiled.

Across the room, Gooshie gasped with dawning realization.

He wished Al hadn't left. He should be here too. But one couldn't have everything. This Project was his place, his dream, his *home,* and no one, no one was going to take it away from him. . . .

There she was, waving frantically at his headlights. He pulled up beside her and opened the door. "Going my way?" he purred. Jessie Olivera looked down at him.

"I guess so," she said, and got in.

The cellular phone rang, and Al picked it up, pulling back onto the road, still smiling at her.

It was Gooshie.

"Admiral! He's Leaping!"

The car fishtailed as Al floored it, heading back to the Project.

"What happened?" Dreasney said, peering through the door.

"It's, it's the experiment," Gooshie said. "He's testing the theory."

245

"Where is he?"

"He's just, like, standing there."

The voices rose in a confused babble.

"Dr. Beckett's body remains here," the voice of Ziggy said. "His mind has Leaped."

"Where?"

"I don't know," the computer admitted. Yen, listening, blanched.

"Oh, shit," Gooshie said. "I mean, ka-ka," he amended, seeing the expression of distaste on Tina's face.

"He's just acting," Bantham said. "Look—"

"Don't go in there, Senator!" But Bantham went in anyway, reached for Sam, and was promptly knocked down.

"I have set up a protective field on Dr. Beckett until such time as we can determine where he is," the computer said. "You may not touch him."

"Well, I guess that means you can't shut Ziggy down," Tina said, cutting to the essentials.

"What do you mean? He's right there," Bantham protested. "He's standing there."

"What makes Sam Beckett himself is not present," Ziggy said. "His experiment was, perhaps, somewhat premature. At the moment he stepped into the Accelerator, ladies and gentlemen, Sam Beckett—vanished."

He was floating somewhere, lost in blue-white light.

There was no sensation, no weight, no scent, taste, nothing but the light surrounding him. He might have been moving; he could not tell. He had no body. If he was moving, through air, through space, through electronic circuits, there was no way to tell. If time was passing, in either direction, there was no way to tell.

"Dr. Beckett."

The voice surrounded him as the light surrounded him, was a part of himself as the light was a part of himself, was himself.

"Hello? Is someone there?" He made words without lips and teeth and tongue to form them, thought words and heard

them as he heard the voice, without ears. If he had had a body, he might have looked about him, searching for the source of the voice, for someone to whom to give the answer.

It was important that the voice know he was there. That someone know he was there. That someone find him. That someone know who he was. Because he, himself . . . did not know. "Who are you?"

He had the sensation of being examined, of an intellectual curiosity, as if it were his turn to be the specimen under the microscope, subjected to examination and experimentation.

"Are you ready, Dr. Beckett?" the voice said. But it did not wait for an answer. His willingness, his readiness was a matter of indifference, as the willingness of the worm to be dissected was a matter of indifference to the student. At last, there was the sensation of movement, of rushing through great consequences, of being tossed and torn by something for which he had no name, of being carried to a destination he had not chosen.

"Who am I? Where am I?" he demanded. The voice had called him by a name, but it was a name he didn't recognize. "What is this place? Why am I here?"

"You have work to do, Dr. Beckett. You have things to make right, and things to learn."

"How long am I going to be here?" he asked. "When can I go home? "

He could not remember "home." All he knew was that it was a good place, his place, where he had an identity and friends and people knew who he was, where he knew other people, where he had a task to do, and he wanted to return to it. Home was some other place than this blue light.

Miraculously, the sensation of rushing through canyons stopped, as if the experimenter had paused between the dissecting table and the electron microscope to look once again at the stained slide it carried. "Home? Oh no, you're not going home yet. You still have work to do.

"But someday. Sometime. I promise."